An Autumn Hideaway

MARGARET AMATT

First published in 2021 by Leannan Press

ISBN: 978-1-914575-92-1

For Ian and Ossian

CONTENTS

CHAPTER 1

Autumn

Hundreds of glass beads shattered with an almighty crash, pinging across the shiny floor of Grantley and Byrde's Boutique in Chelsea. Autumn sprang back, hands clutching her face in alarm. The shelf she'd just finished stacking was no more. Luxury candles lay in tatters and crushed glass covered the floor. An odd aroma of cinnamon, sea breeze, and lemongrass wafted around.

'Oh, my god.' Autumn squeezed out the words, repressing a giggle. Laughing was generally better than crying, though the funny side of this wasn't easy to find. Someone gasped behind her. A customer? Her boss, Mr Byrde? *Shit.* He'd be furious.

A hand pressed her shoulder. 'Autumn, are you ok?'

She glanced around to see her friend and co-worker, Priya. *What a relief.* 'Can you believe this? I don't know how I did it… It just shattered.' Her urge to laugh now bordered on hysterics. How on earth could she fix this?

'Oh, Autumn,' said Priya. 'Let's get this cleared up while the shop's quiet. If Mr Byrde sees it, he'll be mad. We can't afford to ruffle his feathers any more this week. He's on the warpath.'

'What is it now?' Autumn held her fingers to her forehead as she surveyed the damage to the hundred-and-twenty-five-pounds-a-pop candles.

'I haven't told you about our meeting yet.' Priya bent over, picking up a candle in a frosted glass jar. Autumn winced at the crack. *I'm going to be in so much trouble.* This job paid better than the local grocery store; she didn't want to lose it. This was a poor way to repay Priya, who'd helped her get the job in the first place.

'Oh, yes. What happened? Was it about the promotion?'

'No. Nothing like. Do you remember I was off a couple of weeks ago when the twins weren't great?'

'Yes.' Autumn picked up several more fallen candles.

'Well, it's not my fault. They must have picked up something at nursery. But Mr Byrde wanted to talk to me about redundancies. He said they're coming and he hinted I'd be the first to go because I've been off so much.'

'Really?' Autumn scanned around the piles of chaos. The slightest whiff of this and Priya wouldn't have to worry. Autumn could see herself getting the boot before break-time.

'Yup. And I can't lose this job, I need the money.'

'Don't worry.' Autumn brushed up the shattered shards. 'I was last in; I should be first out.'

'I don't want that either.'

'I'm sure I'll find something else if I have to.' She'd missed promotion after promotion at EN-Sure, the insurance company where she'd worked for four years. When it had gone bust, she'd been reduced to this. She smiled at her friend before surveying the woefully impossible task scattered around the floor. How could they ever get this cleared up? Thankfully, it was a Tuesday morning, and business was slow. Priya fobbed off the few customers while Autumn checked around for any remaining glass fragments, suspecting she'd be finding them for weeks on end, probably embedded in her soles. Come tea break, she'd psyched herself up to confessing to Mr Byrde. 'What's the worst he can do?'

'Eh, sack you?' said Priya.

'True. But I'm sure Tesco would have me.'

'Aww, no.'

'It would be a shame though, I'll miss you… and the candles.'

Priya shook her head. 'You and your candles. Maybe that's what you need to do, get down to starting that business.'

'I don't see that ever happening.' Dreaming of making her own candles, soaps and bath products was the dream Autumn fantasised over, but she never got any further than making wishes and Pinterest boards. 'Right, let's see what Mr Byrde has to say.' As Autumn pulled out her phone, several messages distracted her. This influx was not unusual. She had a large pool of friends who messaged her about their travels, wedding plans, children, and the stress of their tough jobs. Her contributions revolved around the continuing Josh-gate saga, most of which was sordid and she preferred not to discuss. She suspected the intrigue she provided fuelled the more gossipy of her friends for months. She could see why it might look interesting to an outsider, but when you were stuck in the middle of it, it wasn't. It was downright soul-destroying in fact. But these messages weren't from friends. 'He's never messaged me before.' Autumn frowned and tossed her long auburn hair over her shoulder, a frown tightening her forehead.

'Who?' Priya peered in the staffroom door.

'Phil, you know, my stepdad.' She used the term in its most woolly form. 'Apparently, Mum's left him.' Autumn glanced at Priya. All Autumn's besties knew the story. Her mum had been with Phil on and off for ten years. She wasn't a settler, showing Autumn at age twelve that life with a bottle of wine was more important than caring for her only child.

'Time to crack open the champagne, I'd say,' said Priya.

Autumn smirked. 'Totally, I never got what Mum saw in him. But read this.' Autumn held out her phone. 'He thinks she's been kidnapped.'

'No way. Isn't it more likely she ran off again?'

With a sigh, Autumn put the phone away. 'Yes, much more likely.' Her mum had a history of doing just that. Looking up, Autumn pulled a pout and held up her hands. 'I'm not sure what to do.'

'Are you worried?' said Priya.

Autumn straightened out her white blouse, checking behind Priya for customers. 'I'm not sure.'

Priya, like all Autumn's friends, knew she and her mum weren't close. 'It's natural to worry.' Priya pulled her in for a side hug.

Autumn tapped her fingers to her lips. 'Even when Mum hasn't been around for me? You know I've tried with her lots of times, but nothing gets closer to her than a cheap wine.'

'Hmm,' said Priya. 'Why don't we go see Phil after work?'

'I can't,' said Autumn quickly. 'The house… You know, it's a mess.'

'That's ok. I won't judge you by it.'

'It isn't just that…'

'What then?'

'Josh's parents,' said Autumn through her teeth. 'They live across the road.'

'Oh, yeah. I forgot.' Priya twiddled her fingers for a few seconds. 'But we probably won't see them. And if we do, so what?'

Autumn shrugged like the moody teenager she'd been when her mum first moved in with Phil ten years ago. After Autumn's parents had split when she was twelve, she'd lived with her dad and his string of girlfriends for four years. For an adolescent girl, it had been trying to say the least, so at sixteen, she'd moved in with her mum, trying to give her a chance, but it hadn't played out.

'I just…'

'Are you going to tell me what's happening with Josh?' Priya folded her arms, looking stern.

'We've split up.' For the umpteenth time. Almost as soon as she'd moved in with her mum, she'd fallen hook, line and sinker for the good-looking guy down the road. But he was older. At first, he'd liked her as a bit of fun. Then he'd moved on, left Autumn heartbroken, and married someone else.

'Good,' said Priya, 'because he wasn't right for you.'

Autumn scoffed. 'Right.' He'd been everything she always wanted… or so it had seemed. When he came back, saying his marriage was crumbling, Autumn had fallen again. And yet he was still with his wife, despite all his assertions that he was leaving her. Every time they met, he promised. She just had to wait. Three years later, she was still waiting.

'Yes, Autumn. Time to forget about him. Come on, let's go to Phil's and get this sorted out.'

*

When they clocked off, Autumn changed into her jeans and pulled on her purple coat. Instead of heading for the tube, she hopped on the ninety-two bus. Priya grinned at her. 'This is like a holiday for me. The kids will have to make do with their dad a bit longer.'

'You're funny,' said Autumn.

'Just wait until you have kids, you'll know what I'm talking about.'

'Speaking of kids, wait until you hear what The Reaper said to me last week.'

Priya laughed at the name. Autumn couldn't help herself. It was the nickname she gave Krystina Ann Reaper, her father's girlfriend, a woman who loved Autumn as much as a fungal infection. 'I dread to think.'

'She said' – Autumn mimicked her thick London accent – '"I hope one day you fall for a guy who already has kids then you'll find out for yourself how wearing and soul-destroying it is".'

'Seriously, the bitch.'

'Oh, yeah. I'm just a drain as far as she's concerned. This was part of her telling me she didn't want to have to buy me a Christmas present this year because it's pricey enough buying stuff for her own two daughters, never mind me. Do I actually want a Christmas present from her? Last year she gave me a five quid gift card for Ann Summers.'

Priya snorted into her hand. 'What did you buy with it?'

'I was spoilt for choice. I could afford a pair of knickers in the reduced section or a pack of condoms.'

Autumn smiled at Priya's amusement, but she wasn't sure it was that funny. She didn't like to read into exactly what message Krystina had been sending with that gift, though she suspected it was to jibe her about her relationship with Josh. No one really understood. How could they? She guessed what people called her behind her back. But she'd believed in Josh, believed his words and his promises. Or had she just wanted to? She craved the security of having someone and if he was there, even just out of reach, there was no possibility of meeting anyone else and having her heart broken. She just had to wait for Josh and everything would be fine. Wouldn't it?

Thirty minutes later, they got off the bus and nipped down the street of redbrick terraced houses where her mum and Phil lived.

Holding her head high to make the most of her five-feet-two and – a very important – half inches, Autumn rolled back her shoulders and pushed open the creaky gate to number 109. The path up the tiny strip of garden at the front of the house was slippery with wet leaves. Priya followed, her nose twitching. A pungent smell hit them. Pools of water sagged on the tops of black rubbish bags piled at the side. Covering her mouth, Autumn coughed. 'Jeez, this is worse than ever. What a mess.'

As she knocked on the door, a fleck of peeled paint fluttered to the ground. An ominous thump sounded from inside. Priya put her hand on Autumn's arm, her eyes widening.

Pushing onto her tiptoes, Autumn's gaze wandered left then right, scanning the terrace. A couple of houses down and across the street was a neatly kept house – Josh's house.

'Shit, there's Josh's dad.' Autumn looked away from the man who was lifting an armful of hedge trimmings into a bin.

'Who cares,' said Priya. 'Let Josh go.'

The theory was plain as day but he'd been such a constant in her life. She kept expecting the call from him to say he'd left his wife for good and they could get back together. Without him, she was lost.

As a huge shape approached through the filthy glass, Autumn fidgeted with the clip on her leather bag.

'Oh, it's you.' Phil's flabby face poked around the door and he rubbed the sleep from his eyes.

'Hi, Phil. I just wondered if you've heard from Mum?'

'Nuffink, like. Come in.' Opening the door, he let her pass. ''ello,' he said as Priya followed.

'Hi.'

Autumn's hand clutched her mouth. She almost choked.

'Mind yourself there.' Phil waddled past and led the way down the corridor, edging past boxes and bags piled high.

'Phil, we don't want to stay for long. Just tell me what happened. Did you call the police?'

'No. I was talking to them across the road. 'er says not to, 'cause Vicky left and doesn't want to be found, like. But I wanna know where she is. I'm dead worried, like. I fink she's gone off with someone who might bc bad for 'er.'

Autumn struggled to remain impassive. Who could be worse than Phil?

''Cause 'er's not well, see.'

'Not well?'

'Not been well for ages. I wouldn't like nuffink to happen to 'er, like.'

'What's wrong with her?'

'Lemme show you the note, like.' Phil disappeared up the stairs, sending a box flying. A jumble of brass objects clattered down the stairs, landing at Autumn's feet. She jumped as a tarnished elephant almost gored her boot. Lurching back, she hit the wall, and an old picture thumped to the floor. 'Ew.' She flicked at a trail of cobwebs on her shoulder. 'Not my new coat.'

'This place…' muttered Priya.

'Is gross.' Autumn ducked through the door to the living room, covering her mouth again as a coughing fit gripped her. 'What the hell has happened here? It was never this bad.' The sofa was buried underneath layers of clothes, bedding, carrier bags, and goodness knows what else. Dirty old curtains at the window hid papers, ornaments, and several lampshades. Frames and pictures hung around the room at odd angles, and stuff was piled everywhere. Clamping both her hands over her mouth, she stared around, shaking her head.

'No wonder your mum left. I don't blame her,' said Priya.

'Me neither.'

Phil returned and passed Autumn a sheet of paper. It looked like her mum's writing, with her big circles dotting the *I*s. It also made it clear she was leaving and didn't want Phil to come after her. Autumn handed it back and turned to Priya to do a discreet air punch.

'Well,' said Autumn, glancing at Phil. 'It doesn't look like she's been kidnapped. I think she's left you. Sorry.'

Leaving Phil staring at the note, they made their way outside.

'It sounds like a good move for your mum,' said Priya, 'but I wonder where she is and what's wrong with her. Who's the person who told Phil your mum didn't want to be found?'

'Josh's mum, I expect. She's the street busybody.'

'Let's ask her.'

'No,' groaned Autumn. As far as Autumn was aware, Josh's mum didn't know her son had carried on seeing Autumn several years into his marriage. She always sensed the woman didn't like her. She certainly hadn't approved of her son dating Autumn when she was a teenager AKA *that girl from the dodgy house across the street.*

But Priya was on a mission: she pushed open the gate. Josh's dad peered up, then dashed up the short path for the door. Autumn struggled not to giggle.

'Am I that scary?' asked Priya.

'No, he's just a wet blanket.'

As they reached the door, Josh's mum appeared on the top step, her arms folded and her jaw hard. 'Why are you here? We don't want any trouble.'

'Me neither,' said Autumn.

Josh's mum raised her eyebrows. 'Yeah? Well, how come I've had Debs on the phone, crying because she found someone called Autumn was calling our Josh?'

Autumn's heartrate increased. Debs knew? His mum knew? Or they suspected, at least. 'I, er… We're friends.'

'I know what you are. I know what you've always been,' hissed Josh's mum. 'Leading my boy astray right from the start. Well, keep away. Debs is pregnant and I don't want nothing ruining it for them.'

The word pregnant rendered Autumn speechless. Before she could gather her thoughts, Priya spoke. 'Have you heard anything about Autumn's mum? Phil said she'd left.'

'What?'

'Yes, that's why I'm here.' Autumn struggled to stop her emotions bubbling out. Josh and Debs were having a baby. That's why he'd split this time. And there was no going back. He'd cheated on Debs, which was bad enough, but a baby. Autumn wouldn't be a homewrecker.

'She's gone,' said Josh's mum. 'And I'm glad. That man is toxic. I hope he moves out. He brings the whole street down.'

'And do you know where she is?'

Josh's mum shrugged. 'Yeah, she told me a while ago, said she was finalising the arrangements, but she didn't want Phil to know. She met a guy on online dating.'

Autumn exchanged a glance with Priya. Mum was online dating while living with Phil? Rewind… Mum was online dating, period.

'She said he was the guy she'd always wanted.' Josh's mum snorted. 'I'd never trust someone from one of these dodgy sites. His name's Mike and she's gone to live with him.'

'Mike? Mike what? And where?' Autumn pressed.

'No idea what his surname is, but wait until I tell you where he lives…' Autumn nudged her head forward, pressing the woman to spit it out. 'On an island in Scotland.'

'What?' Autumn looked at Priya again, who mirrored her shock.

'Yeah, here, Clive!' she yelled inside. 'What's the name of that island Vicky went to? Started with an M, I remember thinking it was Mike from somewhere beginning with M.'

'Mull,' shouted the voice.

'That's it. Mull. Like the wine. I wonder how she's enjoying it,' said Josh's mum with a wicked grin.

If discovering her mum had run off to live on an island wasn't bad enough, the following day made up for it. The shelf smash came back to bite. Mr Byrde agreed with Autumn's point *last one in, first one out* and her mishap was the last straw.

'Clumsy workers do nothing for our image,' said Mr Byrde.

When Autumn changed out of her work suit that evening, Priya looked on, her eyes glassy with tears. 'I'm so sorry.'

'Don't be,' said Autumn. 'In fact, I need the time off.'

'Why?'

'I'm going to go look for Mum. What if she's in trouble? And if not, I can just see the place for myself and maybe relax a bit before trying to find a new job… again.'

'I think you're crazy,' said Priya. 'But I also think it's a great idea. How will you find her though?'

'It's an island. It's not big. Remember when we all went to Lindisfarne and we walked around it in an hour.'

'That's true,' said Priya. 'Just take care. You haven't travelled much on your own.'

'It's an adventure, isn't it?'

*

Autumn waited in Euston Station early on Saturday morning, bouncing on her toes with a coffee in her hand. She checked the departure board. Here she was with nothing to lose, except cash she should be saving for a rainy day. Judging from the grey skies, that day had arrived.

Despite being no stranger to spontaneity, Autumn was used to an exacting group of friends planning their moves and making sure everything ran smoothly. Left to her own devices, she drifted with the flow, picking up fun and friends wherever she went. Maybe instead of doing this, she should have ploughed her paltry savings into renting a shed in Cornwall where she could make her candles and soap by the beach. She stretched and yawned. That dream would have to wait a bit longer. It had never really taken off because it had seemed linked to Josh. When they were together, they could make that big move. It wouldn't be as scary as doing it on her own. Now it was never going to happen.

Safely on the train, Autumn closed her eyes and rested her forehead on the cold glass window. A guilty ache rose in her chest. Josh, Debs, a baby. Heat spread over her cheeks. Why had she wasted so much time on him? That light had been snuffed and she was awash in limbo-land. Waiting around for him had always been like that, but this was worse. Hopeless.

Go away, Josh. She sat up straight and stretched. He was not going to bother her for the next few days; she was determined. Which left her mum. Phil had said she was ill. He hadn't explained. Was there something more sinister going on? Maybe she'd gone to hide because she didn't have long to live. Autumn covered her mouth. She could have done so much more for her mum, but she'd done nothing. She'd never tried to help her escape Phil. At sixteen that was understandable, but at twenty-seven what excuse did she have? Now she was heading north to a place she didn't know the first thing about.

Rain hammered the windows. Autumn jumped from flickers of excitement to moments of silent fretting, making it impossible to settle or concentrate. The weather deteriorated. After googling Mull and seeing pictures of blue skies and beautiful beaches, Autumn scrunched up her nose. What would she do on a remote island for a week? What if her mum didn't want to see her? It was such a real possibility that by the time she'd arrived at Glasgow Central Station, she'd almost talked herself into getting on a train back to London. With a deep breath, she held steady. *Keep going.* She located the departure board and searched for the Oban train. With twenty minutes to spare, she had time to go to the loo and get a coffee.

Platform, platform? She scanned the board but couldn't see the right one. A guard in a bright orange jacket went by and she grabbed him.

'You're at the wrong station,' he said. 'The Oban train leaves from Queen Street. It says so on your ticket.'

'What? Where's that?' She scanned around, sweeping her long auburn locks from her face.

'Here's the map.' The guard pulled a leaflet from a wall rack and pointed out the route. 'You could try for a taxi or you might still make it if you run.'

Her boots weren't made for running, but the queue for the taxis was the length of the street. She jostled people as she hightailed it, dashing across roads, and hoping her on-the-hoof map reading would get her to the right place. She didn't dare google it; Google maps had a habit of going all over the place when she used it, especially if she was in a hurry. Specks of rain peppered her cheeks. She came to a halt as unfamiliar buildings towered around her. Nothing looked right.

'Where's Queen Street Station?' she begged a passer-by.

'Just up there. Turn the corner at the shop with the blue sign.' He pointed.

'Thank you!' She hoisted her bag and ran. Her case rattled along behind. Scrambling into the entrance, she spied the departure board. 'One minute,' she screamed. Her feet ached. She ignored face after face of startled looks as she raccd toward the train. 'Excuse me… Sorry!'

The guard on the platform had the whistle in his mouth.

'Please,' she yelled. 'Please let me on! I have to get on that train!'

With a scowl, he opened the door. 'Cutting it far too neat.'

She threw herself aboard. 'This is the Oban train, isn't it?' she called as the doors snapped shut. The guard nodded. The train rattled off and Autumn staggered, colliding with the wall. Struggling to shove her case onto the rack, she shook with exertion and panic. Only the top shelf was free, and even on tiptoes, she could barely reach. With a giant push, she launched her case onto it. She sensed eyes on her: Mr Nosey and all his relatives peered out from behind books and tablets. Autumn spied an empty seat and made a beeline for it.

CHAPTER 2

Richard

Richard Linden glanced up from his book and pushed his glasses further onto the bridge of his nose. A young woman had tumbled onto the train at the last minute and was making her way down the aisle. Across the table from Richard was an empty seat. His sixth sense, which was his least competent, told him she would sit in it.

'Is anyone sitting here?' she asked.

Just in time, Richard bit back the reply which jumped to his throat, *obviously not, unless it's the invisible man,* and settled on, 'No.'

'Cool.' She slid into the window seat, then stood again to wrestle off her purple coat. Brave woman. The train was arctic and the radiator grille beneath the window stone cold. Richard hadn't ventured out of his jacket. The woman tugged the coat from her arms, then tossed it beside her. Her eyes fell on him. He swallowed, gripping his book tightly. A smile spread over her face and Richard blinked, looking quickly back at the open pages. The moment he saw the print, he realised he should have smiled back. Not that it mattered.

Trying to concentrate on the words, Richard couldn't help watching her every move in his peripheral vision. She messed up her long, spiralling locks of auburn hair, then raked in her bag. A phone landed on the table and slender white fingers, tipped with sparkly bronze nails, scrolled across it. The phone lit up and the woman lifted it to her ear.

'Hi, Bekki. I am, yes. I almost missed it. I was at the wrong station. Can you believe it…? Haha, not funny.'

Putting his head down, Richard tried to ignore her, but she had a chirpy lilt that sang to him like the dawn chorus at four a.m. 'I doubt it'll take me long to find her,' she continued. 'And I need a change. I've booked into a stunning hotel.' Her laugh tinkled. 'I didn't get a chance to show you. I'll forward the link, and you can have a look.'

As she ended the call, she rested the phone back on the table and Richard's eyes strayed, observing what was on the screen. Seriously? Since when did he care about other people's business? *Eyes down and nose out.*

Rain battered the coaches and trickled down the windows. The woman slouched in the corner, her coat pulled over her like a blanket. Lowering his book, Richard observed out his side. The weather matched his mood: grim, gloomy, and tempestuous. This time yesterday he'd been in New York, and the day before, on the banks of Lake Michigan near Chicago. Four days living in the nightmare he'd created. After six years, he still regretted the day he'd given in, signed the papers and agreed to let his wife take their son to live in the US. He retained visiting rights, but what did that mean in real life? Any chance he had of bonding with Adam was long gone. He was a father in name only and travelling five thousand miles for a review meeting gave him nothing except a pain in the chest.

He glimpsed across the table. The woman was looking over, her lips curling into a smile, and he snapped his attention back to his book, shaking his head. *Do not talk to me, do not talk to me.* Words from the page weren't penetrating his brain. His finger was tapping the table. He didn't know how long he'd been doing it for, and he couldn't stop.

So much of his investigation remained, and time was closing in. This trip couldn't have come at a worse time. Four days, when he had a deadline looming, was huge. Working on planes and trains in different time zones wasn't happening for him. When his work phone had gone off during the meeting, his ex-wife's look had almost sent him to an early grave. His workaholic tendencies had wrecked their marriage and he was surprised she hadn't found a way of cutting him out of Adam's life completely with the phone faux pas.

Raking his fingers through his hair, he swallowed back his thoughts. He yearned to get back to Mull, where he could breathe again, and possibly sleep. He hadn't slept well for months.

'The four o'clock ferry's cancelled. The next one is under review,' said a man's voice somewhere in the carriage. 'We might not get there tonight.'

Richard groaned. Delays were part and parcel of island life, but he couldn't handle a night in a B&B, not tonight. Plus, he'd left poor Peppy with Ron Matheson. The dog would be frantic, though he didn't object to company as much as his owner.

The woman opposite tossed off her coat blanket, picked up her phone and swiped the screen while chewing on a cuticle. Was she aiming for the ferry too?

'Excuse me?' she said.

Richard ruffled his dark hair with an irritable sigh. He couldn't help himself. He was jetlagged and exhausted, but something about her held his eye. An unexpected, relaxing sensation spread across his shoulders. Her expression was welcoming. 'Yes?'

'Do you know if Oban is a big town?' She smiled, toying with the edge of her phone.

'Depends what you mean by big,' he said, focusing on a raindrop trickling down the window and merging with another drop. 'It's a reasonably sized town, but it's not a city.'

'Are there hotels and places to stay if I miss this boat?'

'Lots of hotels and places to stay, yes.'

'Thank goodness.'

Having spent the entire journey with his jacket on, Richard felt warm. Standing up, he collided with the overhead shelves. 'Ouch.' He rubbed the top of his head. At six foot four, this was always a hazard, but he usually had the wit to remember. He tugged at his zip. Halfway down, the bloody thing jammed. This was exactly the kind of shit which happened to him when he least needed it. Seriously? On a packed train when people had nothing better to do than watch him. Other people's opinions didn't matter, but it didn't stop him wishing he could evaporate. Maybe if he sat back down, he could unpick the zip from the lining. A group at the opposite table had stopped talking and were smirking. He sunk into his seat and pulled furiously, but it wasn't going anywhere, just making him hotter.

'Here, I can help you with that' said the woman opposite. 'I've got the knack.'

'What?' Before he could object, she'd got out of her seat and sat beside him. She took hold of his zip like he was a three-year-old and folded it round to look at it.

'This happens to me all the time,' she said, fiddling with the lining. 'But if you get this bit out…' She gritted her teeth as she tugged at it.

Richard held his head back, keeping stock still. Sometimes people's astonishing lack of boundaries and personal space infuriated him. But this was worse. Not only was she far too close, but he couldn't avoid her obvious physical attractiveness. Her bright turquoise eyes glinted with determination as she waggled the zip pull. An intense conditioner smell drifted up Richard's nostrils from her very close, glossy hair. It had to be red, didn't it? He'd always had a weakness for red hair. Lorraine had started it. His fiery ex. The woman he'd wanted to marry, but hadn't. He'd married Ruth instead. When their relationship had fallen apart, back to Lorraine he went, and what a mess it had been.

'Nearly got it,' said the woman. 'It's always worse trying to do it on yourself. I got in such a flap one time, I cut myself out of a lovely jacket. I wish I hadn't, I really liked it.'

Her accent sounded like she was a Londoner – not cockney, but a similar twang.

'There you go.' She pulled the tag down to his lap, disengaging her hand before she touched him somewhere he really didn't want her to go without invitation.

'Thanks,' he said, unhooking the end as she nipped back to her seat. He took off the jacket but he wanted to hide. Would she talk to him now? He didn't want to spend the rest of the journey chatting to a stranger. He just wanted to melt away.

'No problem.'

She seemed to get the message he wasn't up for chatting and returned to scrolling through her phone. As the train approached Oban, people shuffled around. Richard flung his book into his backpack and sat upright, holding it on his knee. The woman stood to put on her coat. With a brief smile in his direction, she took her place in the throng of people getting off. Richard waited until everyone had moved past before rising. A crowd blocked the exit. The woman was on tiptoes, her fingers scrabbling on the handle of her case. The doors opened and people jostled off. She put her foot on a ledge, her case just out of reach. She was really short. Richard stretched over, grabbed her case and lifted it down. She caught it, stumbling backwards.

'Thanks,' she said.

'Well, one good turn and all that,' said Richard and he jumped off the step and strode towards the ferry port very glad to be off the train.

CHAPTER 3

Autumn

Autumn stowed her case on a rack in the centre of the ship and ventured outside. After nervously waiting for over two hours at the terminal, she was finally aboard. Dark storm clouds gathered beyond the bay and she shivered. A muffled honking sound made her peer up at a long string of geese. She watched until the clouds engulfed them. A sharp wind whipped her face as the ship eased from the harbour. Warmth and caffeine called. She dragged open a heavy door and stepped in, admiring the well-fitted interior. Nothing like what she'd imagined. She'd expected a small boat with limited seating but she wasn't complaining. This was more like a cruise ship with lounges, a café and shops. She didn't linger after downing her coffee, as many people were waiting for tables.

Close to where she'd left her case, she spotted an empty seat and flopped down. The man on the right shifted at the movement. Him again. The rather grumpy man from the train. She gave him a brief smile. He frowned and she looked away, but something about his presence made her feel less edgy. She didn't know him, but having that prior connection calmed her mind. If changing ferries mid-sail or some other hitherto unknown situation arrived, she'd brave his frown and ask him. Her phone rang with its silly tinkly tune; she really must change it. As she fumbled in her pocket, she knocked the man with her elbow. He moved irritably, rolling his broad shoulders backwards.

'Sorry,' she said. 'Hi, Priya.' Autumn switched ears, not wanting to prod him again.

'How's it going? I can't talk long, Andrew's putting the twins to bed and if I'm not there, it never ends well. Mummy is always best.'

Autumn gave a wry smile. Would she ever be the one putting a baby to bed? She'd dreamed, one day, she and Josh would have a child. Now he was going to be a father, but it was nothing to do with her. 'I'm on the ferry, it's really stormy.'

'I thought you'd be there by now.'

'There were loads of delays.' She skimmed over the crowd of passengers. 'This boat is so busy. How can so many people fit on an island?'

Mr Grumpy scratched his head and sighed softly. Autumn kept her voice low as she chatted.

'Let me know when you arrive,' said Priya, 'I better go.'

Ending the call, Autumn leaned back, pulling in her arms and shifting to get comfy, but it was impossible without touching Mr Grumpy and after untangling his zip, she had the impression he was distinctly freaked out by her. Maybe she should have left him to struggle with it, but she hated seeing people in distress.

An announcement sounded, calling drivers and passengers back to their cars. Autumn moved closer to the foot passenger exit. Waking her phone, she checked her email confirmation from the hotel.

If arriving on foot, you can catch the Tobermory bus, it will stop at the hotel on request.

A bus, right? Autumn imagined herself cramped on a tiny Postbus with several other people for a distance she could probably walk quicker.

A lot of bumping and rocking followed as the boat docked, which Autumn guessed wasn't normal from the conversation amongst the throng waiting to disembark. Thrown forward, she tried to grab her suitcase and narrowly missed colliding with Mr Grumpy as he pulled a bag from the rack. 'Sorry,' she mumbled. He didn't seem to hear.

*

A thunderous downpour clattered on the glass roof covering the walkway on the quayside. Autumn jostled amongst the crowd. No one was hanging about. Squinting through the drizzle and mist, she saw a collection of vehicle tail-lights disappearing into the darkness. Where to catch this bus?

What was that sound? *My phone again.* Not a good time. She fumbled about her pocket and pulled it out. Brian Elworthy flashed across the screen with a truly terrible photo of a rotund man on a deckchair with the full-lobster, British summertime tan. Dad? Stopping abruptly, Autumn answered it. Some people careered into her, cursing as they ducked into the torrent of rain. 'Oh gosh, sorry.' She raised her hand. 'Hello? Dad?' His calls were so infrequent these days, it took her by surprise and always gave her a flutter of panic. Was someone ill?

'Is this nonsense about your mother true?' he said.

'What?'

'I had a ridiculous message from that horrible Phil, saying she's run off somewhere again.'

'She has. I've gone to see if I can find her.'

'Do you know where she is?'

'I have a rough idea.' Autumn glanced around into the falling darkness. A very rough idea.

'Well, when you find her, tell her I need to talk to her about the divorce. Bloody inconsiderate of her to go off now when I need her to sign stuff. We should have done this years ago, but your mother always made far too many demands, that's why I put it off. She's terrorised Krystina with her nonsense.'

'Seriously?' Autumn wanted to laugh. Krystina terrorised by someone! Not a chance. Her stepmother-to-be was a vixen who made children cry just by stalking past them in her leopard print leggings and skyrise heels. She was a cross between Pat Butcher and Samantha Fox, not a good look for someone attempting to play the victim.

'Yeah, so tell her to get back here and sign the papers ASAP. No more nonsense.'

'Right.' Autumn squinted into the gloom, straining to make out the lie of the land. 'Well, I'm stuck on an island in the middle of nowhere, but when I find her, I'll tell her. Talk soon. Love you.' She ended the call, digging her nails into her palm. Now, find the bus stop. The ringing started again. 'What?' she answered automatically.

'What do you mean you're on an island?'

'It's where Mum's living. At least I think it is.'

Her dad laughed. How could he find it funny? Autumn was too cold and tired to be remotely amused. 'This is not real, Autumn. It's your mother's idea of a flamboyant gesture, she likes to make a scene.'

'What are you talking about? I want to check she's ok, I think she's depressed.'

Brian's laughter intensified. So did Autumn's heartbeat. She gritted her teeth. 'Depressed! What nonsense.' Brian guffawed. 'She's a bloody alcoholic. Running off is a smokescreen, she'll be back demanding money for booze before long. Krystina and I have set a wedding date. I probably shouldn't have told her, but that's why I need the divorce completed. We have a new life. But instead of signing, she's made up a mad story and pretended she's off to live on an island. Get on the next bus and come back to London. She'll text in a few days saying it went wrong and shift the attention straight back to her. It's typical of Vicky.'

'Hold on a minute. You and Krystina have a wedding date?' Autumn fiddled with her cuff. Brian and Krystina had been engaged for several years and it seemed to be an arrangement they were both happy with.

An official in a hi-vis jacket spoke into a radio as he closed a heavy metal gate. The rhythmical thump of cars leaving the ferry had stopped, and apart from the rain's steady beat everything was quiet.

'Yes, we've finally set a date, assuming your bloody mother signs on the dotted line in time. And you're invited, of course, my darling.' His voice melted into jovial tones. 'It is going to be an extravaganza like you wouldn't believe.'

Oh, I might. Imagining the type of thing Krystina would want was easy. She was *My Big Fat Gypsy Wedding's* biggest fan. Numbness crept over Autumn. Her dad was marrying that woman and her mum had vanished. Her family didn't get much better than this. Through the haze of rain and spray, a double-decker bus marked *Tobermory* rolled past. 'That isn't the one I'm meant to be on, is it?' She spun around, watching as it vanished into the gloom.

'What?'

Her heart thumped wildly. 'Sorry, I have to go, I need to catch a bus. I'll text you later. Bye, Dad.' She ended the call and stepped out. A tremendous gust almost bowled her over as she battled towards the empty bus bays. With a sinking sensation, she searched for the timetable, squinting at the tiny print through the rain. The hotel she'd booked was near a small village called Salen, and she was in Craignure. Was it walkable? In this weather? Running her glossy nail down the list, she stopped and tapped the last time. *No way, this is not happening. That was the last bus.* Through the downpour, Autumn discerned lights glowing from a long low building. Sandwich-board signs swung violently by the door next to two parked cars. A shop! She ran along the road, suitcase rattling behind, rain slapping her in the face.

A bell tinkled as she entered. Waking her phone, she checked the hotel's exact location. *Thirteen miles!* What? With a shaky hand, she grabbed some snacks and edged between the shelves to get to the till. A middle-aged woman behind the counter watched as Autumn manoeuvred her case into the tight gap between the shelf and the till.

'Hi.' She pushed some wet hair behind her ear and took a calming breath. 'I don't suppose you know how I could get to Salen tonight? I just missed the last bus.' *How stupid must I sound?*

'Oh dear.' The woman drew in her severely plucked brows and fingered a gold name badge emblazoned *Anne.* 'There's an island taxi you could call, though he could be anywhere. He's always busy on Saturday nights. I can give you his number.'

'Yes, please.'

Anne pushed the contactless machine towards Autumn, and she slapped her card on it. 'That's it gone through. I'll get that number.' Anne's focus shifted for a second to the back of the shop before she scribbled a number from a card in the window.

Autumn stifled a yawn. How long would it take the taxi to get there? She didn't want to wait too long, she needed a good long soak to warm up. Taking the number, she smiled her thanks and ambled towards the door. Rain lashed the windowpane as she put the number into her phone.

'Hello. Did you get Peppy all right?' Anne spoke behind her.

'Yeah, thanks,' replied a gruff and vaguely familiar voice.

'He's been good as gold; we love having him. Any time, don't hesitate to ask.'

'Thanks.'

'And how was your week?'

'Fine.'

'I wonder, are you driving straight home?'

'Yes.'

'Maybe you'd give that lass a lift to Salen, she's missed the bus.'

Spinning around, Autumn's eyes glinted. Someone who could give her a lift. Anne was smiling at a tall man. Autumn's heart leapt. There stood Mr Grumpy. His scowling face didn't shout happy or helpful, but again she had a weird sensation; a sort of *everything's going to be ok* type thing. Though she wasn't sure where it was coming from because he didn't exude warmth or friendliness. Maybe she'd used up all her credit in his good books when he lifted her suitcase down. He glanced sideways and fished in his waxed jacket pocket.

'That was careless.' He opened his wallet, keeping his eyes on it.

Autumn bit her lip and approached. Surely this was better than waiting twelve hours overnight in the rain for a bus? Or calling a taxi *that could be anywhere?*

'It's a horrid night to be stuck,' said Anne.

'I didn't realise the buses had left for the night,' Autumn said. 'I live in London, I'm not used to…'

'It's the black Freelander.' The man waved his debit card towards the door, not looking at her. 'It's open.'

'Oh… Thank you.' She blinked at Anne, who nodded encouragingly.

'That'll save you waiting in this.' Anne gestured at the torrent gushing down the window.

'Thanks.' Autumn twisted her hands.

The man glared at the card reader. Autumn left, aware of Anne's reassuring grin. The black Freelander was backed into one of the small spaces in front of the shop. It was so grim Autumn could hardly see a thing. She opened the back door and shoved her case into the footwell before jumping into the passenger seat amongst a detritus of paper, receipts, jackets and hats. She carefully moved them to the floor.

A slight whimper. 'What the…?' Autumn nearly died as something wet pressed into her neck from behind. 'Oh, god, you're a dog.' She took several deep breaths as she stroked the long, pointed nose. 'You gave me a fright.' How had she not seen him when she opened the back door? He was huge, though his dark grey coat was good camouflage. 'I hope you're a friendly dog, are you?' He rested his bristly chin on her shoulder. 'Am I crazy?' she whispered. 'I'd never accept a lift from a stranger in London.'

The car buffeted sideways in the wind and the driver's door flew open before she could change her mind. With barely a peek in her direction, Mr Grumpy shoved the keys in the ignition. The dog nuzzled his neck. 'Good boy, now lie down.'

'This is really kind of you.'

Mr Grumpy clicked his seatbelt. 'So where are you going?' He adjusted his glasses, eyes firmly forward.

'Oh, it's called the Glen Lodge Hotel. Wait a sec.' She swiped through her phone and found the link, angling it so he could read it. 'It's near Salen, though I don't have a clue where that is. I didn't think it would be so far from the ferry.'

'I know it,' he mumbled, not checking the picture and starting the engine.

'You do? That's good. So, you must be a local?' She pushed her fingers under her legs and sat up straight, fixing her smile, aware it probably appeared like a pained grimace. It felt like one.

'Well, I live here.' He turned onto the road.

She waited, eyes about as wide as they could go. For several minutes he was silent. She flopped back. Should she try again? Releasing her hands, she fiddled with the strap on her bag. Her head spun. She didn't need to talk, but the spiralling silence made her frazzled brain ache. Should she get out her phone? Was that rude? But just sitting was awkward. Sneaking a peek out the corner of her eye, she watched him focusing forward, his dark brows closed together in a frown.

'I hope this isn't taking you out of your way,' she said.

'It's not.'

'Oh, good… So, um, what kind of dog is that?' She cocked her head at the giant filling the backseat.

'A deerhound.'

No elaboration? She inhaled, long and deliberate, tapping the window ledge. Mr Grumpy gave a little cough and rubbed his swarthy cheek. Autumn's hand fell into her lap.

'You wouldn't happen to know anyone called Mike, would you?' If only she'd thought to ask at the shop.

Mr Grumpy's forehead contracted; his brows drew together in a dark line. 'What?'

'I'm trying to find a man called Mike.' Now she was talking, the words tumbled out as they always did. 'Actually, I'm looking for my mum, her name's Vicky, but you won't know her. She's moved here to live with him. I don't know exactly where. We're not close.' She twisted in her seat to face him. 'I just know she's with a man called Mike and he lives on Mull. I googled it but nothing came up. And I tried the phonebook, but without a surname, I'm pretty stumped.'

With a shake of his head, Mr Grumpy adjusted the temperature dial. Autumn peered at him through the approaching darkness. His grim profile stared unwaveringly at the road.

'It's not you, is it?' She grabbed the chair. Was it possible? Vicky was still young, this guy was possibly around ten years younger than her. 'Is your name Mike?'

'No.' He tugged at his sleeve, resting his elbow on the windowsill. 'My name's Richard. And I don't know anyone called Mike.'

'Ok, good.' She dropped back into the seat. 'That would have been too weird. I don't mean you're weird.' She looked at him quickly. 'Just, well, you know.' This was getting worse. She needed to get to the hotel and switch off her brain, or at least her mouth. She was emotionally exhausted and her nerves were like raw meat, she couldn't control the crap she was spouting forth.

The windscreen wipers worked overtime. Richard pushed his glasses further up his nose and Autumn tilted her head to scrutinise him. He was dishevelled and his expression was grim, but he wasn't unpleasant. That inexplicable aura of reassurance hung around him, like someone in total control. Perhaps that was why he'd seemed so helpless when his zip jammed; a man with such composure wouldn't take well to being flustered.

She closed her eyes, hoping when she opened them, she'd be back in her tiny flat in London. The one she could be evicted from at any second if she didn't find another job. And how could she do that when she was here, spending her last savings on what was probably nothing but a wild goose chase?

'Do you know,' Richard began in his low Scottish accent. Autumn's eyelids flicked open. 'Almost three thousand people live on this island?'

'No, I, um, didn't.'

'I expect a few of them are called Mike. How will you find the right one?'

'I guess I'll ask about a bit.'

'Ask about?' His tone was beyond incredulous. 'There are three hundred miles of coastline, you can drive over a hundred miles of road, and you're going to ask about? When you don't have a car?'

She nodded in silent contemplation at the information overload. 'I hadn't quite grasped the size of this place.' *A minor complication.*

'Evidently.' He stooped forward, peering into the darkness.

'I thought it was tiny… Oh crikey.'

He shook his head. 'This is the fourth largest island in Britain.'

'Is it? Oh, my.' She rested on the window. Make that a major complication. 'But there are buses, so I can get about.'

'Can you?' He raised his eyebrows at his wing mirror. 'You're the girl who almost missed the train, and you've just missed the last bus, even though it takes less than a minute to walk from the ferry to the bus stance.'

'Not one of my better days.' The mirror on her side shared her dismay as she stared at the tiny bedraggled reflection, just visible in the last remnant of light. 'I guess I didn't really think this through. I just wanted to see my mum and check she was ok. I've never been a brilliant planner.' No wonder her life was such a mess.

Richard squinted sideways and his expression softened. 'Buses will get you about the main roads, but if your Mike lives in a remote farm or in an out of the way village, then you'll need a car.'

Autumn let out a sigh. 'Perhaps I could hire one somewhere, do you know of anywhere—'

He slammed on the brakes. With a sloshing sound from the road, they came to a halt.

'Jesus!' She grabbed her seat, clinging to it.

Another car whizzed past in the opposite direction.

'Bloody maniac,' said Richard. The dog stuck its nose through the gap. Autumn reached instinctively to pat it. Her fingers landed on warm skin. Richard had got there first. She withdrew quickly.

Richard pulled off, returning his elbow to the windowsill. He glanced sideways for a fraction of a second. Was that a tiny smile? With only the light from the dashboard, it was hard to tell. Save what was lit by the headlamps, outside was now completely dark.

'The garage in Craignure might hire you a car.' Richard slowed as they approached a split in the road. 'The owner has one or two he lets to visitors.' He pulled on the indicator and rolled across the road into a gateway.

'Where are we going?' Why was he driving down a dark driveway? He pointed as the headlights flashed on a large sign, Glen Lodge Hotel. 'Oh, we're here. I thought it was in a village.'

'The village is about a mile along the road. I didn't think you'd fancy walking it.'

'No, I don't. Wow, thank you, I really appreciate this.' A surge of water rose as he pulled up at the grand entrance. A glowing light illuminated wide stone steps and a half glass door into a bright vestibule. 'Can I give you money or something?' Autumn fumbled with the belt clip.

'No.' Richard shook his head, briefly making eye contact. A miniscule smile twitched, relaxing his features for a split second before he looked away.

Opening the door, Autumn jumped straight into a puddle. 'Oh no.' Water seeped through to her socks. 'I'll get my case.'

Autumn ruffled the dog's head, then shut the back door. Dumping her case, she fished in her handbag.

'Can you close the door?' said Richard.

'Wait.' She swallowed. It was worth a try. 'Before I go.' Leaning on the passenger seat, she scribbled out the number for Grantley and Byrde's Boutique on a business card, wrote her name and number and passed it over. 'Take this.'

'What's this for?' Richard squinted at it under the light. 'I don't need any luxury home goods.'

'No, no, not that. It's my number, you can contact me if you find out anything.'

'About what exactly?'

'About Mike. You're local, you might hear something.'

He stared at the card. 'Right.'

'Thanks for the lift.' She waved and shut the door.

Before the light went out, she caught him glancing at her for a fraction of a second before pulling off. The Freelander sloshed through the puddle and the rear lights faded into the thick darkness.

Relief flooded her. She was here at last. But at the same time, she felt abandoned and alone. She drew in a deep breath through her nose and pulled her suitcase up the steps, her legs wobbling, weary from the travelling. Raindrops trickled across her face and somewhere in the blackness beyond, waves crashed. The tickle of excitement she'd experienced that morning returned as she touched the door handle. A magical hook behind her navel pulled her into the warmth and she shut the door to her worries.

CHAPTER 4

Richard

Early morning rain washed over Richard. He welcomed it, tossing back his head, closing his eyes and letting it cleanse away unwanted thoughts. Sleep had eluded him. His time in America had been fraught, as always. He shook his hair and rubbed his cheeks. Memories gnawed at his brain, burrowing deep. His meeting with Adam hadn't been the father to son meeting he'd dreamt of. It was the nightmare version where Adam threw himself into a wall and had to be restrained by his carer. Trying to talk to him in such conditions was impossible. His son no longer recognised him. Richard was worse than a stranger. His presence caused nothing but injury and pain.

The wind ruffled his hair and the waves' tempestuous crash played like an orchestra. *It's ok, I'm home*. Routine would kick in; he'd be back to normal. His own brand of normal. The previous week would sink into oblivion, eventually. But when his own flesh and blood was concerned, it made everything more difficult. Being a father had never been what he had imagined, and now it was a needle pricking his side that he couldn't remove. Any chance of a regular family life was gone.

'This way, Peppy,' he called as the dog loped across the slick black rocks. Richard removed his glasses. They were so wet, he could barely see a thing anyway. He thrust his hands into his pockets and roved along the shore, glancing at the rock pools where tiny beads peppered the surface, their imprints ricocheting into wide rings.

He navigated the jagged boulders, inclining his head against the wind and making his way among the barnacles, his boots crunching into the shingle. The familiar sound soothed him. He tried to focus on it, but too many thoughts plagued his guilt-ridden mind, buzzing like flies around the rotten carcass of his aching brain. Eight years ago, when Adam was born, Richard could only have dreamed about living in a place like this with his family. Now Adam lived in his grandparents' estate on the shore of Lake Michigan, Richard's ex practised law in Chicago, and he was here, five thousand miles away.

He snatched a stone and hurled it far into the ocean, sighing as it dropped with a heavy slosh. Peppy made a half-hearted run after it.

After a mile or so, a squat, portly figure emerged in the distance wrapped up heavily in a long overcoat, hurrying towards Richard. A labradoodle scurried alongside her. Could he turn and go the other way… or hide? Options were limited. The beach was wide and long with no cover. 'Just say hello and keep walking,' he intoned. But he wasn't sure where to look now she'd spied him. Stuffing his hands deeper into his pockets, he focused as best he could on a large boulder, but the figure was getting too close to ignore. Peppy nuzzled his leg, then bounded forward.

'Morning, Richard,' said the muffled voice from inside the coat. Peppy was almost nose to nose with her as she leant to give him an affectionate clap on the ear.

'Morning,' he mumbled.

The woman bustled straight for him, pulling down her muffler. Richard edged sideways, trying not to stumble on a sharp rock. The two dogs sniffed around each other, wagging their tales.

'Terrible weather,' boomed the woman. 'The wind blew the bins over last night. Got the fright of my life. I sent Neil out to check what had happened, he wasn't best pleased.'

Richard skimmed around, desperate for an escape route. *Small talk – no!* This was exactly the thing he wanted to avoid.

'How are you? Have you been away? Your car wasn't there.'

He nodded, scratching his neck. The nosey woman may be considered a neighbour – however distant – but he didn't even know her name.

'Still working out and about?' Her bulging eyes peered from under the heavy layers of waterproofs.

'Yes.'

'Good, good. Have you heard about Sarah's husband from Dervaig? He's been asked to work on one of those dreadful dredger boats.'

'Eh… Who?' His gaze darted around. Was there no way out? Why must she always quiz him about people he didn't know or want to know? He was here for peace and even listening to her was more than his nerves could stand right now.

'Terrible, isn't it? But oh my, what a palaver I'm having with my daughter. Can't make up her mind whether she wants to come back here for Christmas or not. I suspect she has a new man. Oh, my goodness. Be thankful you don't have children. What a nightmare.'

Richard drew in a breath and held it, counting inside his head; the air might soon release from his ears. *Actually, I do have children. One child, anyway.* He'd told no one on the island and he wasn't going to start with her.

'Honestly, if I'd known what trouble they were, I'd have stuck with dogs.'

'Right.' Richard clenched his fists. Was she trying to be funny? Because he wasn't in the mood. An outlying boulder lined with cormorants became incredibly fascinating. He stared at it, hoping she'd walk on, but she carried on talking. Richard needed to switch off. He had to. Shutting down to external pressure was his speciality. But sleep deprivation made it impossible. The woman's words droned, and his mind shifted. Something else stirred.

Long red hair, turquoise eyes, and a mission that wasn't his. All there, nagging and gnawing. If he didn't do something about it, it would bother him. He wouldn't be able to put it to rest, but it was so darned stupid. Reading people wasn't his strong point but something about that redheaded woman was unforgettable. The look on her face wouldn't easily fade.

'Right, better get on.' His neighbour pulled up her muffler. 'The sooner this walk is over the better, then I go back and try to sort out my daughter.'

'Do you know anyone called Mike?' asked Richard, still staring seaward. He had to. He couldn't have it buzzing around all day, knowing he'd seen someone and hadn't asked.

'Mike, did you say?' she yelled over the wind. 'Mike who?'

Richard shrugged. The question was insane, worse than the needle in the haystack. *That* he would find, but *this?* 'Anyone on the island called Mike.'

'I don't think so. Why?' She furrowed her brow.

'Someone asked me yesterday.'

'Hmm, let me see.' She rubbed a mole on her chin. 'There could be a Michael Anderson down Fionnphort way. I think that's the name, can't be sure. He's some relation to the Crichton-Leiths from the Ardnish Estate.'

Richard raised his eyebrows. He'd worked with the Crichton-Leiths in the spring and not found them particularly helpful. 'So, how old is this Michael?'

'Let's see, forties, fifties maybe? I really couldn't say. I'm not sure I have the right name. There was definitely a Michael who worked on the boats there years ago. Was it Anderson? Or Robertson? Anderson, I think.'

'Ok.' Richard wiped his glasses and put them back on. 'Thanks.'

'No problem. Who wanted to know? One of those family history types? An American, was it?'

He shook his head. 'English by the sound of it.'

'Oh well, I'll keep my ears open. Best get on.'

Whistling Peppy, Richard nipped up the beach and onto the road. He hastened back, hoping to avoid meeting his neighbour on the return, in case she'd remembered several other Mikes or more stories about people he neither knew nor cared about. He'd done what he'd been asked. He could file away the notion.

Perched ahead was his house, Creel Lodge. Its splendid isolation flooded him with comfort. He climbed the steep incline to the drive and grabbed a couple of logs from the store at the back door. Behind the house was a flat yard with the garage and a large shed, both modern and made from timber which had settled into a natural pale grey tone. Beyond that was a sheer embankment, leading to a rocky coastal bluff. In the summer the vegetation was bright green, but the colours had changed to a rich autumnal reddish brown, dripping and saturated by the recent rainfall.

Banging the sand from his boots, Richard crossed the threshold, feeling the warmth on his cheeks. The flush of solace from seeing his beautiful house was short-lived. One man and his dog were too few for a place built for a happy family. The rooms were bright and airy but sparse. He'd never bothered to properly decorate, there didn't seem much point when it was only him. As he spent most of his time at home in his study, it was easily the most lived-in of the rooms and contained his precious book collection. The other rooms either resembled a holiday home or lay empty.

He donned a pair of thick socks and cast some logs onto the wood burner before sinking into his wing-backed armchair. His phone rested on the grey tartan arm, beside a small blue and white card.

The name *Autumn Elworthy* was scribbled on it, alongside details for an upmarket department store in Chelsea. Was that where she shopped? She'd been well-dressed and smartly turned out. Richard sighed. He'd had his share of entanglements with power dressing women. None of them had ended well. Autumn Elworthy hadn't seemed power crazy. She was too scatty. How had she missed that bus? Maybe talking to some other random strangers or assisting them with caught zips.

Richard lifted the card and tapped it on the seat, gazing out at the tempestuous ocean. The thought hadn't gone: he'd only done part of it. What was the point in him knowing about someone called Mike? He couldn't care less. But he should tell Autumn, shouldn't he? It was none of his business. He didn't do things like this. Contacting strangers and getting involved with people was way out of his comfort zone. Especially young attractive women like her. What if she got the wrong idea?

His hand hovered close to the wood burner. But a seed of curiosity had dropped into fertile soil. If he burned the card, he'd never know. A tingling intrigue crept up the back of his neck. One message wouldn't hurt, just one, and he'd be well-prepped. He would tell her the facts and let her do with them what she pleased. No need to see her. He could pass on the information and leave it there.

CHAPTER 5

Autumn

Opening the curtains, Autumn gazed over a mystical scene. Low clouds lingered over the sea beyond. Glittering raindrops fell from the saturated trees and bushes in the garden like in a fairyland. She couldn't help but smile. Making her way to the dining room, she admired the beautiful décor. This was a proper Scottish pile with gorgeous furnishings and a sumptuous finish, new and shiny, and beyond her budget. Though thanks to Wow-Deals.com, she'd bagged herself an off-peak bargain. Even if she didn't find her mum, she craved a break before hunting for another job. Her job in insurance had seemed secure, if not exactly fulfilling. If anything, she preferred the shop. At least there she had people to talk to, and if all else failed, she could sniff the candles. When EN-Sure had gone bust Autumn had been left to fend for herself. After growing up with parents like hers it was nothing new, but it wasn't pleasant either. Often, she had a drifting sensation, like life was going on around her and she was simply dipping in and out, never wholly taking part or getting anything from it.

A young waitress showed her to a table by the window in the large dining room. Autumn's boots clicked across the shiny floor. Before she sat, she turned to the waitress. 'This might sound mad,' she said. 'But I have to ask, do you know anyone called Mike who lives on the island?'

'Oh, um.' The waitress looked around. 'No, I don't. I'm not from the island, I'm Dutch, I'm only here to the end of the month, but I'll try to find out.'

'Don't worry.' Autumn took a seat. 'It's ok.'

A few minutes later, a different woman appeared at her table with a tray. 'Hello. I heard you're looking for someone.' She brushed a long sheet of ice-blonde hair over her shoulder.

'I am. Are you from the island?'

'Originally, yes. I'm the owner's daughter. I'm hotel-sitting this week with my fiancé. He knows more people than me, so if you tell me who it is, I can ask him.'

'Well, I'm in a bit of a fix because I know nothing about him, only that he's called Mike.'

'Just Mike? Nothing else?'

Autumn pulled a sorry face. It sounded worse than ridiculous when she said it out loud.

'I'll ask Carl, and then I'll get back to you. He's gardening just now. What was your name again?'

'Autumn.'

'I'm Robyn. I'll see what I can find out.'

'Thank you. I've been really stupid,' confessed Autumn. 'I didn't look at maps or anything. I had no idea how big this island was.'

Robyn smiled. 'That's quite common around here. A lot of people assume because it's an island it must be small. When I was a child, I remember a woman collapsing when she arrived here. She'd come on the Fishnish Ferry. It's a much shorter crossing, but it's a very long drive over some crazy back roads to get to it. It was too much for her.'

'Oh crikey, it is daunting,' *and I have a bad habit of rushing into things.* Autumn's eyes strayed to the window. A few leaves rustled by, breaking the misty view to the sea. 'I'm not sure where to start.'

'The island can take weeks to explore, but if you want to ask about for this man, you could try Tobermory. It's the main town, but it's Sunday, so some of the shops will be shut.'

'Ok. I'll go there and have a look round. Is it easy to get to without a car?'

'Without a car? My goodness. Nowhere here is easy without a car. If you walk to Salen, you can catch a bus. We have timetables at the desk, but take care. It's about a mile to the village along the main road. Carl might give you a lift if he's at a point where he can stop.'

'It's ok, thanks. I'm not sure how long I might need, and a walk will do me good.'

Autumn's boots had dried. Hopefully, they'd hold water for another day or two. Her coat was cosy from the radiator and she pulled up the collar as she made her way outside into the crisp air. Craning her neck, she could see the shore nestled under the low lingering mist. As she strode up the drive towards the village, she inhaled the clean air. Taking care along the roadside, she stepped in as a few cars passed, rushing through puddles, giving her a wide berth. She half hoped a black Freelander would go by; she wouldn't hesitate in flagging it down.

It was further than she'd expected, and she was glad Richard hadn't dumped her in the village the night before. The roadside walk in the dark would have been horrendous. Gorgeous colours glowed around, and beads of rain dripped from the leaves and branches. A small waterfall cascaded over rocks, rushing into a verge-side stream. At the bus stop, Autumn checked her messages, waiting. The pretty little village was clustered along the main road with mostly Victorian-looking buildings either in natural stone or painted white, and a few more modern houses. A shop resembling a low cabin-like warehouse with a small parking area in front drew a steady bustle of shoppers both on foot and in cars. Autumn considered going in and asking about Mike, but it would be just her luck the bus would arrive when she was inside. The wind shaved across her hair. She fished in her bag for a hair-claw, loosely sweeping wild curls off her face and clamping them back. Checking the time over and over, she bounced on the balls of her feet. Where was the bus? She couldn't have missed it again.

It arrived twenty minutes late and Autumn hurried on. Her stomach churned as the bus buffeted about. The layers of cloud lifted, clearing the sky and her brain. The sheer size of the place was overwhelming. Finding her mum would be next to impossible. Rugged coasts rushed in and out of view, gusts whipped horizontal trees and torrential rain lashed. Autumn huddled beside the window. Why would her mum want to live in such a wild place? Mum, who'd rarely been as far as Brighton. They crested a hill and the sea burst into view. White breakers chased each other over the surface, racing to the shore. This was escapism all right, but it wasn't Mum. Not unless Mike had a cellar full of wine. Autumn swallowed and rubbed her cheeks. *Could I have prevented this? If I'd been more helpful and considered my mum's needs?* But she'd spent the last few years playing out her part in Josh's miserable life, clinging to the one person who'd shown her some kind of love during her formative years. A man who used her. How clearly she could see it now. Never once had he considered her, helped her, or shown her any concern unless it affected his needs.

Stepping off the bus in Tobermory, Autumn raked her fingers through her hair, trying to contain the tangled mess in the claw against the biting wind. Heavy clouds threatened more rain as she ambled along the promenade, admiring colourful houses lining the street. On the other side, a railing barred off a pretty marina filled with boats of all shapes and sizes. Was this it? Her street in London had more buildings than the entire town.

Robyn was right: a lot of the shops were shut. A display of bright plastic toys and postcards led Autumn to a newsagent; it was a relief to get out of the wind. Scanning around, she waited until the short queue dwindled, but the assistant didn't know anyone called Mike.

She tried the small supermarket, the hotel and two pubs, but nobody could think of anyone called Mike. Cold drips pelted her from above, getting heavier. A small café in a gift shop was open and packed with people. She squeezed her way in. All the tables were full. Avoiding rucksacks and wet jackets, she hovered amongst the crowd, perusing the various knickknacks and handicrafts. A neat set of candles caught her fancy, and she inhaled the exquisite scent named Sea Kelp and Water Mint. Her eyes closed. *I need one of these.*

After buying it, she returned to the bus stop and rubbed the rain from her face, completely at a loss. Passers-by had hoods pulled right up and zips over their mouths. Autumn hadn't brought waterproofs, and she didn't own wellies. A text pinged in. She almost dropped the phone, her hands were so cold. An unknown number displayed on the screen. For a second, she thought it might be Krystina. She had a habit of changing phones, and Autumn was expecting a message after her dad's call the previous evening. Her stepmother-to-be always had to throw in her tuppence worth, making sure Autumn knew how annoyed she was. A flicker of irritation needled her. Did those threatening texts send her mum over the edge? If her dad was pestering her for papers, what might Krystina have done?

Autumn raised her hand to her mouth as she read.

A man named Michael Anderson might be living near Fionnphort. It could be the person you're looking for. That's all I know, but it might help. Richard.

She stared at it, thrown off course. Richard? Seriously? She read it several times, her brow slowly furrowing. It was beyond unexpected. She hadn't anticipated hearing from him ever again, but with this text, a balloon of hope expanded in her chest. Biting her lip, she tried to work out how to reply. Did she need to? He said clearly that was all he knew. But still, she wanted to find out more. Like where he'd got this information. Her thumb hit the green icon.

'Hello?' Answered an abrupt voice.

'It's Autumn.'

'I know. I, er, recognised your number.'

'So, I got your message. You found a Mike?' She looked out over the harbour. A broad crack opened in the clouds, letting in a blue sky. A rainbow climbed high, ending in the cabin of one of the boats. 'How did you find him?'

'I haven't found him. I asked my neighbour, and she told me about him. It might be nothing,' he said with a little cough.

'Wow, thanks.' He'd asked someone. A twig of hope dangled before her. He'd remembered her mission. 'Honestly, right now, even nothing is better than what I've got.'

'That makes no sense.' He sighed. 'But, um, I'm glad it helps.' A momentary pause. Autumn held the phone to her ear. 'You didn't say what age he was or anything.'

'I assume he's about the same age as my mum. She's forty-four.'

'*Forty*-four?'

'Yup, she had me when she was eighteen. That's part of her problem,' Autumn mused aloud. 'I guess having me so young deprived her of life.' Why had she just told a stranger that? Richard didn't reply; he was probably cringing. The rainbow faded. Had he hung up? Autumn peered at the screen. 'Sorry, I didn't mean to say that.'

'I, er, well, yes.'

'Listen, I assume buses go to Finny… What did you call that place?'

'Oh yes, there are always buses going to Fionnphort.'

'Great, I'm going now, that's brilliant.'

'Yeah, well, it might be nothing.' His voice trailed away.

'It's a place to start.' She wanted to leap for joy. 'I've been hanging around Tobermory all day not knowing what to do.'

'You're in Tobermory?' he said. 'It takes over two-and-a-half hours to get to Fionnphort on a bus from there.'

'What? Does it? Oh.' She checked the time: almost two. 'Ok, so there's no way I can get there, ask about and get back,' she rattled. 'Especially if the last bus leaves at some crazy early time. I suppose I should go tomorrow. Listen, thanks.' A bus turned the corner and approached the stance. 'I really appreciate it.' Autumn hoisted her bag onto her shoulder.

'Well,' he cleared his throat. 'If you want, I, um, well, I'm working in Fionnphort at the moment. If you wanted a lift tomorrow,' he mumbled.

'You'd give me a lift?' Her voice blurted out more like a squeal.

'Well, yes. If you want, but it's not compulsory.'

She stifled a giggle, aware she should be utterly freaked that a grouchy stranger had offered her a lift. Why then, did she feel like dancing? Hopping onto the bus, she raked in her bag for her ticket; the phone pressed to her ear. She'd uncovered a friend in the most unexpected place and, grumpy or not, Autumn was ok with it. 'I would love a lift, thank you. That is so kind.' The bus lurched and Autumn crashed into a pole. 'I don't fancy another bus journey if I can help it. These buses are like roller coasters.' She struggled up the aisle to a seat. 'And I've never had the stomach for them, especially after my friend went on one and forgot to put the bar down. Thankfully, he has a very strong grip.'

'Right. So, I pass the hotel at eight o'clock. If you want a lift, wait at the door.'

'I will, thank you.' A long silence followed.

'Yeah, well, see you.'

'Thanks, Richard. Bye.' Taking a seat by the window, Autumn rubbed her hands together, warmth flowing into her veins. Resting back, she smiled. What would her mum make of it if she turned up at the door? *Who cares?* That was a bridge to cross after she'd found her. Right now, the search was on and it was enough.

When Autumn returned to the hotel, Robyn was at the front desk. A handsome man with thick forearms leaned on it, talking to her. He ran his fingers through long blond curls as he looked up.

'Oh, hello,' said Robyn. 'How did you get on?'

'Not bad. I have a sort of lead.'

'Oh, that's good. This is Carl, my fiancé,' said Robyn. The man shook Autumn's hand. 'I asked him about Mike.'

'Yeah,' said Carl. 'I can think of two guys called Mike. There's a Mike Young who's about twenty-six, but I'm not sure he lives here any more.'

'That's too young,' said Autumn.

'The other one was an odd-job-man, he worked with my dad years ago. I don't remember his surname. I can find out, my dad'll remember.'

'That would be great, thanks. I met a guy yesterday when I arrived and he's found out about someone in Fionnphort, so I'm going there with him tomorrow.'

'Great,' said Carl. 'What's it all about anyway? Is it a relative, or are you with an insurance company or something?'

Autumn explained.

Robyn's brows drew together. 'You have my sympathy. I never had a great relationship with my mum until recently. I see Carl with his mum and I'm so jealous.'

Autumn nodded as she observed Robyn. 'You and I have a lot in common.'

'It's so hard when you've grown up not having that. It's my mum who owns the hotel. We… Well, we made up earlier in the year. I came back to help update the hotel.'

'Wow, you did a great job. It looks amazing.'

'Thank you.' Robyn checked the clock.

'I'll take the desk for a bit,' said Carl. 'If the two of you want to grab a drink or something.'

'Really?' said Autumn.

'Yes, sure,' said Robyn. 'If you like.'

'Oh, yes. I'd love that.' Autumn smiled her thanks.

Making new friends was always fun and chatting to Robyn turned out to be just that, but the meeting the following day preyed on Autumn's mind, leaving her unsure if she was apprehensive, petrified, or excited.

CHAPTER 6

Autumn

From the top of the hotel's front steps, Autumn scanned the panorama of blue. 'It is so beautiful here. Yesterday was so misty, I didn't see it properly.' After spending an enjoyable evening getting to know Robyn, Autumn was pleased to have her company again as they waited. Cool morning air played on her face.

Robyn gazed over Autumn's head into the distance. 'It is pretty, but this is just a tiny part of the island. Carl and I have a house at Carsaig now, which is several miles south of here. Maybe I'm biased, but the scenery there is incredible.'

'I bet it's lovely. Is that a seaplane?' Autumn squinted towards the jetty.

'Yes. It belongs to a man who used to be an RAF pilot. He's planned air tours for next year. I'm scared to go up in case he forgets he's not flying warplanes any more and tries some fancy manoeuvres.' Robyn smiled. 'Oh, look, is this your man?'

A black Freelander rolled down the winding driveway past the woodland and the track to a little cabin nestled close to the trees. 'Yes, it is. I hope this isn't another rash move of mine.' Autumn straightened her coat. 'I know nothing about this guy.'

Robyn pulled a side pout. 'I'm not a very trusting person, so I think you're brave. But if he's offered to help, that sounds promising.'

'I get a good vibe from him.'

'Do you read auras? I used to work with someone who did that. It's not something I understand at all.'

'No, me neither.' Autumn grinned. 'I'll stick to vibes for now and leave auras to the pros.'

The Freelander pulled up in front of them. 'Oh, he's handsome,' said Robyn, 'but don't tell Carl I said that.'

With a giggle, Autumn jumped down the stairs. 'I won't say a word and I'll see you later.'

She meandered to the passenger door, covertly examining Richard. Robyn had a point. He wasn't bad on the eye, in an unpolished kind of way. As she opened the door, she admired how tidy the car looked before continuing her visual appraisal of Richard. His grey top, hanging loose, coupled with dark cargo trousers didn't look like workwear, more like he was off for a casual wander. His thick dark hair was more kempt than before, and he had an altogether more composed air. Robyn waved from the top step.

'Hey.' Autumn jumped into the seat.

'Hi.' Richard's features tightened, and he scratched his eyebrow. 'Are you good to go?'

'Yes.' Autumn clicked her seatbelt.

'Good.' Richard swung the Freelander around and Autumn waved to Robyn before peeking into the backseat, where the dog lay sprawled. Aside from him, the car was very tidy and clean.

'Hey, Mr,' she said. The dog raised his head good-naturedly. 'What's his name? Is he even a he?'

'Yes, he's called Peppy.'

'Sweet. And what's your surname? I guess I should know who's driving me.'

'Linden.'

As talkative as ever. Still, that bubble of security formed around her again and she forgot all her lingering worries. She was determined to keep speaking, suffering as she did from a desire to fill every silence. Even if Mr Linden lacked conversational skills, she didn't. She could do this. After spending time in the company of her stepsisters, she was practised in the art of waffling, even if she knew her words were falling on deaf ears. How often had she gone into the room where they were sitting and chattered on, only to realise they were either wearing headphones or deliberately ignoring her?

'So, tell me something else,' she said.

'Such as?'

'Anything, your job, your background, your family.'

With a tug on his collar, he said, 'I'm a consultant in marine ecology.'

'A what?' Autumn tilted her head forward.

'A marine biologist, focusing on consultancy work.'

'Wow.'

'Indeed.' He fidgeted with a loose button at his neck.

'So, do you dive and stuff like that?'

He nodded. 'Sometimes I dive, yes. And other times I do "stuff like that".' He raised two fingers from the wheel to air quote.

A very different picture of him entered her mind. Autumn grinned. How good would he look in a wetsuit? Now she'd thought it, she couldn't unthink it and she didn't want to. Instead, her naughty eyes roamed over his broad shoulders, his chest and down to where his cargo trousers gripped firmly across his thighs. *You're a fit guy… nice.* Josh had been fit when they first met, but after his marriage he'd let things slip and latterly had put on a bit of weight. He obviously thought he was made, having two women batting for his attention, so he didn't bother exercising. The git. 'Em…' She cleared her throat and mentally chastised her eyes. 'How long will it take to get to Fionnphort?'

'About an hour, maybe longer.'

'An hour? Wow, so long.'

'Have you even looked at a map of this island?' Richard stared at the road like he was blinkered.

'Not exactly.' She flicked him a brief glance. 'Ok, no.'

He rolled his eyes at his wing mirror, but he was almost smiling. Silence resumed. Autumn crossed her feet, admiring her long brown boots and humming. She was making inroads, small ones, but better than nothing. The silence wasn't too awkward, in fact, it was rather enjoyable. The view wasn't too shabby on either side. *Naughty me.*

'Have you always lived here?' she asked.

'No.'

'So, where—'

'Listen,' he cut in. 'Can I ask you something?'

'Shoot.'

'You don't have any details about Michael Anderson. So, how do you plan to find him?'

'Hmm. You might have noticed I'm not a great planner. I just go with the flow. Everything happens for a reason, so I suppose the answer will come to me.'

'Right.' Richard rubbed his forehead. 'You really believe that?'

'Yes.'

'Wouldn't it be better to have some kind of plan?'

'Ok, so… How about I go ask around the shops?'

Richard nodded slowly. 'Great.'

The sarcasm wasn't lost on her. 'But?'

'Well, it won't take you long, there is only one shop.'

'Is there?' Autumn chewed her lower lip.

With an incline of his head in her direction, Richard raised both his eyebrows, his answer clear. Autumn smirked and looked away. He had the air of a disgruntled teacher.

Tall trees blocked the view on either side now. Hardly another car passed until they reached Craignure. Autumn sat up straight, taking it all in. A ferry glided in, looking super-smooth as it turned slowly towards the docking area. 'I hardly recognise this place. It was so gloomy the other night. What a difference some sunshine makes.'

'That's the garage.' Richard pointed without lifting his hand from the wheel. 'If you still want to hire a car.'

Peering out the window, Autumn wrinkled her forehead. 'I'm not sure. It looks a bit old-fashioned.'

Richard shuffled in his seat, pulling in to allow a couple of cars to go by. Autumn tapped her fingers, glancing at him every now and again. He scratched his wrist, resolutely watching the winding, narrow road for several miles. The scenery panned out to new views of the sea, boats, and trees in their splendid autumn hues; little snapshots and dramatic scenes appeared around every bend.

'Why don't you just call your mum?' Richard rubbed his neatly shaven cheek. 'Wouldn't that be the simplest thing?'

Autumn shifted to face him. 'Mum left her phone with Phil, the man she was living with, and a note saying she doesn't want to talk to anyone. She has a history of going off. She always comes back eventually, but she's never gone this far before.'

'So, how do you know she's here?'

'Her neighbour told me.'

'It all sounds a bit strange to me.'

'It is. We're not close,' Autumn huffed. 'In fact, I reckon Mum resents me.' Sighing, she trailed her fingers across her brow. She'd always been a disappointment. Vicky hadn't really wanted kids, definitely not at eighteen.

'So why do you want to find her? Why don't you let her go?'

'I can't.' Autumn gazed out the window. 'I guess I still cling to the fragment of a dream that one day I'll do enough to earn her notice, her approval, her love maybe.' The words came out more to herself.

'Does that still matter? You're an adult now.'

'I just want a chance to prove I'm worth something.'

They swung around a wide low bay; the sea lapped at the edge. 'I'm sure you're worth something to someone,' said Richard. Autumn caught his eye, and he didn't look away as quickly as before. 'Don't you have other people in your life?'

'I have a dad.'

'So, doesn't he…?'

'He's pretty wrapped up with his girlfriend and her daughters. I'm kind of the forgotten one. But it's ok, I have lots of friends who make up for it. Thing is, I lost my job and I… well, I think I had a midlife crisis.' Or maybe a post-Josh crisis would better describe it, but she didn't want to mention him.

'You're a bit young for a midlife crisis, surely.'

'I know, so a mid-ish-twenties crisis kind of thing. I had this need to do something for myself. And this is where the universe sent me.'

Richard adjusted his glasses. 'Well, I hope your mum appreciates it when you find her.'

'I guess everyone deserves a chance.'

'Do they?' Richard slammed on the brakes as a bus hurtled round a bend on the other side.

Autumn jolted forward, her hands snapped to the edge of her seat. 'I'm not sure I want to drive here, these roads are terrifying. Don't they ever get wider?'

'Not really.'

'Oh crikey, I haven't driven for years. Not since I borrowed Dad's car for a trip to Brighton about two years ago. I hated that too, I can't stand motorways.'

'So, what do you like? A nice, wide, empty road?'

'Pretty much.'

His eyes darted sideways, and he conceded half a smile. But it was gone in an instant. Autumn returned it, hoping it would come back, but he just carried on leaning his elbow on the windowsill and minding the road as they wended down a twisty section. Tall mountains towered around. The scenery was vast and rugged, stunning enough to keep Autumn quiet. She whipped out her phone and snapped purple hillsides and waterfalls. Without meaning to allow it, her mind wandered. Where was her mum in this vastness? Why had she gone to the extreme of living in such a remote location?

Richard steadied the wheel with his weather-worn hand. No wedding ring – not that it mattered, but still. He was of an age where he could easily be married and have a family, but something about him said *unattached and keeping it that way.* Autumn looked him up and down. 'Are you, um, diving today?'

'No, I'm doing shore studies.'

'Is it too cold to dive?'

He raised his shoulders. 'I've dived in colder than this. I might have to go in, but not too deep. All the deeper studies were completed last month. It's never going to be hot here even in midsummer. Not like the Mediterranean or the Pacific.'

'Have you been to the Pacific?' Autumn's mouth fell open.

He nodded. 'Yup. I've dived all over the world.'

'Cool.' She sank back into the rest. 'I've never really been anywhere. Unless you count Ibiza, and I didn't exactly see much except the inside of a bar.'

'Sounds like my idea of hell.'

She laughed. 'You're funny.' For a fraction of a second, he caught her eye and smiled dryly. It made her stomach flip. His smile transformed him, rendering him ruggedly handsome rather than grim.

As the car descended into a valley, the terrain opened out. The sea appeared again, in a flat expanse between two landmasses. Autumn imagined romantic scenes of days gone by. Every view framed something new, remote and wild. On a low-lying strip of land between the road and the sea was a herd of highland cows, shaggy coats thick with mud.

'Shouldn't they be in a field?'

'Most of the livestock roams free here. That's our rush hour.'

Autumn smirked. 'Nice one.'

Richard pulled on the indicator and drove over a narrow bridge. 'Just don't get too close to them if you're out wandering. They're usually ok, but don't test that hypothesis.'

'Are you serious?'

He tilted his head to the left, curling his lip. Of course he was. He was always serious. She was learning.

'The views are stunning, but it must be a tough place to live.'

'Oh, there are lots of good things about living on an island,' mused Richard. 'Peace is number one.'

She shook her head. 'Don't you like company?'

'Not especially. People are fine as long as I'm not with them and they don't talk.'

Autumn mimed zipping her mouth shut. Richard's lip twitched. A ping caught her attention and she pulled her phone from under her leg and checked through her messages.

'The signal is patchy, but it gets better at Fionnphort. Lots of places have no signal. At my house, I only get reception near the front window. You were lucky when you called yesterday, I was standing right there.'

'That must be a pain.'

'Not at all,' said Richard, with the tiniest hint of a smile. They caught up with a bus and followed it around several bends. In the distance, another coach was snaking its way along the edge of a rocky outcrop. They continued for several miles until they reached a long straight road, with scrubby fields on either side, still following the two buses. Autumn checked her phone again, attending to a message from Priya. The car slowed, but she was engrossed in her message. Sensing they'd turned, she looked up. Gravel crunched beneath them as the car drew to a stop.

'We're in a car park? I thought this place had a beach.'

'It does, you missed it when you were messaging. I'm walking back that way. If you're going to the shop, it's that way too.'

Heading for the boot, Richard opened the back door for Peppy. His dark hair ruffling in the wind, he pulled out his backpack and equipment. Autumn followed, absently stroking Peppy's bristly head, her eyes travelling over Richard's kit. 'What's all this stuff for?'

'It would take weeks to explain.' Glancing at her, his brows lifted. 'Possibly longer.'

'Oh, right.' She smiled. 'Maybe another time.'

'The shop's down there.' He hoisted a large backpack over his shoulder.

'I'll wait for you.' She placed her hands in her pockets as a gentle breeze tickled her neck. The longer she could prolong their moment of parting, the better. Once he'd gone, she wasn't sure what she'd do. Her confidence was ebbing away.

The car park was half full and newly tarred. An exhibition centre was on one side and some modern white houses lined the road to the sea on the other, but no other people.

'Let's go.' Richard balanced the last pack on his back, resembling a hiker heading for a month in the wilderness. Peppy trotted in front as they marched down the hill to the main road. Opposite was a long, steep grassy bank, leading to a wide grey sandy bay with an enormous, cracked boulder in the middle of it. 'That's where I'm going.' Richard pointed to a hill on the far side of the beach. Peppy was halfway down the embankment, sniffing. 'There are some bays and rock pools. I'll be there all day. Are you coming back with me? Or getting a bus?'

'I eh… I'm not sure. I don't know how long it'll take.'

'Well, let me know when you decide. You have my number. The shop's right there.' He indicated across the road.

'Thanks, Richard.' Autumn tilted her head, suppressing the mad urge to hug him. Where were thoughts like this coming from? A reaction to Josh? Meet a nice man, go from friendly chat to hugs in sixty minutes? Where would that lead? By the end of the week, they'd be married with two kids at that rate. Smiling at her craziness, Autumn added, 'I appreciate this.'

He blinked rapidly but held eye contact. 'You're welcome.'

'Bye,' she said, as he turned towards the beach.

'Bye,' he muttered.

Autumn sighed and made to walk across the road.

'And good luck.'

Spinning back, she caught the end of his wave. Instead of crossing to the shop, she stepped to the edge of the verge, watching him striding down the hill. He made short shrift of the rabbit holes and mounds. Soon he was on the beach. Peppy bounded around, showing off his gangly legs.

Richard's long, lean figure diminished as he made his way to the other side. 'What a curious man you are.' With everything unfamiliar surrounding her, she wished he was still there. She scanned the eclectic mix of buildings, old and new, on a low hill descending to a slipway in a small harbour area.

The shop stood out with its signs swaying about in the wind. Edging her way past a couple of people inside, Autumn lingered at the shelves. The queue dwindled. She sensed she was one of the few people remaining. Grabbing a newspaper, she dropped it on the counter. 'I wonder if you could help me,' she asked the man at the till. 'I'm looking for a Michael Anderson. I believe he lives around here. I'm trying to get in touch with him.'

The man scanned the newspaper. 'Never heard of him, sorry.'

'Is there anyone around here who might know?'

The man shrugged. 'A pound, please. Maybe someone at the pub? It opens at twelve.'

Leaving the shop with a sinking sensation, Autumn flopped onto a bench beside the road. So that was it? All this way for nothing? What to do now until twelve o'clock? Her thumbs slipped across her phone as she ran a search for Michael Anderson, adding Mull, Fionnphort, and lots of other combinations. All came back with nothing useful. With a sigh, she gazed over the turquoise sea. The sun edged out and the wind eased, making it quite pleasant. Further down, some people waited at the slipway for a small ferry. Where was it going? Perhaps it was drifting out to sea. She knew the feeling.

Pushing her hands under her legs, she scanned around. Barren rocks jumbled with patches of green and little white houses were scattered around. The place had an end of the road remoteness about it. *Is this the end of the road?* How much further could she expect to get with so little information to go on? A line of coaches and cars parked across the road didn't fit. Where had the people gone and what were they doing? Autumn swung her head to keep her hair out of her face. Should she knock on some doors? She balked at the thought of explaining herself over and over without sounding idiotic.

'Are you the girl who's trying to find someone?' A voice spoke behind her. Autumn spun round. A woman with a large carrier bag came out of the shop, adjusting a scarf under her chin.

'Yes.' Autumn jumped to her feet. 'Michael Anderson, do you know him?'

'No, can't say I do, but you see that little house down there, the one with the blue door?' She pointed towards a higgledy-piggledy cluster of white cottages perched on the hill beside the shore. 'If you call in, old Mary MacLean lives there. She's lived around these parts forever and knows everybody. If your man is around here, she'll know him.'

'Oh wow, thank you so much, I'll go straight away.'

'By the way, she's in her eighties, a bit deaf, and she likes cakes.'

'Brilliant.' Autumn turned back to the shop. 'I'll get some.' Ten minutes later, she knocked on the blue door, bouncing on her feet, praying it would open.

A tiny white fluffy head poked around and smiled at her. 'Hello? Are you lost?'

'Eh, not exactly. Are you Mary MacLean?'

'I am. Should I know you, dear?'

'No. I just heard you were the person around here to ask about other people. I'm looking for someone, you see, and I wonder if you can help me.'

'Come in.' Mary opened the door. 'I'll boil a kettle.'

It was such a warm welcome, Autumn's spirits lifted. 'Thank you. I brought these.' She held up a box of French fancies.

'Oh marvellous, I can see you're my kind of girl.'

Taking off her boots, Autumn followed Mary into the hallway; the bristly beige carpet tickled her feet. 'What a view.' She navigated the small but bright living room, edging past a brown armchair. Mary indicated she should sit at a tiny table wedged into the space in front of the window.

'Never tire of it,' said Mary. 'But it's not like it used to be. Cheeky so-and-sos come knocking on this door asking me if I'll sell the house, I thought you might be one of them. Been offered good money but I've had this cottage for years, I'm not giving it up now; they'll be taking me out in a box.'

'Quite right, this is a lovely spot.'

'Certainly is, but it's packed with tourists, worse than ever. All heading over there, of course.' Mary pointed with her thumb to the little island beyond. 'Stream through this village like nobody's business. It's a bit better now the summer rush has died down. I'll just pop out and put on a cup of tea, hope that's alright, don't keep coffee, never liked the stuff.'

The sea lapped at the beach, mesmerising Autumn with its slow rhythmic beauty. Mary returned and laid the tea, fetching a plate from a small sideboard.

'Oh, what a treat.' Mary eased into the chair opposite. 'Very few people visit me these days, the village has changed so much. So many incomers, you hardly meet anyone from the island now.'

'That's a pity.' Autumn opened the packet of cakes and arranged them on the plate.

'So, who are you after? Tell me about the person you're looking for and I'll see if I can help.'

Where to begin?

Mary stirred her tea, nodding her encouragement.

'It's my mum…' Autumn began the story. The little ferry dotted back and forwards as she told Mary everything.

'Dear oh dear,' said Mary through mouthfuls of cake.

'That's how I ended up here.'

'Yes, you need to find her, it'll be good for both of you.'

'Maybe.' Autumn bit her lip.

'Hmm, now Mike.'

Autumn screwed her lips into a sideways pout. 'There was possibly a Michael Anderson. I heard there's someone around here called that.'

Shaking her head, Mary nibbled on another cake. 'The only Anderson around these parts I can think of is William Anderson. He used to work on the boats but he must be retired now, lives over the hill, in a croft Knockvologan way. His wife died, oh, a long time back.'

'Hmm.' Autumn pursed her lips. 'It doesn't sound right. It's definitely not William.'

'I'll keep thinking, though I'm not sure how to get in touch.'

'No problem.' Autumn fished in her bag and pulled out a business card. 'This is my phone number.' She scribbled it down.

'Wonderful. Oh, is that your name? Autumn.'

'Yes. Sorry, I should have said.'

'What a beautiful name, suits you with the red hair and all.'

She tossed it over her shoulders, cheeks a little pink. 'Thank you. My birthday's in October, I guess my parents thought it was cool.'

Mary smiled. 'And it is. Now, where will you go after here?'

The view drew Autumn's attention again. 'I should go and ask in the pub and if I get nothing there, I suppose I'll get the bus back and try something else.'

'Did you get the bus? I thought you came with somebody.'

'I did, but he's working all day. I wouldn't like to ask him to do any more. I don't know him well enough.'

'I'm sure he wouldn't mind, you're a very pretty girl.' Mary lowered her head and raised her eyes.

Autumn gazed towards the beach. 'Thanks, I can see what you're driving at, but really, he isn't like that.'

'He must be a kind man, and I'm sure he wouldn't mind.'

The carriage clock on the mantelpiece chimed 12 o'clock as Autumn left. Had she talked for that long? Glancing to the beach, she half hoped to glimpse Richard striding back, but the sand was bare.

A stream of people wandered through the village, aiming for the pub. She followed, ready to ask her question again. But after spending an hour there for lunch, she left with nothing new. Nobody could think of anybody called Mike. She'd been offered Callums, Duncans, Roberts and a Douglas but not a single Michael.

CHAPTER 7

Richard

Seabirds circled high above the hidden beach. Their distant cries blended with the gentle rush of white horses chasing each other ashore. Peppy sniffed around boulders and investigated the waves as Richard placed samples into a small tank, enjoying the endless tranquillity. A high-pitched ringing broke the sound of the waves, the birds, and the putt-putt engine of a fishing boat. He guessed who it was. Why had he suggested she call him? He didn't need that kind of interruption. The work phone was bad enough. Managing a team of seven stationed around the Hebrides was adequately challenging without this. At the same time, he couldn't abandon Autumn. He'd thrown himself smack bang into someone else's business and this was the result. *Only myself to blame.* No one ever called him on his personal phone. His work colleagues knew better. Emails were always a safer bet.

The ringing stopped. Richard scratched his cheek, trying to focus. His muscles tensed. After gazing at his sample for several minutes and seeing nothing, he straightened up. What if it was an emergency? He couldn't concentrate without knowing what she wanted. Marching across the sand, he pulled out his phone from the front of his backpack and hit call. 'Hi.' Peppy joined him, sliding his wet nose under Richard's hand.

'Hi, how's it going?'

'Ok.' He flexed his fingers, then patted Peppy. 'I'm really busy.' His tank lay woefully empty; so much still to do, and the deadline was getting perilously close. So unlike him. Bad weather had already hampered progress, not to mention the trip to America. 'So, what's up?'

'Well, I've hit a brick wall. I'm not sure what else to do,' Autumn said. 'I think I'll get the bus back.'

'Right, ok. Just check the timetables.' He scratched his eyebrow, pacing, the phone glued to his ear.

'Haha, yeah. I will. Listen, thanks so much.'

'Yeah. No worries. And good luck.'

'Thanks… Well, bye.'

'Bye.' He slung the phone into his back pocket and reverted to his samples, ignoring the pain in his chest. Was that it? He searched his backpack for the iPad. 'What happens now?' he asked Peppy. 'I just let her walk away? I should. I mean, she's a stranger, just someone I was giving a lift.' He sat on a jagged piece of rock and let out a long sigh. Peppy rested his head on Richard's thighs and peered up with his big brown eyes. 'I should message her,' Richard said, trying to shake his brain into action. 'It's not her fault she fell in with the most anti-social bloke on the island.' He tapped a quick text.

Will be leaving 4ish if you miss the bus or change your mind.

Returning to the tank, he carefully removed small pieces of seaweed and photographed some specimens, adding notes and willing his concentration back. If any unwanted subject threatened to break in, he recited the seventeen times table. It had worked at school in the bad old days to zone out the bullies, so quick to tease the lanky geek with the spots and outsized glasses.

He lost track of time, as he often did when immersed in his discoveries, and determinedly ignored his phone. His research teams' work had been described as impeccable, meticulous and ground-breaking. He'd built a reputation. Now it had been said it couldn't be unsaid, and the pressure was always on to live up to it, again and again. When the time came for discussion and team analysis, he'd be ready. But social interactions distracted his mind from the facts. Coupled with his appalling sleep pattern, he wasn't getting on half as well as he wanted.

Finished with his latest batch and ready for the next, Richard glanced towards the sandbank. Someone was coming. Red hair tangled around in the wind, gold buttons glinted, a neat, petite figure in long boots and a smart purple coat. *She found me.* Hot tension spread in his stomach. Peppy darted forward, greeting Autumn with a wagging tail and a nose rub. She giggled and patted him.

Here she was in all her glory. Now he was in trouble. Helping a stranger was one thing, finding her attractive was another. Her card should have gone straight in the fire, but he'd thrown himself in instead. He'd never been a great lover of company. His previous relationships had been born out of an inability to say no rather than a desire for companionship. Autumn's company was a whole new ballgame. She'd filled his normally long dull drive with laughter and light. Annoying questions and chat too, but it was bearable. Maybe even enjoyable. To the point where he couldn't let her walk away. Not yet. But to what end? *Just helping, that's all. She's not staying. There's nothing to worry about.* Ruth had told him years ago he'd never find anyone who would put up with him again and he shouldn't inflict his company on anyone. Lorraine had used him for her pleasure and laughed when he'd expressed his hope of furthering their relationship past the *sex whenever she wanted it* stage. He was a serious mess when it came to women, so he'd jumped off the bus and was doing just fine on his own. Absolutely damned fine.

He loosened his jacket. The wind had eased, which was why he felt warm. A perfectly logical explanation. Autumn had obviously decided on a lift. On the way home, if she asked questions, it didn't mean he had to reply. He was at liberty to keep himself to himself. She was leaving at the end of the week, so it wouldn't matter if he made up a pack of lies to get rid of her. It wasn't as if they were going to be seeing a lot of each other. *Seventeen times five is eighty-five,* he recited. Where should he look? *Seventeen times six is one hundred and two.* There was no escape. She was heading straight for him. Stumbling over some boulders, she pulled her hair off her face. *Shit.* She was so damned beautiful; it was like watching a TV commercial for expensive perfume.

'So, you found me.' He folded his arms, his jaw stiffening as he attempted a smile, but it was embarrassing. He wanted to see her as Autumn the stranger again, not Autumn the stunning woman who was distracting him just by existing.

Autumn beamed, raising both her eyebrows. 'I did. I tracked your footsteps all the way here, and I didn't get lost.'

He swallowed and rubbed the back of his neck. 'Is that some kind of achievement for you?'

'It certainly is. I've lived in London all my life and I still get lost there, especially at the Seven Dials. Nightmare.' She fake-smacked her forehead.

'Hmm, I know the place you mean. It's a bit of a maze.'

'Not half.' She cast her eyes over his equipment. 'This all looks so professional.'

'I am a professional.' He pulled a fake smirk. 'It's my job, remember.'

'So, what's it for?' Autumn patted Peppy, beaming at the dog as though he was a precious child.

Richard shook his head. This stuff took years to learn. How could he summarise in a few seconds? 'It's, well…'

'Yes.' Autumn's expression lit with curiosity.

Richard's arms stayed staunchly folded. 'It's for surveying coastal and inshore ecosystems. I'm examining the impact of kelp dredging in the area.'

'Kelp?' Autumn repeated, but her expression said it all. She may know everything about luxury home goods, but this was so obviously out of her field. She peered into the tank resting on a large flat boulder. 'Ooh, what's that?'

'Don't knock it over.'

'I won't, I'm just curious. What's kelp dredging?'

Richard knelt beside his tank. 'I can tell you later. I'm really busy. What time is it anyway?'

'Just after two.' She checked her phone.

'So, I guess you're not getting the bus.' He didn't look up. It was best not to. What he saw made him feel things he didn't want or need, emotions he'd shut away for years, for his own good.

'Didn't you get my message?'

'I haven't checked yet.' He raised his eyes to see her smiling sweetly. 'Sorry.' He couldn't imagine a way to make her look more perfect. *Seventeen times seven is… one hundred and nineteen.* She didn't belong here. She belonged to the city with its fashionable ways and bright young people. 'I had lots to do.' Why was his heart thumping so hard? 'If you don't mind waiting until I finish.'

'Sure.' Pulling some strands of hair from her mouth, she sat on a large boulder.

'But not here!' he protested. 'Why don't you go for a walk or something?'

'I won't interfere.' The corners of her lips tweaked up. 'I'll just sit here quietly.'

'Is that even possible?'

'Let's see.' She crossed her legs and stared out to sea.

He swallowed, his mouth dry. The waves crashed loudly on the craggy rocks, breaking and gushing white foam about them. It was not distracting enough. His gaze wandered to the boulder. Autumn perched on the edge, her slim legs crossed like a model on a photo-shoot. Peppy lay at her feet, quite content. Richard dropped back to his tank. He had to focus. *Seventeen times eight is… one hundred and… thirty-something-or-other.*

'What island is that?' asked Autumn.

'I thought you were being quiet.' Richard scoffed. 'And are you for real? That's Iona, one of the most famous Scottish islands.'

Autumn gave a pert shrug. 'Why is it famous?'

'Look it up on your phone. It's the birthplace of Christianity in Scotland. Thousands of people come here every year on a pilgrimage.'

'Oh, that's why there were so many buses, and Mary said lots of people flooded through the village. I get it now.'

'Who's Mary? And are you going to stop talking?'

'Do you want me to answer that, or stop talking?'

He glanced up; surges of energy spiked through his nervous system. Stretching her legs, Autumn smiled an innocent smile. Richard pulled a fake one in return. 'I suppose I have to resign myself to this for the next few hours.'

Autumn swung her legs and hummed in agreement. The wind whipped around, wiping the grin from her face, and she hunched over. Richard could barely hear what she was saying. Her soft voice blended with the beat of the waves until he realised she was behind him. 'Kelp is seaweed, right?' she said.

'Yes, in the simplest form. It's an algae seaweed.'

'It's really good for candles. Does it grow here?'

With a frown, Richard stood, towering over her. He pointed towards the sea. 'Out there.'

'Underwater?'

'Yup. Huge forests of it. But if you want to use some to make candles, you can pick it up all over the beach.'

'Show me what it looks like.'

He walked a few metres down the beach and picked up a long slimy brown piece of kelp. Autumn screwed up her nose. 'I haven't a clue how it goes from this to candle form,' said Richard. 'That's your domain. If you want to take some with you, I'll give you a sample bag and you can collect it.'

'Ok, cool.'

He pulled out a clear bag and handed it to her. She wandered down the beach, combing around with Peppy sniffing at her feet. Back at his tank, Richard tried to keep focused, but his eyes strayed over the top of the tank. He forced them down. He had to stop looking; it was pointless and distracting, but also impossible. He couldn't look anywhere else. Autumn bent over, examining the kelp, then sat on the boulder and checked her phone. She shivered as she scrolled.

'Take this.' Pulling off his jacket, Richard offered it to her.

'But you'll freeze.'

Not a chance. He was burning up. 'I'm fine.' Turning his back to her, he ignored the wind biting his neck and the twisted knot growing in his gut. He was assisting a helpless stranger, as anyone would. Nothing more to it. Nothing at all. The fact she was the most attractive woman he'd seen in… Well, a long time, was an unfortunate coincidence. Convincing? Not in the least. He was at the top of a slippery slide. One push and he'd be straight down, but he wasn't sure how to walk away now he was here.

CHAPTER 8

Autumn

Wrapped in Richard's forest green Trespass jacket, Autumn observed him as he worked. This jacket had a fragrance all its own. She wanted to capture it and make it into a special candle just for her. It would be something to curl up with on a chilly night and keep her safe from harm. She pulled the jacket close around her and whiled away a few moments trying to think up what she would call the fragrance. Sea Spray? The Heart of the Hebrides?

Maybe she could weave it in with something in her bag of kelp. Why was she doing this? Picking up random bits of seaweed and googling everything she could do with it? It was useful stuff but not in her world. Only in her dreams. Her mind wandered to her mum. What had ever attracted her to a place like this? Or was it, like her dad said, all a piece of nonsense? She dropped her hand and stroked Peppy. 'Is my mum on the island?' she mumbled. Peppy nuzzled into her. 'Or should I just forget about trying to find her here?'

Richard stood and stretched, holding his hands high. His grey top lifted an inch from his belt line. Autumn trailed her finger along her lip. What tight obliques he had. Not bad for a scientist. But he must be a powerful swimmer if he could free dive. What else was he hiding? Not that it was any of her business, but it didn't stop her from wanting to find out. *Reckless, impetuous and impulsive.* She bit her lip. 'I should be sensible,' she whispered to Peppy. 'But he's fit.'

Richard checked his watch and Autumn dropped her eyes to her phone.

'That's enough for the day,' he said.

She jumped off the rock, shaking her hair away from her face. Peppy leapt to his feet too and padded towards Richard. 'I can help,' said Autumn. 'I can't stand idly by while you lug all this equipment back to the car.'

'I do this on my own all the time, I don't need—'

'I know you don't *need* help.' She swung off his jacket and held it out. 'I'm just offering.'

He nodded. 'Keep the jacket, you need it more than me.' Busying himself with the packing, his gaze stayed down. When everything was stowed, he lifted a bag from the sand and handed it to her. She shouldered it and started walking. As the bag strap held his jacket tighter around her, the sense of being protected and secure clung to her.

'Just don't drop it.' He hoisted the rest of the baggage onto his back.

'I won't.'

He flicked her a small and ironic smile before setting off.

Despite the layers, a shiver ran through Autumn. Out of the cove, the wind was ferocious. Richard strode off, his long legs carrying him at a pace quicker than she was used to. Peppy bounded on ahead. Autumn ran to keep up. How could anyone walk that fast? Heads down, they battled across the boulders and scrubland towards Fionnphort. 'I can hardly stand. This wind.' Her boots sank into the stubbly grass as she jogged along, her breath cut by the heavy blasts.

'We're nearly there.' Richard's words swirled away. Moments later, he stopped and waited, scanning over her. 'Sorry, it's brutal if you're not used to it. Walk behind me.' He set off again as soon as she drew level. Easier said than done: he could take part in a land speed race with those strides. But he was a good windbreak; Autumn cowered in behind. 'Are you ok?' He turned back, slowing so she could keep up.

'Yes, but you walk so fast.'

'It's my legs versus yours.'

'Well, can you pretend to be a dwarf or something then?'

He gave a little smile and slowed his pace. Peppy waited at the hilltop beside the road. Richard hopped up beside him and put out his hand. Autumn curled her fingers around him and held on. He pulled her the last bit and didn't let go. 'Thanks,' she gasped.

'Let's keep walking. When we get to the road between the houses, it's more sheltered.' His thumb grazed the edge of her wrist before he released her hand and strode off again.

What a relief to get out of the wind. Autumn's hair felt like a tangled rug. 'Do you think I'll ever get a comb through this again?' She teased out some strands, peering at it.

'It looks… fine.'

'Does it?'

Autumn bit her lip as Richard skimmed over her. 'It would benefit from the services of a brush, but no one will mind. It's a fairly common style for around here.'

'I bet.'

'Just leave that behind the car.' Richard pulled off his pack and indicated Autumn to do the same. 'And can you let Peppy in, please?'

'Sure.' She opened the door and Peppy hopped onto the backseat. Once he was settled, she took off Richard's coat plus her own and got in the front. 'It's cold in here now.' She pulled the coats over her legs like a blanket.

'I'll put the heating on.' Richard started the engine. 'There's a warmer jacket in the back.' Swivelling round, he stretched through the gap and his face came close. He blinked. Autumn smiled, unsure. It was an attractive face, but she shouldn't really be looking. He might be spoken for, and here she was eyeing someone else's husband or boyfriend. He hadn't said one way or another. Maybe another half was waiting at home, not appreciating his helping a lost stranger. Unwanted visions of Josh and his pregnant wife interrupted her train of thought. Richard grabbed a blue checked shirt with a thick sheepskin lining and passed it to her. 'There.' Turning away quickly, he adjusted the heating.

'Very snuggly.' She wrapped it around herself, closing her eyes for a second and nestling into it.

Richard clenched the wheel tightly and pulled off. Loosening the neck of his top, not looking left, he coughed. 'So, do you still want to know about kelp dredging…'

'Oh yes.' She smiled at him from her dreamy nest.

'Well, the Hebrides are surrounded by huge kelp forests. They're some of the most amazing habitats in the world. Diving there is incredible. I've had some indescribable experiences and made some remarkable discoveries in there.'

Autumn's eyes widened at his animation. This was like a different man.

'Kelp is a useful and increasingly lucrative product,' he said.

'I know. It's in lots of candles and soaps.'

'So you see why companies who make these products on a grand scale would be interested in these forests.'

'Yeah, I get where this is going.'

'Exactly. Kelp harvesting has become a big thing. In Norway, it's wiped out huge sections of their kelp forests, because not all companies are sensitive to the environmental importance of the forest ecosystems. Some companies use industrial dredger boats to cut it. This system is quicker and more cost-effective than traditional and less-invasive methods, but it's highly damaging.'

'And you're trying to stop it?'

'My team is investigating the impact.'

'Oh, I thought you worked alone.'

'There are eight of us, including me. I'm managing the project, but we have research stations all around the Hebrides.'

'That's good then.'

'It is, but people will do anything for money. And some experts will overlook important facts to secure their inflated pay cheques. Even former acquaintances of mine have been ensnared. They don't fake the results, they just omit certain parts.'

'Yikes. I don't like that. I'm glad you're one of the good guys.'

'Hmm.'

'So, who do you work for?'

'I'm working for an environmental group. They want me to prove it's damaging enough to ban it. I have to quantify it with conclusive evidence. It's not easy, and it takes time. I'm presenting my team's findings to the Scottish Parliament at the end of the year, so I don't have long to complete it.'

'Well, I suppose they asked you for a reason. You must have the right credentials.'

'I do.' He stared at the road, then cast her a little wink.

'Of course you do.' Autumn grinned before gazing at Fionnphort as it disappeared. The wind swirled and the waves chopped about, colliding in great peaks. It was cosy to watch from her warm bubble.

'So.' Richard gave a little cough. 'What are you going to do with the kelp? Do you make candles for a living?'

Autumn let out a giggle. 'I wish, but that's just a crazy pipe dream. No, I don't have any exciting skills like that. I just work in shops and that kind of thing.'

'You should try making your own. Lots of people here use kelp in island-made products. Soap, seafood, even gin.'

'I'd like to try, someday.'

'Do it. You'll never know otherwise. If you start as a hobby, you can learn as you go along and minimise the risks. Just see if you enjoy it. You already have experience in selling products, so you have a head start. A lot of people go into craft and creative businesses but don't know much about the selling part.'

'Maybe, but I was just working in a shop, not exactly setting up online retail or anything.'

'It still counts. You'll understand more about it than most people and you can adapt your skills if you have to.'

'I suppose.' She smiled at him, a little puzzled at his faith in her, but her chest inflated with a sense of possibility she'd never known before.

'I assume you didn't find your mum,' he said.

'No.' Autumn raked her hair in a bid to detangle it. 'I met a sweet lady called Mary, but she couldn't think of anybody called Mike. I asked in the pub, and the shop, but it was all a blank. So here I am, still with nothing more than I had this morning.' *Except for an ever-increasing crush on a stranger.* He'd just given her more encouragement to follow her dreams than anyone in her life ever.

'Weren't you going to knock on every door?'

Snuggling deeper into his jacket, Autumn said, 'I couldn't, it didn't feel right.'

As he pulled in to let a car pass, Richard tapped the wheel. 'You realise it could take ages to find her like this? How long do you have?'

'A week.'

'It'll be a miracle if you pull that off. You could join an online forum and ask on there. There are lots of groups for locals. Or google him.'

'That's a good idea about the forum. I did google him, but there was nothing.'

'Well, don't be too blunt on the forum about who you're searching for. If your mum doesn't want to be found and sees your messages, that won't exactly help you.'

'Oh, yeah. Good point. You're smart.'

'Thanks. I think.'

'I'll consider what to say. You know, I do appreciate this, really.'

'I haven't done anything.' He adjusted his glasses. 'Except listen to you talking non-stop for the last few hours.'

'Fine, I'll be silent for the rest of the way.' She mocked being put-out.

'You expect me to believe that?' His smile suited him so much. His shoulders relaxed momentarily. He had barriers, enormous brick walls and it wasn't her business to know or care why, but having him there to talk to was such a relief.

Autumn's stomach rumbled. 'Pardon me. Must be the sea air.' She rubbed her midriff. 'I wish I'd bought a snack. I don't suppose there's a takeaway on the way home.'

'No. But there's an Inn at Craignure, they might give you some chips.'

'Great.' She beamed.

'I mean, I'll stop. You can go in and get some.' He made it clear: no way was he going in. But she wasn't about to quit that easily. He'd laid the gauntlet neatly at her feet and she was ready to pick it up.

'Really? You don't want to come in? I'll buy, as a thank you.' She cocked her head.

'Eh no, I don't need a thank you.'

'Why not? I mean, I don't want to keep you from anyone if you have other plans, but a meal would be nice. You can tell me more about kelp.'

He flexed his fingers on the wheel, his neck reddening. 'Actually, I do have plans. I'm resting my ears.'

She quirked her eyebrow. 'That's not good enough,' she teased.

'Sounds great from where I'm sitting.' He assumed an innocent expression.

'Nope. Not good enough. Chips with me is much better.' She smiled. 'Unless someone really is expecting you home. If there is, just say.' No way did she want to end up with another Josh-gate on her hands. If Richard had any kind of partner, she was out of here. The disparity in their lives wasn't lost on her, nothing could happen here in the long term, but she wasn't about to risk anything, not even for one day.

He considered his wing mirror and nodded. 'Hmm,' he muttered. 'The fishing expedition.'

'Maybe it is… So go on, bite.' She trained her focus on him, unwavering, waiting until he glanced back.

'Ok, well, it's my mother.' He gave a little cough. All trace of humour faded. 'She has my tea ready at six every night. I don't like to keep her waiting.'

Autumn's eyes almost popped out their sockets. *No way!* Worse than anything she'd suspected. Living at home with his mother! Dinner on the table? *Really?* 'I'm sorry.' At his age, that couldn't mean anything good. Had she stumbled into some kind of Norman Bates reality?

A smile welled on his left cheek. 'That was actually a joke.'

'What?' She slapped his thigh, making him jump. 'Really?' Mr Deadly-Serious-the-Grouch had pulled one over on her? He shook his head with a proud grin. Autumn couldn't believe it. 'That's it. Now you have to go.' She folded her arms and stared.

'Or what?'

'I'll think of a suitable punishment.'

'Oh yeah?' Laughing, they looked at each other for too long before Richard swerved into a passing place just in time to avoid a white van.

*

Forty minutes later, Richard pulled up in front of the Inn and grabbed his jacket. Autumn followed him across the car park, watching as he scratched his neck and fidgeted with his collar. Peppy loped along at his side.

'Looks cute,' said Autumn. Richard pushed open the thick wooden door and ducked under the low beam, holding the door. Autumn headed straight for the bar and picked up a menu from behind two locals. 'Is the food any good?' she whispered to Richard's chest. He was so tall. Everyone was tall to someone of her lowly height, but he towered above her. The sea breeze still lingered on his loose grey top. She inhaled it. *Mmm, better than any luxury candle anywhere.* It embodied a relaxing sense of calm and safety.

'No idea, I've never been in here before.' He took hold of Peppy's collar.

'Are you serious?' She gaped at him. Was this another of his 'jokes'?

'Quite.' He squinted over her shoulder at the menu, hugging his jacket in his arms like a shield.

'And do you really live with your mother?' His incapacity to lie had seemed absolute. Had that been a covert cover-up in the shape of a joke?

He tilted his head. 'No. I most certainly do not. Anyone who's met my mother would understand why.' His dark eyes twinkled as she peered into them.

'So where does your mother live?'

Letting go of Peppy's collar, Richard lifted his glasses and rubbed his eyelid. 'Do you need to know?'

'No, but you could tell me anyway. It's just a friendly question.'

A large hand clapped him on the shoulder. Richard almost dropped his glasses as he spun around. Autumn was wedged between him and the bar.

'A'right, Richard mate, I've no' seen you in here before,' said a man's voice. 'And Peppy. Where's my favourite big boy?' He clapped the dog all over. 'You want to come back and stay with your uncle Ron, aye?'

'Hi, Ron.' Richard replaced his glasses and Autumn edged out from behind him.

'How's it going? What you doing in here? Come and sit wi' me. In fact, you owe me still.' Ron grinned at Richard.

'For what? I settled up fair and square after the last job.'

'Not work. Remember that little wager we had on who would win the rally? Loser buys the drinks. I'm still waiting for my beer.'

'What? Oh… that.'

Ron chortled, his broad belly shaking under his black heavy metal t-shirt. 'Aye, now you remember.'

Autumn peered around, smiling. Ron goggled between her and Richard, his grin broadening. Richard pinched the bridge of his nose.

'Pardon me,' said Ron. 'Who have we here? Hello there.' His left eyebrow wriggled towards his bald scalp, and he stretched out his heavily tattooed arm.

'I'm Autumn.' She shook his thick hand.

'Autumn, well, well.' Ron glanced at Richard and turned down his lips. With a little wink, he nodded.

Richard looked away, his jaw clenched. 'She's um…' he muttered.

'No need to explain.' Ron fake punched his shoulder. 'I'll let the two of you get back to your business. Don't mind me, my drink can wait, I see there are more important matters at hand. Very nice to meet you, Autumn. See you soon, Peppy.' Ron gave Richard a huge thumbs-up before joining a large group in the far corner.

Keeping his head low, Richard muttered, 'This was a bad idea.'

Autumn squinted at his reddening cheeks. What did that mean? Was this Josh-gate starting over? 'Please tell me you're not married,' she said. 'Does he think I'm your bit on the side?' The phrase made her wince. She'd been that for far too long.

'God knows what he thinks, and no, I'm not married. Let's order,' said Richard.

After they'd chosen their food, Autumn lifted the drinks and beelined for a quiet table in the corner, far from Ron and his friends. With a chuckle, Ron raised a glass from his table. Autumn sent back a small toast and took a seat. 'Who is he?'

'Not the master of subtlety.' Richard sagged into a seat with a sigh. Peppy huddled under the table. 'He skippers my boat if I need someone to take me out and he dog-sits when I travel.'

'You have a boat?' Autumn stared wide-eyed.

'Yes.' Richard dropped his head, running his fingers through his hair. 'A cabin cruiser named the Silver Moon.'

'So, do you travel a lot with work?'

'Not as much as I used to.' Richard's gaze darted towards Ron's table and back.

'Why does he want you to buy him a drink?'

'Because he made some silly bet with me. I don't know one rally driver from another, so I was never going to win. But that's Ron for you, he's always up to something. He borrowed some books from me ages ago and never returned them. Now, he's sitting over there sniggering at me.'

'I'm sorry.' Autumn smirked. Richard was sweating this. 'I don't think he's sniggering at you. He's happy for you.'

'Why would he be?'

'Because he thinks you're on a date.'

'I know he does.'

'So, what's the problem? Let him think that. What's the worst he can do? If he spreads a rumour about you, so what? I don't see why you wouldn't be allowed to go on a date.'

'No one said I wasn't allowed, it's just… Well, this isn't a date.'

'I know.' Autumn smirked.

Richard took off his glasses and placed them down. His eyes wandered to Ron and he frowned. Autumn crept her fingers across the table and tapped the top of his hand.

'Hey,' she said. 'Thanks for today.'

'Yeah, no worries.' Seemingly absent-mindedly, he lifted his thumb and brushed it over the soft spot between her thumb and forefinger. Each stroke trebled her heartrate. Richard stared into the middle distance, apparently oblivious to the seismic eruptions he was causing inside her. She let out a little whimper. Had she died and gone to heaven?

'Ohhh,' she moaned, forgetting herself and he jerked his hand away with a sudden realisation at what he'd been doing. 'Yeah, better stop.' She giggled. 'If you carry on like that, we might have a *When Harry Met Sally* incident.' Only it wouldn't be fake.

'What?' Richard shook his head. 'I think I left sanity behind when you arrived on this island.'

'Must be in the air because I did too,' she smiled, raising her glass. 'Cheers!'

'Cheers.' He raised her a toast.

Raucous laughter from across the room pulled Autumn's gaze back to Ron. 'He looks like the type who knows lots of people. Maybe he could help me find Mike.'

'Why not go ask him? I'm sure he'd love to help you.' Richard cast her a wry smile.

'What, as much as you?' Autumn imitated his sarcasm.

Turning to the window, Richard gave a lop-sided grin. 'Yeah, that much.'

'Well, ok, how about I take him a drink and say it's on you? That'll pay your debt.'

Richard gave her a searching look, then pulled out his wallet and handed her a tenner. 'Take that, then it really is on me. Thanks.'

Autumn crossed to the bar and ordered a beer. Ron roared with laughter, shaking everything on the walls. With a deep breath, she took the beer and headed towards his rowdy table. A few moments in Ron's company yielded loads more laughs, but no useful information. Some of his drinking buddies shook their heads, brows furrowed, expressions of great concentration as if working out some tricky calculations. Maybe they should phone a friend or go 50/50?

'Ok, great,' said Autumn. 'And, Ron, now Richard's paid his debt, you can give him his books back.'

'Aha! Yes!' he roared. 'I forgot. I'll drop them off in a couple of days. Naughty me. Feel free to give me a good spanking.'

'I might pass on that,' said Autumn, returning to Richard.

He glanced up. 'No luck?'

'No.' She slumped into her seat.

'Your phone just rang.'

'Oh.' She woke the screen. 'I don't recognise the number.' She held it up. 'Someone wanting me to buy insurance, I expect.'

'That's an island code, maybe it's your mum.'

'You think? That would mean a whole new level of organisation on my mum's part. Like she'd have to have my phone number with her, which seems highly unlikely.'

Richard took a sip of his soda water. 'I begin to understand where you get your planning skills.'

'Very funny.

'So what did Ron say?'

'Nothing sensible, but he's going to return your books in a couple of days.'

'You asked him.'

'Sure.' Autumn spun her phone around. 'Oh, look, there's a voicemail, so it can't have been Mum, she never leaves messages.'

'Why not listen to it and find out?'

Autumn put it on speaker and waited.

'Hello… it's Mary… Oh dear… I, eh… I'm not good on these message things. I remembered somebody, a Michael from Fionnphort… I think you could call me… no, what time is it? Oh dear, no, best not. I don't answer the phone after six, always get these funny things. I'll call you tomorrow morning and let you know… Right… how do I stop it? Er, goodbye…'

'Oh my. Should I call her?'

'Wait until tomorrow,' said Richard. 'She said she never picks up after six.'

'I guess, but how about…' Autumn peered up with a grin. 'Are you going to Fionnphort again tomorrow?'

'I am.' He raised his left eyebrow.

'Maybe I could come with you?' She fluttered her lashes.

Richard slowly nodded. 'You could.'

'Yay.' She clapped her fists together.

With a vague smile, Richard drew back as a dinner plate landed in front of him. 'So, what will you do?' he asked.

'Go and see Mary, find out what she knows, then go hunting I suppose, if she has an address.'

'Here's hoping you find the right person.' Richard raised

his glass. Autumn clinked it and smiled, focusing on him. It felt like she was looking at exactly the right person, just not the one she was searching for.

CHAPTER 9

Autumn

'You're up sharp again,' commented Robyn from the reception desk, as Autumn strolled to the front door. 'Did you have any luck yesterday?'

'Sort of. Well, I have a lead.' She leaned on the desk. 'I went to the pub last night with Richard.'

'Oh?' Robyn's eyes widened. 'That's nice.'

If Autumn could find a way to transfer Richard to London, she'd ask him out. Not that she'd ever asked anyone out before, but she'd brave it for him. So much about him appealed to her in an abstract and inexplicable way, but he was in the wrong place at the wrong time.

'Oh, I forgot to mention this,' said Robyn. 'You might have seen the flyers for our quiz night here tomorrow evening. You're welcome to come along, and feel free to invite Richard.'

'Thanks. I might ask him, but I don't get the impression he enjoys that kind of thing.'

'I know how he feels. I don't enjoy big social things either.'

'Really? You seem pretty sociable to me.'

'I've had a steep learning curve this year.'

'Oh.' Autumn glanced out the door. 'There's Richard, I better go.'

'Good luck,' said Robyn.

Autumn nipped down the stairs and jumped into the passenger seat, adjusting the waistband of her white jeans.

'Morning,' said Richard.

'Hi, and hey, Peppy.' She leaned around and patted him before smiling at Richard. 'And how are you today?'

He pulled off before Autumn had fixed the seatbelt. 'Fine, you?'

'Good, thanks. Have you recovered from last night?' Autumn clicked the buckle and looked up.

'Me?' He turned out the drive onto the main road. 'I wasn't the one knocking back the wine.'

'I know, but you didn't want to go for food originally. I thought maybe it had traumatised you.' Autumn peered at him. He seemed to be struggling not to smile.

'I'll live.'

'Are you mad at me?'

Richard's eyes darted sideways. 'Should I be?'

'No. In fact' – she clapped her knee – 'you are going to be proud.'

'Why?'

'Because look how prepared I am. I have a map and a compass, I found them in my room.' She held them up.

'And do you know how to use them?'

She laughed. 'Not really. Well, I can read a map… Sometimes.'

Glancing sideways, he gave her a *seriously* smile. It made her laugh. 'Will you need them for walking around the village? It's tiny.'

'Best to be prepared.'

'And what happens if you find her? Are you going to try to persuade her to go home with you?'

'I don't know. I just want to talk to her and check she's ok.'

'Will she want to see you?'

'Maybe not, but I'm trying to focus on the positives. Even in the mess of life, there's usually something to laugh about.'

He frowned. 'Interesting idea.'

'It stops me panicking too much about the future. I feel so lost sometimes. I blame my parents,' she joked, though maybe it had more than a kernel of truth. 'They weren't great role models.' And then she'd had Josh and clung to the idea he'd lead her somewhere sensible.

'You aren't defined by your parents,' said Richard.

'But sometimes… I guess I just feel lonely. I know it's silly because I have lots of friends, but no one really to guide me.' The reason she'd wished Josh would provide stability, and security. How wrong had she been?

'Yeah, it's hard when there's no one to confide in.'

'I just muddle along with friends mostly. I had a yoyo childhood. My mum's been addicted to alcohol since I was twelve. I lived with my dad until he got his latest girlfriend. She didn't like me, so I tried back with Mum again.' Always to and fro, never really belonging anywhere.

Richard slowed the car, approaching a bend.

'My dad's getting married in December.' Autumn tapped her finger on the windowsill. 'I'm surprised it's taken him this long. That's why I missed the bus, because I was on the phone to him. So technically it's his fault you're saddled with me too.'

'How thoughtless of him.'

'Indeed. So, there you have it. Now you know everything.'

'A physiological impossibility. But I am now in possession of a lot more facts about your private life than I expected to be after knowing you all of two days.' He swung the car into a passing place.

'Knowledge is power, Richard. Think of how you can use that information.'

He smirked. 'So I can blackmail your mother if it turns out the Mike she's run off with is a billionaire ex-rock star?'

'Exactly. Now you're getting with the programme.'

'Who would have thought it?' He side-eyed her and shook his head. 'After thirty-seven years of being a social outsider, I'm finally getting with the programme, though I'm not sure I know exactly which one.'

'You're funny.'

'Me? I think you've mistaken me for someone else.'

'You definitely have a hidden joker, which is good because being miserable doesn't help anyone.'

'I guess not.'

'But I do sometimes wonder why my mum left the first time. It's something that never goes away. How could she leave me like that when I was only twelve? Life's tricky enough at that age.' Autumn picked at a thread on her white jeans.

'It is.' Richard seemed to weigh the information with a slight sway of his head. 'Maybe she had a breakdown.'

A string of cars whooshed by as they waited. Autumn let out a long sigh and rubbed her forehead. 'Maybe she did. And I know people say it's never the child's fault, but what if it was? I can't help feeling somewhere along the line I messed up. I've never been academic or anything like that. Maybe I was a disappointment to her. Those times I didn't do my homework, went to friends without asking and stuff like that.'

Richard looked over as another car passed, then laid his hand over hers, pressing it into the seat. Autumn inhaled as the pressure of his palm increased. It was like he'd discovered a secret route to her soul and held the key to a magic door. A tingling warmth spread through her limbs. 'None of this is your fault. It's just…' His brow crinkled. 'Don't let the sins of your parents affect you.' The wipers swished, streaking the windscreen. 'Be proud of who you are.' After a brief squeeze of her hand, he let go and pulled out of the passing place. 'Not everyone's academic. And those of us that are, don't have the skills you have.'

'Like what?'

'Practical skills like buying and selling. People skills like kindness; smiling; putting people at ease; talking…'

'Funny.'

'And true.'

With an appreciative smile, Autumn glanced at her hand. The skin was warm where he'd touched her. His words flowed into her veins and her heart blossomed like someone had nurtured it from seed and it had finally flowered. Whatever he saw in her, he believed she was someone worthwhile. It made her want to fling her arms around him and hold him tight.

'You know what I did when I got back last night?' said Autumn.

'No.'

'I looked up ways of getting kelp into candles but the information isn't very clear.'

'I've got a lab in my shed, I'm sure we could find a way of doing it.'

'Are you serious?'

'Deadly. Though I'm not sure when we'll have time.'

'Hmm, yeah.'

'I need to do some analysis later this week. If you find your mum and you want to come round, well…' He gave a little shrug.

'Wow. That would be great but it's not that important.'

'Sure it is. If it's just a matter of drying the kelp, it shouldn't be too difficult. I'd rather kelp was used to fulfil your dreams than to line the pockets of the industry CEOs.'

'Thanks.' She clasped her hands under her chin and did an internal dance. This was too good to be true. He was offering to help her turn her dreams into reality. Even if it was just a little step, it was better than anything she'd achieved so far.

As they approached Fionnphort, misty clouds eclipsed the views from the day before. Richard parked and Autumn got out, pressing her lips together and thumbing her ear. The wind bit into her. Huddling up to Peppy, she watched Richard take out his equipment. Going to the beach with him was what she really wanted to do. They could talk about kelp, or anything really. She just wanted to stick with him, get to know him some more, and enjoy his company. When he was around, she felt whole.

He took a step back and almost stood on her toe, she hadn't meant to get quite so close, but he was like a magnet. 'Sorry. Do you want to borrow this?' Holding up a black waxed jacket, he looked her up and down. 'It's more waterproof than, well, the thing you're wearing.'

'Ok, thanks.' She put it on over her coat and it fell to her knees. Glancing at Richard, they exchanged a smirk.

'Just watch, the zip jams. Though you've got the knack so it should be ok.' He flicked her a tiny wink before hoisting on his last piece of equipment and slamming the boot.

'I thought I'd freaked you out with the zip incident.'

'You did. But you also fixed the zip. Another of your skills.'

'A dubious one.'

Together they walked down the little street to the main road and across to the embankment edge, neither one talking, Peppy trotting ahead. Autumn bit her lip. What to say? Since their exchange in the car park, Richard had gone closed and quiet. 'That's Mary's house there.' She pointed. 'I wonder what she's remembered.' She was back at the end of the road. Everything was dull, gloomy and hopeless. Gazing over the empty beach, she scanned the scattered rocks and cottages. Her focus fell on Richard. He was watching her. The temptation to throw in the towel and stick with him almost overwhelmed her.

'Well…' He swallowed.

Autumn fiddled with the hem of the waxed jacket as she studied him. Should she hug him? It would give her reassurance. But she doubted he'd appreciate it. 'So, I'll see you later. I might have to walk somewhere depending on where this person lives, but I could meet you back at the car, or would you prefer me to get the bus?'

'No, meet me. And text me, let me know what happens.'

'I will.'

They faced each other and Autumn's heart raced. With a slight nod, Richard turned towards the hill. Autumn swung her bag over her shoulder.

'And Autumn.'

'Yes?'

He walked back. 'Why don't you take Peppy? If you need to walk somewhere, he'll be company. If not, come to the beach, I'll be close to where I was yesterday.'

'But will he come with me?' Autumn bit her lip as the dog frolicked on the embankment.

Richard called him, fished in his pocket and put him on a lead. 'Peppy, you're going with Autumn. Be a good boy, take care of her.' He handed the lead to Autumn and Peppy panted like he was laughing, wagging his tail. 'There, that's better.'

Autumn clutched Peppy's lead, then stepped towards Richard and landed a playful punch on his arm. 'Thank you.'

With a small smile, he raised his fist in return. She knocked her tiny knuckles against his broad ones. 'Take care,' he said, giving Peppy a quick pat before starting down the hill.

A hollow pang ached inside Autumn as Richard descended the embankment. She wished he would come back. Peppy nuzzled his head under her sleeve and she snuggled him. 'I feel like I've just said goodbye to an old friend.' Not someone she hardly knew.

Rain dripped off her hood and played a rapid rhythm on the rocks at the side of the path. Finally she tore her eyes from Richard's retreating back and strolled with Peppy towards Mary's cottage.

'Goodness, what a surprise.' Mary beamed, letting her in from the rain. 'I was about to call you. Who's this?'

'Peppy. Is it ok for him to come in? He's Richard's dog, but I'm borrowing him to keep me company.'

'Oh, what a lovely idea. Yes, he can come in, though there's not much room. Maybe he could lie in front of the fire.'

Autumn took off Richard's jacket and hung it behind the door, feeling like she'd shed several pounds. Mary pottered around, fussing Peppy and making tea. 'What a good dog, but what a lot of room he takes up.'

Sitting in an armchair, Autumn held out her feet to the cosy blaze. Peppy licked her toes and she giggled. 'This is lovely.'

'So, after our chat yesterday.' Mary laid out the tea tray and sank into an armchair. 'You set me wondering. I was thinking about William Anderson, and I remembered he had a son. Now I can't be sure, but he might have been called Michael.' Mary shook her head, staring into the fire. 'Of course, he might have left, most young people do. I don't always hear about it these days.'

'What age is he?'

'Oh dear, let's see, William is probably ten years younger than me, so Michael could be forty, maybe fifty.'

'Thank you.' Autumn tapped her finger on the table. 'This could be it. I wonder if he has a phone number?'

'I can check the phone book.' Mary bustled off and came back with it. 'I suppose there's a way of doing this on fancy computers these days, but I like good old paper.' She scanned down the page and shook her head. 'No, he must be ex-directory. A lot of people are. I am, otherwise, I get all these calls about selling the house.'

'Oh dear, yes. That's not good. Is the croft somewhere I can walk to from here?'

'Yes, you can, but it's a long way over a hill. It'll take you at least an hour each way, maybe longer. I haven't done it for years. Well, I can't walk to the shop these days without feeling like I've hiked about a hundred miles.'

'Oh, Mary, bless you and thank you so much.' Autumn leaned over and held the old lady's hands. 'I have Peppy to look after me.' Autumn's eyes wandered to the clock on the mantelpiece. 'So, I'll give it a try, and if it gets too much, I'll just turn back. I enjoy walking.'

Mary's wrinkled forehead puckered in the middle and she drew in her thin lips. 'Take great care.'

'Thank you, I will.'

Swamped in Richard's jacket, Autumn left the house with Peppy. Rain drove into her as they advanced towards the car park. Passing the Freelander, they continued up the track towards a wild hillside. 'Here.' Autumn unclipped Peppy. 'You won't run away, will you?'

A vibration caught her attention. Drips fell on her phone screen as she checked it. She tapped out a quick response to Priya's wondering how she was getting on.

AUTUMN: Following some leads. I met a man who's been helping me out with lifts. I'm setting off to look for a possible Mike.

A pain rose in her chest. What was she doing, disappearing into the wilderness when she should be in London, looking for a job, and a new flat? She didn't want to face it.

'I guess I shouldn't take any selfies, no one should see me in this state.' Her horror the previous night when she'd caught herself in the mirror was enough. *I went to the pub like that!* Laughing at the recollection of her wild hair and wind-burned face, she ploughed on through a gate and beyond, pulling the jacket collar close to her cheeks. She was glad to have it, not just because it provided some relief from the cold driving rain, but because she had a piece of Richard. If only he could have come with her. She stroked Peppy as a message pinged back.

PRIYA: A man is helping you? What kind of man?

Autumn couldn't help grinning. What kind of man indeed? Stopping to shelter her phone from the rain, she tapped a reply.

AUTUMN: A kind one! He's lent me his dog and his jacket. And he's going to help me dry some kelp to make candles with. So even if I don't find Mum, I've got something to look forward to.

She hummed what she thought sounded like a Scottish tune. It carried far out to sea on the prevailing wind with a melancholy air. Pulling up her hood, she trudged along the path, head bowed, tapping out a text to Richard. He'd want to know and she may as well, while she still had reception. Would the phone still work out in the wild? A text came in.

PRIYA: Holy crap, sounds like you're crazy about each other. I hope he's young and handsome, not a sixty-year-old with no teeth.

Autumn grinned, feeling like a high school kid with a crush as she replied.

AUTUMN: Yeah, he's nice and I like him, but I'm only here until Saturday so I better be sensible!!

Short blasts of wind whisked the sea to her right. No cars, no signs of life. The vegetation was limited to low shrubbery clinging to craggy rocks. Autumn clapped her raw hands, wishing she'd brought a pair of gloves. Plodding up a hill, she squinted through the rain. Angry blasts drove her back, and she stopped, gulping air as she read Priya's latest message.

PRIYA: To hell with sensible! You get in there, girl!

Laughing, Autumn climbed a small ridge at the side of the path and surveyed the huge expanse of emerald scattered with jagged rock clusters. Peppy nudged up beside her and she rested her hand on him. The clouds thinned; the driving rain eased. The scene unfolded as she inhaled the salty air. Her hood fell back, and the wind plumed and tangled her long curls out behind her. After a few seconds, she hopped down and carried on along the rising track. Ahead were the outlying signs of farm buildings. She could ask someone there. Relaying this to Richard, she clipped Peppy onto the lead and quickened her pace.

A rumbling sound attracted her attention as she approached the large stone barn. Peering around the doors, she smelt silage and the pungent aroma of cattle. A man hung from a tractor, shouting. 'Bring it in, I'll set it up in here.' He looked around as Autumn approached. Was she allowed in here? It probably breached all health and safety regulations, especially with a dog in tow.

The tractor engine rumbled to a halt. The man jumped out. 'Are you all right there? Can I help you?'

'I'm sorry to bother you, I can see you're busy.'

'No problem, what can I do for you?' He took off his woolly hat and ruffled his shaggy white hair. 'Are you lost?'

'I'm trying to locate someone called William Anderson. I was told he had a croft up here. Do you happen to know where?'

'Aye, Wullie! Yes, I know where he lives. Are you walking?'

'Yes.'

'You've got a fair bit to go but keep on this path for half a mile or so, then there's a shortcut. Here, let me draw you a map.' He clumped over to a workbench covered in objects Autumn couldn't imagine a use for. Maybe just as well. Some of them looked like torture instruments. She winced. From the chaos, the farmer pulled out a grubby reporter's notepad and a biro. Scrawling on it, he produced a little diagram of how best to get there. He ripped it from the notepad and passed it to her.

'Thank you, that's helpful.'

'Are you a relation?'

'Not really, it's actually his son I'm looking for. You don't happen to know him, do you?'

The farmer scratched his head, scrunching up his features. 'Wullie's a bit of a recluse, I don't see him about. Someone visits him with shopping, it could be his son, but I'm not sure, sorry.'

'That's ok, and thanks for this.' She waved the drawing.

'When you cross the field, some of it's a bit boggy, just go round the wet patches.'

Armed with the little map, she set off, avoiding a huge muddy puddle on the track. The tractor thundered back into action and Autumn set Peppy free again.

A further message pinged to Richard. What would he be doing? Autumn threw back her head to inhale the clear air. It was good to know he was somewhere back there in the distance. Ploughing towards the top of a hill, she stared about, suddenly warm. She took off Richard's jacket and draped it over her arm. Was it remotely likely she was going to find her mum here? If Vicky had agreed to live somewhere this isolated, she would regret it. There was nothing for miles.

Cresting the incline, Autumn gazed over another stunning vista of the wild sea far below. White birds circled a tiny fishing boat, dotting between the rocky outcrops, miles away. Breathtaking. She took out her phone and snapped a picture, which didn't do it justice. Revolving the camera, she took a selfie with Peppy, sending it to the only person she didn't mind seeing her in her current state.

She checked the scribbled map and made her way along a little path to the left. It entered a scrubby woodland via a rickety stile. Peppy scrambled over. Autumn followed, jumping off the bottom step and squelching into the wet ground. 'Yuck.' Her boots were half covered in mud. 'Maybe a shortcut isn't a good idea, and what possessed me to wear white jeans?'

Peppy bounded ahead, sniffing excitedly. Unbuttoning her coat, Autumn sploshed along the path while the sun sat high above; it had turned warm. Carrying her bag, Richard's jacket and her own coat was a pain; collectively it felt like they weighed more than she did. She patted her back pocket, checking her phone was still there.

Crossing another stile and pushing through bushes and low branches tangling over the path, Autumn came to a large open field. On the far side was a ridge; bent, gnarled trees grew along the edge. She made her way across, following Peppy, his nose to the ground. 'So, where now?' No paths were visible. She checked the scribbled map. 'I think this is right, but how do you get down?' She scrambled along the ridge until she came to an opening. 'Is this it?' *So steep.* Stray branches and broken twigs littered the way. At the bottom, it looked like another field. Peppy nosed forward, sniffing around the undergrowth. Tentatively, Autumn picked a path down, speeding up only to keep her feet. Momentum carried her further and faster than she intended.

With a gut-wrenching jolt, she tripped. The world flipped upside down, Autumn's hands flailed, her breathing stopped. She couldn't make a sound. It was like she'd been put in a barrel and shaken until she landed with a splash. Lying face down at the bottom of the hill, she peeled herself from the marshy, wet ground.

Kneeling in the soggy patch, limbs aching, she held her cheeks. A wet nose prodded her in the shoulder. 'Oh, Peppy. Help.' A low snort made her peer up. Beyond a row of bushes, three mud-caked highland cows clumped towards her. 'Oh my god.' She gasped, scrabbling around desperately to reach her phone.

CHAPTER 10

Richard

Sun shone on the hidden beach at Fionnphort. Richard searched the shoreline with his trousers rolled up, and the cool clear water lapping at his ankles. Taking his time, he looked carefully, examining the area, stopping at regular intervals and hopeful places, but nothing was right. The clear water may as well have been filled with thick mud. His stomach muscles gnawed and contracted. He couldn't concentrate. How ridiculous! It had to stop. 'Seventeen times nine is… one hundred and something,' he muttered, bending over and lifting a net full of seaweed.

Maybe not having Peppy was bothering him. The sense something was missing wasn't unusual. In fact, he couldn't be sure if this pain was new or an intensification of the chronic guilt that attacked him every day. The ache of wondering if he'd made the right decision regarding his son.

Returning to the pop-up tent with his samples, he spied his phone flashing, *6 new messages.* Why had he checked? Six? Discounting them, he emptied the contents of his net into a tank. But it was impossible. Now he'd seen the messages, he couldn't ignore them, and he had told her to text him, though he should have specified to stick to important updates. Lifting the phone, he swiped it open, sitting inside the tent door.

AUTUMN: Hi, how's it going? Mary told me William Anderson has a son possibly called Michael. I'm walking with Peppy to the croft to look. It's in a place called Knock-vol-au-vent or something… I can't spell it and definitely don't ask me to say it!

Knockvologan? Richard pinched the bridge of his nose and squeezed his eyes shut. *She's walking there on her own, in those boots, with her sense of direction?*

AUTUMN: Thanks for letting Peppy come with me. What a good dog he is. I might have to steal him.

Richard sighed. *With my track record, I'll end up letting you walk away with him.* Just like he'd done with his only child.

AUTUMN: It's wet and chilly, just as well I have your jacket!

AUTUMN: Can see a farm, will ask there. Some amazing views up here.

AUTUMN: Guess what! They know where William lives! But it's miles away, going to keep walking. The farmer told me about a shortcut and drew me a map.

'Shit, no.' Richard dropped his head into his hand and massaged his forehead.

AUTUMN: It's pretty here but flipping heck… don't think we're ever going to get there… how do we look!!??

'How do you look?' He stared at the smiling photo of Autumn and Peppy's huge nose too close to the screen. What answer could he give without opening a trapdoor and falling straight through? Why was she asking him that? Did she want the truth? *You look bloody gorgeous.* He'd never met anyone who caused such cataclysmic eruptions inside him with just a smile.

He put the phone back on the floor and rubbed the nape of his neck. After writing a few notes, he lifted it again. Should he reply? Would that just encourage her? He'd never finish if she kept up like this all day. His thumb hovered over the screen. What to say? He put the phone down again. Maybe she'd find her mother and after the reunion, she'd leave the island for London and that would be that. Back to the daily grind, no more disruption, he'd be alone, the way he was used to. *Seventeen times ten equals one hundred and seventy.*

At the shore, he adjusted one of the posts he'd used to mark out the area he was surveying. A tightly tied rope showed him a perfect rectangle. The camera. How had he returned to the sample area to photograph it without bringing the go-pro? *What is the matter with me?* Jogging back to the tent and unzipping it, he fished around, spying the phone again. Snatching it up, he replied quickly.

RICHARD: How's the shortcut?

After about half an hour, he gave up. Nothing was going right. He couldn't make head or tail of his finds. He needed a break. Packing everything away, he jogged back to the village and deposited the bags in the Freelander. He would work on some analysis on the iPad until he heard back from Autumn. Coffee would help, so he headed towards the shop. An elderly lady approached him at the door. Richard tried to look elsewhere but she was examining him.

'You're the man who brought Autumn here.' She peered at him through her sharp discerning eyes. 'I saw you with her on the beach yesterday. You're Peppy's owner.'

He rubbed his neck. 'Yes.' How did she know that? Sometimes people on this island knew someone had sneezed before they'd had time to wipe their nose.

'I'm Mary, Autumn might have mentioned me. She brought your lovely dog to see me this morning. What a gorgeous boy he is.'

He nodded. 'Yeah, he is.'

'Autumn's walking to William's croft, you know. I really wish she hadn't, I know she has your dog to keep her company, but it's such a long way and so difficult to find if you're not familiar with the area.'

'Maybe I should go and look for her.' Richard searched the horizon.

'Yes, please do. I'm very worried about her.'

Back in the Freelander, Richard started the engine and drove up the hill. The Bluetooth was on. He called, but it rang out. Where was she?

CHAPTER 11

Autumn

Sitting on a sharp boulder, Autumn didn't care it was cold and painful. Head in her hands, she let tears fall. Totally pathetic, but she couldn't stop. Her body shook, awash with emotion and discomfort. Peppy hung his head until Autumn opened her arms. He rushed to her, and she sobbed into his neck until it turned to almost manic giggles. 'Oh, god. I'm covered in mud. It's up my leg, it's in my boots, and my ankle aches. I hope it's not broken. If those cows come over, I need to get away.' Though outrunning them was out of the question – especially now.

She looked up, trembling and pulling herself together. 'Where's my coat? And Richard's jacket? And my bag? I must have dropped everything.' Her teeth chattered. The flimsy fabric of her striped navy top stuck to her horribly. Peppy nosed her as she rubbed her hands together; they were black with mud. Her ruined, formerly white, jeans clung like she'd wet herself and her feet were numb. The thick cake of mud coating her lower leg brought back the tears. 'They're my favourite boots and I don't have any more with me.' Using her fingertips, she prised down the zip and massaged her ankle through her sodden socks. It stung.

'I need help,' she shouted to the treetops. 'Possibly psychiatric. Why else would I be here? Oh, Peppy.' He lowered his head again. 'I've been so rash. I can't blame Mum, Dad, or anyone else this time. It's no one's fault but my own. How am I going to get out?' The ridge was steep and her ankle throbbed. She hobbled on it, as the cows lumbered along behind the row of gnarled bushes and low trees. 'And of course, my phone has no reception. This is a disaster. Peppy! Oh, no.'

Peppy took off up the embankment at breakneck speed.

'Come back! Oh, god.' *If I lose Richard's dog too.* 'Peppy! Come back!' She scanned around. Where had he gone? He must be at the top, he could be through the field by now, anywhere. 'PEPPY!'

Tremors shook Autumn all over. With a racing pulse, she forgot the pain in her ankle and made a desperate lunge towards a tree root, if she could tug herself up, she could reach a flat bank just above and maybe get up from there. Blackspots clouded her vision as she strained to put weight on her ankle. She collapsed back. This was hopeless. 'PEPPY!' She yelled so hard her lungs might explode.

There he was, at the top of the ridge amongst the wind-battered, horizontal trees like something from *The Hound of the Baskervilles.* 'Oh my god!' Autumn crumpled with relief. He wasn't alone. Richard stood behind him. Autumn waved both her arms above her head.

Richard scrambled down, slipping on the muddy slope, but it didn't hinder his progress. Peppy bounded on ahead, reaching Autumn in seconds and greeting her like a long-lost friend. 'Oh, god, you are the cleverest dog in the world. You found him.' She swallowed as Richard approached, shaking his head as he closed the gap between them. 'How did you know where I was?'

Staggering forward, she put her arms about him. She needed a hug, whether he wanted it or not. Her eyelids dropped as she leaned on his chest, the waffle texture of his top soft on her cheek.

Stiffly, he splayed his fingers on her back. 'I tracked where you must have gone from your messages. I was crossing the field when Peppy bounded out. I followed him. Did you fall?'

'Yes.'

'How did you not break your neck?' Richard's hands slipped away; he stepped back and stared.

'I don't know. I sort of ran the first bit. It got so steep, I couldn't stop. I tripped and rolled into the marsh. Look at me. I'm covered in mud, I hurt my ankle, and I dropped my bag and the coats somewhere.'

Richard shook his head; his brow furrowed in either disbelief or relief.

'I've been so stupid.' Autumn held her hand to her forehead.

'You're tenacious, I'll give you that. The shortcut didn't sound like a great idea. I thought I should come and help.'

'Thank goodness you did. I'm so out of my depth.' Autumn threw back her head, shaking her damp, tangled mane. 'I feel totally useless.'

'You're not useless, you're just not used to this island.'

'I'm so glad of all the people I could have met, it was you.' She stared at him, taking him in properly. He was so tall, dark, and ruggedly handsome. He really was. But above all, he was kind. Tugging at her soaked top, she flapped the edges, hoping to dry it, but it was so cold.

'It's a miracle you haven't broken any bones.' Richard surveyed the hill.

'Maybe I have. My ankle aches. I shouldn't have done any of this.' She scanned her mud-caked boots and jeans.

'It's just dirt.' Richard looked her over. 'What about your ankle?' Do you want me to check if it's broken?'

She stared at him, taking in his firm jaw, his well-proportioned nose, his dark eyes glinting. 'Can you do that?'

'Well, I am a doctor.' He raised his eyebrows. 'Now, sit down and let me see.'

'Are you? I thought you were a marine biologist?' She sat back on the boulder, frowning.

'Yes, and I have a PhD in Marine Ecology, though it's unlikely to be much use if your ankle's broken.'

A tiny smile escaped the corner of her lips. Richard crouched and unzipped her boot. She held her breath as he put his hand on her ankle, then flinched, but not at the pain. He pressed it gently with his thumb and she bit into her bottom lip. 'Nothing is sticking out and you can put your weight on it, so let's assume it's not broken.' He pushed his glasses up his nose and peered up.

'Is that your professional opinion?'

'It's as good as it gets.' He stood. 'Zip your boot back up, that'll support it.'

She did as he suggested before standing to test it. He hovered around, perhaps wondering if she was going to fall over. 'Ok, you're loadbearing, that's good, but I need to find your coat, or else you'll freeze.' He scanned the hill.

'This top is ruined,' Autumn muttered, flicking her fingers down it.

'You could wear mine. I don't think it smells.' He pulled out the neck and sniffed it.

'What?' Autumn's heart thudded, threatening to crack open her ribcage.

Before she could say another word, Richard tugged off the top. Autumn wanted to look away but she couldn't. The tight white t-shirt he had on underneath accentuated well-rounded pecs, a powerful chest, and broad shoulders. *Oh, no. Stop drooling.* As he passed her the top, her fingers trembled.

She clutched the soft fabric, caressing it gently. *Should I strip off too?* Richard was contemplating the hill. He was ridiculously fit. Freckles covered the muscles of his upper arms, highlighting every curve.

Turning to consider her, he rubbed his jaw. 'Somehow you have to get up there.'

'I think I can do it, slowly. But you might have to help me.'

'What do you think I've been doing for the past two days?' He raised his left eyebrow.

She held his gaze, feeling butterflies.

'Put that on, I'll find the coats.' Peppy, sensing they were on the move, roamed off, sniffing.

'Richard.' Autumn grabbed the taut sinew of his arm. An electric shock surged through her, forcing her to let go, but she really wanted to touch him again.

'What?' He swallowed. They stared at each other.

He was on the verge of moving when Autumn pushed onto her tiptoes, and unable to resist, slipped her hand round his neck and pulled him towards her; just for a grateful peck on his cheek, nothing more. What harm could it do? She caught the edge of his lips. 'Thank y—' She froze, incapable of getting the word out. He'd moved slightly and was returning the kiss, softly but enough to send a buzz zipping through her chest. This was beyond everything she'd imagined. Autumn was almost lifted off the ground as he supported her back and her head. He tipped her gently, deepening the kiss. Lingering, slow, intense, and wonderful. Autumn's heart stopped; she didn't want to let go. A cloud of bliss encircled her.

Richard pulled back and planted Autumn's feet on the mossy undergrowth. His eyes roamed around.

'I didn't mean, you know… I just wanted to thank you,' she mumbled.

Richard turned away, placing his fingers over his lips. 'Me neither, I just… Well, yes… Sorry.' He swallowed. 'Come on, look, there's your bag.' He trekked up the hill and lifted it. Groping around, he shoved the fallen contents inside. The back of his neck was red. He swung the bag over his shoulder and searched around for the jackets.

With shaking hands, Autumn took off her wet top. *Please don't let him look round now.* She pulled on his top. It did smell. His sea breeze aroma was now all over her and the fabric on her chilled skin felt unhelpfully sensual. Wallowing in it, she hugged herself.

He scrambled back wearing his waxed jacket and handed over her coat, not focusing anywhere near her. 'Let's move. If we walk along here, it's not as steep at the other end.' He whistled Peppy, keeping his gaze fixed forward, his weather-worn cheeks redder than usual.

Autumn followed, trying to keep her thoughts level. Her fingers were numb and quivering, making it impossible to fasten her coat. *What the heck just happened?* Richard was striding away at a speed she couldn't keep up with anyway, never mind with her aching ankle. She didn't dare call him back. Her face was hot. What an idiotic thing to do. She wanted to stamp her foot until the earth quaked, but the pain in her ankle increased at the thought.

Richard stopped; Autumn continued to struggle along until he hurried back. 'Sorry, I just wanted to check ahead. Here.' He didn't look at her but took her arm. She kept her eyes low. The cold clag of wet clothes against her wasn't as unsettling as the thought of what had just happened. Not because she hadn't enjoyed it… She had, maybe just a bit too much. It changed everything. No more pretending they were just two strangers rubbing along. They were two people with a hefty crush and a powerful attraction. Autumn could vouch for both on her side, but what about him?

'We can get up here.' He held her tight under the arm. 'Come on, you can do it. You might need to scramble.' He squinted sideways, not meeting her eyes.

Inhaling sharply, she put her best ankle forward and allowed him to drag her up the steep ridge, fingers scrabbling for roots and branches to aid her. The pain in her ankle smarted. 'Ow,' she gasped.

'Here.' With a swift movement, Richard swept the feet from under her. Another shock of electricity zipped through her as she clung tight around his neck, her head bumping his shoulder. He carried her the rest of the way, and deposited her on the firm, flat ground at the top. 'There,' he said, 'take a rest, you shouldn't overdo it.'

Dazed and confused by pain and everything that had happened, Autumn forced her breathing back to normal. 'Richard, I have to apologise, I—'

'Don't apologise.' He shook his head. 'I understand.'

'You do?'

Nodding, he adjusted his glasses. 'Sure. People do unexpected things in tough situations. It's mostly adrenaline and cortisol. Sometimes they get us out of trouble, sometimes they don't.' He thrust his hands into his pockets and peered around.

'Or maybe I'm just an idiot.' She dragged back her hair and held it on the top of her head. 'I mean, what am I doing here at all?'

Richard's eyebrows snapped together. 'You're not an idiot. You're a loving daughter who's prepared to give your mum a second chance.' He searched the skyline. 'I'd like to think one day my child might do the same.'

She stared at him. 'What? You have a child?'

He looked her straight in the eye. 'Yes, I do.' His voice trailed off into the wind.

Autumn blinked rapidly. Her mouth fell open, the numb cold in her limbs extended to her brain. 'But…'

'Yeah,' he nodded, 'it's a game-changer, isn't it?'

Autumn swayed, gawping at him. He was a father? That had never been a possibility in any of her musings. She couldn't stop the ringing in her ears, as if walls were crashing in around her. Her chest tightened. 'Why didn't you tell me?'

'This is me telling you.' He flipped his hair and turned away. 'And as I've only known you a few days, this is pretty quick for me. It's not something I'm especially proud of.'

'Why not?' Autumn's brain had gone from numb to overdrive. Peppy darted towards her and she absent-mindedly stroked him.

'Because I hardly see him. He lives near Chicago with his mother.' Richard stalked off, closing the gap to the scrubby woodland, Peppy trotting after him.

'Why Chicago? And what's his name? What age is he?' Autumn couldn't come to grips with any of it.

Richard rubbed his hand down his face. 'His name is Adam. He's eight.'

She was almost running, her numb feet and sore ankle forced back to life. 'I didn't think, well… I don't know what I thought.'

He stopped, and she collided with him. 'You see, I'm as bad as your mum.'

'What do you mean?'

'I abandoned my son.'

Autumn pursed her lips. 'Why?' How could he? Not someone as kind as him.

'It's a long story, and not one I want to tell.'

Autumn reached out and took his arm, tears in her eyes. 'You can tell me.'

'Can I?' He pulled out of her grip and strutted off. 'So you can judge me like everyone else? You'd have every right to. You know first-hand what it's like to have an absent parent. Look at me now. Here I am gallivanting about with you, doing whatever I fancy and people don't know.' He threw his arms out. 'No one knows I have a son. I saw the look on your face back there and I'm not surprised. Of course, it's a shock. I might not be the best at reading the subtleties, but I know what you were thinking. Who wouldn't? People suppose they know me, but they don't. What you see is not what you get.' He kicked a stray branch off the path and Peppy chased after it.

Her ankle throbbing, Autumn limp-jogged to keep up. 'Richard, please. I was only shocked because it was unexpected, but I want to hear your story.'

'No, I can't.' His voice trailed off.

It hurt that he couldn't share with her. Despite their brief acquaintance, they'd developed a bond. Autumn felt it anyway. He stormed ahead, stopping at the stile. Peppy scrambled over first. Autumn held her breath as Richard lifted her down, releasing her quickly and setting her on the muddy path. Trudging through the woodland behind him, she struggled to process everything he'd said. They reached the second stile, and he held out his hand, looking the opposite way. She took it, swallowing as she used his arm to balance on. The Freelander was parked in the lay-by.

Autumn caught Richard by the arm. 'Richard, listen.'

'What? Is your ankle sore?'

'Yes, it's agony, but that's not the point.'

'Then what?'

'I just.' Autumn blinked. 'I trust you. Whatever happened, you had a reason. I hope sometime you'll tell me because I know you're a good man.'

'You don't really know anything about me.'

'I know what you've done for me.' And how he made her feel – not just about him but about herself. He'd given her a spark of belief that she could do something new and different.

Richard held up his hand. 'Yes, let's leave it there.'

'Ok.' She rubbed at her muddy sleeve.

He stared at her for a long moment, then sighed, his voice lowering. 'Come on. Let's get you off your ankle.' Advancing to the car, he opened the back door and let Peppy into the back seat.

'I can't get in the car like this, I'll ruin it.'

'Here.' He pulled out a large black sheet. 'I use these for Peppy.' He covered the seat with it, then helped her in.

She buckled up as Richard jumped in and started the engine. Sinking her head into the rest, she tugged at the wet jeans clinging to her legs, wanting to curl up and cry. Richard turned the car the opposite way from what she expected.

'Where are you going? Fionnphort is the other way.'

'But this is the way to the croft, isn't it?'

'Yes, but…'

'We've got this far.' He revved up the hill. 'We're not stopping now.'

Her vision blurred again. Why was he doing this? It didn't tally with a man who'd abandoned a child. This was the real him. Why wouldn't he tell her the truth? Could it really be that bad? Peppy nosed through the gap and rested his jaw on her shoulder.

'I'm just sorry you had to fall in with me,' Richard muttered to his mirror.

Autumn shook her head. 'I'm not sorry. I'll never be sorry about that.'

Richard crunched the gears up the path. Autumn clasped his hand over the gearstick. He slid out from under her grip, placing his hand on top and holding her tight for a few seconds until she collected herself. 'That's another of your skills. You look for the best in everyone,' he whispered, then pointed. 'That must be it.'

A gate barred the entrance to a rough track. He jumped out and opened it. They continued to wind around bends before the track peaked and rambled downhill. Hitting the brakes, he stopped behind a small cottage. A vast panorama of blue opened out before them. Row upon row of white horses punctuated the sea. A solitary fishing boat wound its way back.

'This must be it, there's nowhere else.'

Autumn swiped at her mud covered clothes. 'Ok, here goes.'

'I'll come with you.' Richard unfastened his belt and followed her out.

'How do I look?' She gave a dry laugh as she straightened herself out, raked her matted hair, and smiled, ignoring the penetrating chill and the muck everywhere.

Richard raised his eyebrow, his gaze roaming upwards from her filthy boots until it settled on her face. Stepping forward, he hesitated, then with a shaky hand rubbed his thumb across her cheek. Autumn's heart missed several beats. 'Apart from the mud?' Richard held out his thumb, which was now black. 'Other than that… Very, um, nice.'

Blinking rapidly, she swallowed.

'Let's go.' He folded his arms tightly.

Trudging around the side of the house, Autumn's fingertips tingled. Was it possible her mum was inside? She knocked on the door, brushing stray twigs off her coat. Her jeans were ruined. They stuck to her everywhere they shouldn't, and they chafed. Shuffling awkwardly, she waited. The door opened, and a wrinkled old face peered round.

'What's this? Who are you?' said the elderly man.

'My name's Autumn Elworthy. I'm looking for a William Anderson. Is that you?'

'Yes, it is. What do you want with me?'

'It's actually your son I'm trying to find, Michael Anderson.'

'Michael? My son isn't Michael. He's called Mitchell, he lives down south.'

'Mitchell, not Michael?' Her heart fell to the soles of her mucky boots.

'That's what I said.'

'I'm sorry, I must have the wrong person. Sorry to bother you.'

'Dear, dear,' grumbled the man, snapping the door closed.

Autumn's eyes returned to Richard. 'So, this was a big fat waste of time.'

Richard closed the gap between them, and Autumn swallowed. 'At least you know.' Leaning over as if to hug her, he stopped and chapped her shoulder with his fist, before turning back to the car. Yes, she knew her mum wasn't here, but she also knew Richard had secrets. Her head burst with questions and a desire for answers, but not the ones she'd wanted when she'd arrived.

CHAPTER 12

Richard

Richard drove Autumn back to Fionnphort. He was at a loss for words even more than usual. Of course, Autumn was disappointed at not finding her mum, but it was far worse. She was disappointed in him. He shouldn't care, but he did. A squirming sensation niggled in his gut. He couldn't tell her the details. They changed nothing.

What was seriously messing with his head wasn't any of that though. He'd kissed her. *Jesus, what was I thinking?* With her beside him, there was no shutting down. He couldn't close off enough to think. He'd reacted to her peck on the cheek with a raw emotion deep from within. It had satisfied something, while at the same time leaving him dangling on a thin rope of temptation. Now he'd kissed her once, the desire to do it again was potent.

Autumn needed coffee. He didn't blame her. He left her sitting on a bench outside the shop while he went in to get it. When he returned a few minutes later, Mary had appeared. Richard coughed to announce his presence and Peppy looked round from where Mary was fussing him.

'I was telling Mary about my misadventures,' said Autumn. 'Honestly, my jeans have dried a bit, but I think they'll have to be surgically removed.' The wind swept her hair as she unthreaded it from her lips.

Mary stooped, leaning on her walking stick, and Richard caught her ice-blue eyes scrutinising him. 'Autumn's had an interesting message,' said Mary.

'Oh?' Richard glanced at Autumn.

'Yeah. Robyn from the hotel messaged me. Her partner's dad used to work with a Mike and she's sent me the information. Mike Robertson, he lives in Croggan, wherever that may be.'

'It's a tiny village, very out of the way,' said Mary.

Autumn bounced to her feet. 'I'll try it tomorrow.'

'I hope this one is the right one,' smiled Mary. 'Do you want to come back to the house and clean up?

'That's kind, but I should get going.'

Mary gave Peppy one last pat before waving them off.

*

'I love Mary,' said Autumn as they drove away, leaving Fionnphort behind.

'She's nice.'

'And she gave me a good lead.'

'Technically, I gave you it first,' Richard informed his wing mirror.

'Are you jealous?'

'No, I was just stating a fact.'

'Ok, so you did and you know I appreciate it.'

'Yes.' He shifted his focus to her, clenching the gearstick as he weaved in and out passing places. Seeing her sitting there, still wearing his shirt, made him want to kiss her again. He tried not to growl as he stared at the road, but the desire building inside him was hard to ignore. She'd affected him. That was why he'd blabbed his story. Part of it anyway. He'd been through years of depression, blame and regurgitation, but nothing would ever acquit him fully, not in his own mind. Here he could do his job and live in peace, but it was a surface calm. No one knew the turmoil inside. What would be the point of burdening Autumn with that? In a few days, she'd be gone. Their kiss and everything else they'd shared would be nothing but a speck of memory.

He rubbed his eyebrow and flexed his neck, his gaze flickering towards Autumn. Her eyes travelled over his t-shirt, his arms, and down… He steadied his breathing. Was she eyeing him up? If she was, it was a crazy game. Though he wasn't clear on the rules. What was she hoping for? Another kiss? A one-night stand? Something more? Because if it was option three, her luck was out. She couldn't think they had any kind of future, could she? The deep hollow in Richard's chest hadn't felt so full in a long time. If he dared to creep out of his box and imagine a future with Autumn, lights dazzled him. Was it possible in any shape or form? Or was he misinterpreting the signals completely and letting his thoughts run wild, turning a two-day acquaintance into something it could never be.

'So.' He cleared his throat. 'How will you get to Croggan? There are no buses.'

'Where is it?' Autumn smiled.

'Check the map, it's around the middle, close to Craignure, out on a little peninsula.'

Autumn opened the map. Richard pointed vaguely, keeping his eyes on the road.

'How did you find it without even looking?' she asked.

'Skill.'

She grinned. 'So, can you walk there or do you have to drive?'

'Drive, Autumn, please. I'm in Fionnphort again tomorrow, there's no way I can come and rescue you from a bog and some highland cows.'

'I suppose I better hire that car then.' She closed the map.

'Sounds like a good plan.' He stared out the windscreen. That was what she had to do. This was her mission, not his. He had to work and his deadline was approaching fast. He couldn't surrender any more time. But he couldn't abandon her. 'I'll drop you at the garage in the morning… if you like?'

'You know I do.'

He returned her smile without looking at her. Where was this heading? An impatient vibe wrestled with his common sense. Something was teetering on the verge of happening and it could go either way. He might easily fall into the trap unless he held off long enough for the danger to pass. Just a few days more. The thought wasn't cheering. A dark ugly cloud sat over the remainder of the week and he couldn't see into it or past it. But like it or not, Autumn was going to leave the island and he would go back to normal. He just had to minimise the potential fallout. It might turn out to be the toughest assignment he'd ever had.

They arrived back at the hotel in what seemed like no time. As he pulled the Freelander alongside the steps to the front door, Autumn peered at him. 'Richard, are we ok?'

'What do you mean? I'm ok. I told you, I don't want to talk about—'

She held up her hands. 'I know, I get that, I still want to hear, but I respect your wishes. I just meant…' Her eyes strayed to his lips and his heartrate spiked.

'Oh, that.' He pulled back and swallowed. 'Yes, we're ok. Yes.' Though in all honesty, his brain was about to explode. 'I told you, it's fine. Tomorrow morning, eight o'clock. I'll be here.'

CHAPTER 13

Autumn

Autumn was thankful she'd squeezed the straighteners into her case. Separating sections of hair, she smoothed them down, relaxing as each strand fell lightly over her shoulders. Personal satisfaction, that was all. She wasn't trying to impress anyone or look good. *Really*. Just because she was in a wild place didn't mean she had to let her hair follow suit.

Her reflection appeared normal. *Phew!* She tweaked her rosy cheeks in the mirror. The sea air must be doing some good. Anything was better than the night before. She'd spent half an hour in the shower with mud trickling down the plughole and steam filling the room. All she'd been able to think about was Richard. Did she really care about finding her mum any more? She'd rather spend the day on the beach chatting to him. Unresolved tension buzzed through her veins. Was there any chance of seeing him again after today?

She finished off her hair and checked her phone. What was she hoping for? A message from her mum? From Richard? Yes, but saying what? The memory of their kiss was jammed on repeat, and not just the kiss. All his warmth and kindness had stirred emotions in her she wasn't sure what to do with. Sitting on the bed, she held her forehead before taking a deep breath and heading downstairs.

The reception desk was empty, but as Autumn passed through the foyer to the dining room, Robyn came out of the lounge with Carl and a woman in a dazzling red coat.

'Good morning,' said Robyn.

'Hi.' Autumn waved.

'This is Georgia Rose,' said Robyn. 'She's an artist, and she's putting on a mini exhibition at the quiz tonight. We're just setting up.'

'Oh, I forgot about the quiz.'

'Everyone's welcome,' said Robyn with a little smile.

'I better get moving,' said Georgia. 'Sorry, I can't stay and chat. I heard about your mission from Robyn. I don't know any Mikes, not on the island anyway, but it sounds intriguing. I'd love to hear more, let's chat later. It sounds right up my street.'

'Nice to meet you. See you later.' Autumn went outside to wait after hardly touching her breakfast. Richard arrived promptly at eight. Was this the last few minutes she would share with him? 'Hey! Peppy, you're such a lovely dog.' She scratched his neck.

'Hi.' Richard pulled off. He seemed to be trying harder than ever not to look at her.

She pushed her bag onto the floor. 'I think I got all the mud out of it. But it took me half an hour to get it off me. The shower was black.'

Richard did a double-take. 'Mission accomplished, I'd say.'

Autumn blinked rapidly. 'So, I've, eh, checked how to get to Croggan.'

'Good.'

'Have you ever been there?'

'I have, it's a good place for sea eagles.' He steered with one elbow on the window edge.

'Well, I might see one then, but more importantly, is it a good road?'

'Not particularly.'

'Are you serious?' She narrowed her eyes.

He pulled his answering face.

'Ok, how bad? Because I am not a great driver.'

'It's narrow and twisty, take it slowly.'

'I hope this is the right Mike.' Autumn ran her fingers through her hair. 'Though I'm not sure what I want to say to Mum any more.'

'I'm sure you'll find the right words once you're there.'

'You think?'

'Well, you're very good at talking.' He flicked her a look.

'Haha.'

When they arrived at Craignure, a ferry rolled into port, the great prow lifting as it approached the pier. The Freelander slowed. 'Here you go.' Richard pulled into the roadside car park next to the garage and dragged on the handbrake.

Autumn gazed at him and he matched it. The look could have lingered much longer, but with a conscious effort, Autumn opened the door and hopped out.

'By the way, there's no phone signal in Croggan.'

'Why are you smiling about that?' Autumn squinted over the seats, her stomach flipping at the look on his face.

'I'm off to have a peaceful day,' he said with a wink.

'What a cheek.' Leaning her head to the side, she mimicked his sardonic smile. 'I bet you miss me.' She would definitely miss him.

'Just look out for yourself.'

She raised her eyebrows. 'You better not say things like that, or I might start thinking you care.'

'Nice.' He cast his eyes heavenward. 'Bye-bye, Autumn.' Peppy gave a little whine.

'Byeee.' Shutting the door, Autumn shouldered her bag, suddenly bereft, like she'd lost a limb.

Before she could move, Richard got out of the car. 'Autumn, I forgot.'

'What?'

'Take this.' He handed her a folded bit of paper. 'Just in case. And I mean it, don't do anything crazy. Be safe.'

She glanced at the note, then into his eyes. 'You big softy.'

'Come here.' He beckoned, and not needing any more encouragement, she hurried straight to him. He embraced her with a crushing force. Autumn held her breath as she clung to him. A pleasurable, tingling warmth crept over her, making her lightheaded. If she could stay like this, everything would be fine. This was the sensation she'd wanted forever. It was like love. Someone who cared. She almost cried. It couldn't be love, not here, not now. 'Just take care. Really,' he whispered onto the top of her head. 'And let me know what happens. I want to hear, ok?'

'Ok,' she said in a shaky voice. Richard gave her back a fortifying rub before releasing her. She stood stock still, giddy inside.

'I have to go but message me.' He gripped her shoulder, then let go and strode back to the Freelander.

'I will.' Still standing like a statue, Autumn watched the car climb the hill and disappear around the corner. For a few seconds, she hoped without genuine conviction he would come back. She hugged herself, trying to preserve some of the feelings he'd just infused her with. Her focus slipped to the note, containing his scrawled email address and home phone number, *in case you need me. X*

She did but she had to be sensible.

The door to the garage office creaked open, not filling her with confidence. Surely they had lots of oil in a garage?

A man in grease-stained overalls appeared through a side door. 'Can I help you?' He wiped his hands on a paper towel.

'I'm looking to hire a car. I heard you do that here.'

'Yes, I have the tariff if you'd like to read.' He pushed a laminated sheet in front of her. 'And I have some forms to fill out. I'll need to see your licence.'

Autumn froze, eyes moving from the greasy fingerprints on the laminate to the man. 'Oh no. My driver's licence is in London.'

After leaving the garage, feeling like an idiot, she traipsed along the pavement beside the shore towards the main part of the village, watching the ferry make its way out. She held her hair off her face. What now? She couldn't walk to Croggan. As she watched the ferry moving slowly out of sight, she decided to call the island taxi. It wouldn't be busy on a Wednesday morning, surely? She sighed, head down, searching her bag for the number Anne had given her that first evening. As she passed the bus stances, she gave a wry grin. How had she missed that bus? Maybe fate? How different things might have been if she'd got it.

'Oh, hello again.'

Autumn looked up, recognising the chatty artist from the hotel. 'Hi.'

'I'm Georgia, we met this morning.' Georgia was standing beside a minibus with the words Hidden Mull on the side.

'I remember. Is this your minibus?'

'No, it belongs to my friend, Kirsten. She runs the tours. This group has hired me to make sure they get some good wildlife shots. What are you up to? Are you still searching?'

'Yes, but your trip sounds more fun. I was meant to hire a car to get to Croggan but I don't have my licence. I'm just going to see if I can get the taxi, though it might be too pricey.'

'Oh, it's Croggan you're after. Kirsten sometimes takes tours there. Shall I ask her if we're going there today?'

'That would be great, but I don't want to make a nuisance of myself.'

'Just let me ask her.' Georgia nipped along the road to where a young woman with a long dark plait was talking to a man in a bus driver's uniform. After a few minutes of chat, Georgia headed back with the other woman. 'This is Kirsten, my friend.'

'I can go to Croggan,' said Kirsten. 'I often take wildlife tours there.'

'I don't want to put you out of your way,' said Autumn.

'It's either there or Loch Buie and they're six and half a dozen. So if you want to tag along, that's fine. There's plenty of room.'

'I'll pay for the ride,' said Autumn.

'Don't worry about it,' said Kirsten with a smile. 'Just leave me a good review.'

'Ok, I'll do that.'

Strapped into the minibus beside Georgia, Autumn enjoyed the views and stunning scenery whizzing by as Kirsten spoke through her microphone to the group of tourists. 'She's brave driving this thing on these roads,' said Autumn.

'Don't I know it,' said Georgia. 'She's cool. Did you see the seaplane at the Glen Lodge?'

'I did, yeah.'

'Her fiancé is the pilot. So they're quite the dynamic duo when it comes to super-crazed driving antics.'

Kirsten flicked a glance over her shoulder, switching off the microphone. 'I can hear you,' she muttered.

'It's amazing you can even live here, it's so remote.'

'Exactly,' said Georgia. 'It's wonderful and free. But it's tough in the off-season. I'm trying to keep things afloat until the spring.'

'What kind of art do you do?'

'A bit of everything. Photography is my main thing but I love painting, drawing, sewing, woodcraft, anything really.'

'I've always wanted to make my own candles and soap,' said Autumn. 'Until this week, dreaming was as far as I got, but I've been learning about how to put kelp in candles.'

'Oh, cool.'

'Do you think there's a market for that kind of thing here?'

'Definitely. Tourists will buy anything made on the island,' said Georgia with a grin.

'These last few days have been quite a culture shock for me.'

'I was like that when I first arrived, but that was part of the thrill. I love a challenge.'

Croggan was only a few miles from the main road, but it took ages to get there. As the road twisted and the bus turned around tight corners, Autumn was flung from side to side. She held onto her seat, glad she wasn't driving. The road cut close to the sea, terrifying and stunning. If her mum was here, even the journey would freak her out. Maybe she was stuck in a house, too petrified to go anywhere.

'Do you know which house it is?' asked Georgia as Kirsten drove the minibus onto a flat band of land in front of the sea.

'Yes, it's in Robyn's message.'

'Cool,' said Georgia. 'We'll be away walking for some time but catch up when you're done. If it's the right house, I guess you'll want to stay for a while with your mum.'

'Thanks. I'll do that.' Autumn waved goodbye to Kirsten as she assembled her party together, then turned towards a cluster of houses. She passed a large farmhouse and a small croft before reaching a gentle hill. The cottage matching the name on the message nestled beneath. It had a falling down picket fence and wild plants crept round the garden. Untidy piles of wood and empty oil cans lay about. Autumn approached the door, shuddering. This place was like a countryside version of Phil's revolting house. Had her mum gone from one horror to another? A black Civic, with a dented passenger door, sat beside an ancient caravan with no wheels.

Autumn knocked on the door. A dog barked, and she stepped back, waiting, toying with her cuffs. A placating voice quietened the dog and a young man opened the door. Autumn's mouth fell slack; she couldn't help staring. The young man smiled through a slight frown. His eyes were a gorgeous icy blue set in a ruggedly handsome face, but what really had Autumn's attention was his hair, which he wore in thick blonde dreadlocks tied back in a low ponytail. He looked like he'd strayed from the set of *Vikings*. As he pushed a black Labrador back from the door, Autumn swallowed. Those were some biceps. She caught the edge of a tattoo under his t-shirt sleeve. 'Stay back, Jet,' he said. 'He's a friendly dog, a bit over-friendly sometimes. He'll jump all over you.'

'Oh.' Autumn fiddled with the latch on her bag.

The young Viking straightened up, smiling a crooked but winning smile. 'Sorry, what can I do for you?'

'I'm looking for someone.' Autumn adjusted her collar.

'Me?' He grinned with a cheeky quirk of his eyebrow.

'Eh, I'm not sure.'

'Well, tell me who it is, and I'll see if I can help.'

'I, um, this will probably sound really strange, but do you know a Mike Robertson?'

'Yeah, he's my dad.' Young Viking nodded and his brow furrowed.

'Really?' Autumn's heartrate increased. What if Mike and her mum were having an affair? Should she say anything else? If she told the truth, she might have a Jerry Springer style bust-up on her conscience.

Young Viking scanned her over. 'Why are you looking for Dad? Has he done something?'

'No. I just…' This was hopeless. Autumn bounced on her toes. 'I don't suppose…' She swallowed hard. Young Viking stared, looking concerned. 'Um, is your dad married?'

'What? That's an odd question. What's going on? Are you some kind of relative?' His expression transitioned through curiosity to worry.

'I don't think so. It's just… My mum ran off with someone and all I know is that his name's Mike and he lives on Mull. I've been searching for them all week and it's led me here.'

Young Viking let out a long sigh. 'Wow, that's quite a predicament. But Dad doesn't live here any more. And unless he's hiding your mum under the floorboards, she's not here either.'

'I'm sorry. He's probably a happily married guy, and the last thing he – and you – need is me coming along with something like this.'

'If only that were true.' Young Viking ran his hand across his remarkable hairstyle. 'My parents are divorced, but I'm pretty sure Dad's not seeing anyone.'

'I know how hard it is when parents split.'

'Do you?'

Autumn looked into his cool blue eyes. 'I've been through it with mine.'

'Yeah, it's a toughy on the old heartstrings. What's your name?' he asked.

'Autumn.'

He gave an appreciative nod. 'Suits you. I'm Blair.' He pushed out his hand and Autumn shook it, admiring his thick forearms. 'So, your mum,' said Blair. 'Sorry, I can't help.' He glanced at his feet and patted the dog, which had reappeared by his side. Despite the Viking tendencies, Blair had a sweet expression. 'So, what will you do now?'

'I'm not sure. I came with the tour party. I don't have a car so I've been hijacking lifts all week.'

'You don't have a car? On this island? You're mental.' Blair burst out laughing. 'Sorry, I shouldn't laugh.'

'No, you're right. I've been so stupid.' She giggled at her own idiocy.

'Well, I'm not working until later and I'm almost finished here. How about I drive you back if you don't want to wait for the tour? And if you don't think that's creepy and forward of me. I mean, just to help out.'

'Would you? That would be great.'

'Sure, if you don't mind going in my bashed car. I got hit by someone going far too fast. Honestly, there are some maniacs on the roads here.'

'Wow, thanks. I'm staying at the Glen Lodge Hotel.'

'Cool, I live and work in Tobermory, so it's on my way. Do you want to go and tell the tour people while I get sorted? I need to feed Jet here, he's Mum's dog, then I'll get my coat.'

As luck had it, Georgia was back at the minibus, raking about. Autumn ran towards her.

'I forgot my tripod. Did you find your mum?' said Georgia.

Autumn explained about Blair.

'Oh, is that him?' said Georgia, peering over Autumn's shoulder. 'Oh, wow, he looks tasty.'

'I guess. And he seems like a nice guy. Listen, thanks for today.'

'No worries,' said Georgia. 'You have my number and I'll see you later at the quiz.'

Autumn hurried back and jumped into the car via the bashed door. Blair took off.

'It's weird,' he grinned, 'I was convinced you were going to say you were some long-lost relative.'

Clinging to her seat, Autumn frowned. 'Yeah. That's not possible, is it?'

With an uncertain smile, Blair eased around a bend. 'I really don't know. I'm pretty sure my parents are genuine and don't have any skeletons. They had me quite young, but that's no reason to suspect anything odd.'

'I hear you,' said Autumn. 'My parents are young too. I think I was a mistake.'

'Yeah, my family are quite a bunch. My mum had an affair with a guy on the mainland and my brother has had lots of problems. So far my dad seems the most normal.'

Autumn grinned. 'So he's not started online dating then?'

'No way. My dad wouldn't have a clue about stuff like that. He thinks I'm going to meet a girl in a bar; he has no idea how things work these days. He just had enough with my mum and all the hoarding and the mess. I'm helping to make Mum's place a bit more respectable so she can sell up.'

'Parents,' huffed Autumn. 'They're supposed to be the ones looking after us.'

'Ha! Tell me about it. We're probably not related but I think you might be my soul sister.'

Autumn smiled and nodded. The week just got stranger and stranger.

CHAPTER 14

Richard

Finishing his work at the hidden beach, Richard threw himself onto the rock where, only a couple of days before, Autumn had been. The vision of her sitting there, auburn locks twisting in the wind, was haunting. *Seventeen times eleven is one hundred and eighty-seven.* 'Why did I get involved?' he asked Peppy. 'Look what I can do without distractions. I've finished the job I should have done by midday yesterday.' It was easy. *Though not half as much fun*, the devil on his shoulder reminded him. Peppy nuzzled his hand. Richard glanced at his blank phone. The same phone which before Sunday had floundered at the bottom of his rucksack, uncharged for weeks on end. He'd used it more in the past few days than he had since he bought it.

'I bet you miss me,' said the voice in his head.

'I do.' He stood, raking his fingers through his thick hair, shaking the thought away. 'But what can come of it?'

Since his divorce and the affair with Lorraine, Richard hadn't been with anyone. How could he trust himself not to be exactly the same all over again? Nothing had changed.

You won't be the first or the last to be tempted by a pretty young thing, soothed the angel on his shoulder. *So deal with it*, said the devil, *and get on with your business.* But why? Did work always have to win? Was giving in to the attraction what he wanted? It certainly wasn't sensible. Autumn had been a breath of fresh air. She had a way of making him feel valued. But what were his expectations? He could open up to her just for the relief of sharing some of his regrets, without hope or thought of anything else. Would that be enough?

He didn't remember feeling this way about Ruth. She'd all but told him they were getting married and he'd gone along with it. On paper, they were perfect. Both high-flyers in their careers, workaholics and perfectionists. But it didn't make them suited to married life or parenthood. When Adam's autism had come to light, Ruth's way of coping was to go home to the place she could get support and security, and it wasn't with her husband. Richard's way had been to fall back into bed with Lorraine, the woman he'd dated before Ruth, hoping she'd have changed her mind regarding a long-term relationship. She hadn't. They'd enjoyed several months of what turned out to be meaningless sex.

No one on the island knew about Adam, not because Richard was ashamed of his son, no: he was ashamed of himself. He hadn't been up to the job, so he'd let go. He hadn't even told Ron and Anne, the only two people he'd formed a relationship with. He'd entrusted his dog to their care, but not his secret. When they thought he was off on work business, he was actually halfway around the world, attending his son's assessment meeting.

Having to sit through the meeting while Ruth and her new husband held hands and spoke as one was sickening. He didn't begrudge her the happiness, but to have another man talking about Adam as though he was his father was beyond humiliation. But Richard had no grounds to complain, he'd agreed to everything. If only his heart could adjust as easily to the arrangement as his brain had. Ruth had propounded it as the perfect plan, but since that day, Richard had lost something fundamental in himself. Any trust in his own judgement and worth was gone.

Did Autumn need to know all this? They'd clicked and had a connection, but it was just a fleeting moment. He grabbed his equipment only to thrust it haphazardly away. He needed to walk or better still swim, but neither would solve his immediate problem: the desperate desire to see Autumn again, talk to her, kiss her, hold her, anything. She was the only thing he could see. *Bloody infatuation.*

'Come on, Peppy. I can't concentrate.' Setting off towards Fionnphort, he patted the phone in his pocket, volume on full. What was he expecting? Croggan had no phone signal. Autumn must have arrived, otherwise it would have been ringing all day, wouldn't it? *That's what you want to believe, but why? She doesn't like you especially. She likes the fact you can drive a car, that's all.* The devil smirked.

It was almost two o'clock. Autumn could easily have been to Croggan and back. Maybe she'd found her mum. How would that go? Richard couldn't imagine a time Adam might come looking for him. He would grow up thinking his mother's new husband was his father, and – for a boy with Adam's needs – if he made that kind of connection to anyone, surely that was to be applauded.

Richard stopped and grabbed his phone, seized by a thought. What if… What if Autumn was lying in a ditch beside an overturned rental car? His insides flipped. How could he forgive himself if something had happened? 'I should have gone with her. Why didn't I?' *Because it's none of my business!* She was practically a stranger. *One you happen to like rather a lot,* the angel reminded him. Richard quickened his pace. Yes, he liked her, he couldn't deny it. Being with her released an oxytocin overload in his brain. That was all it was, a chemical imbalance – or was it just the perfect balance? 'Seventeen times fourteen is two hundred and thirty-something… eight,' he muttered. The chemical cocktail shaking up in his mind had caused yesterday's kiss. She was an attractive young woman who'd messed with his equilibrium. After Friday, things would plateau and everything would be normal again.

Phone in hand, Richard's fingers poised over the screen. He could text her and ask how she was. She wouldn't mind, after all, she'd plagued him with texts the day before. No. He put it away. She was probably busy. He would find out the result soon enough, and that would be that.

Shoving the equipment into the back of the car, he half expected to turn and see her, her face alight, brightening the gloomy day with her hair blowing in the wind, catching in her lips as she chattered. But the car park was empty. *Just like me.* Richard strolled back to the village, unencumbered by equipment, staring at his blank phone, Peppy trotting along beside him.

'Hello.'

He heard a faint voice as he reached the main road. Checking around, he spotted Mary hobbling up the hill.

'I saw you crossing the beach, I hoped I would catch you. Where's Autumn?'

'She's gone to Croggan.'

'On her own? I thought you'd go with her.'

'I'm working.' Richard rubbed the back of his neck, but nothing could assuage the sickening sensation in his gut. Work? Did his whole life have to revolve around it?

'Of course. Oh, poor Autumn.' Mary shook her head and shuffled her feet. 'I liked her a lot. She's got a lovely smile. Once you've met her, she's hard to forget.'

So true, so damned annoyingly true. His head was full of her, but his phone was woefully blank. Tapping out a text, he deleted and rewrote it several times before sending.

RICHARD: Hi, how did it go in Croggan? I hope if you found your mum it went well, and if not that you're feeling ok. I can only imagine how hard this is for you. Your mum is a lucky lady to have such a loyal daughter, and I hope she realises that when you finally find her.

'Now, Peppy, we have to wait.'

CHAPTER 15

Autumn

Autumn looked at Blair as he drove by the shop at Craignure, and they both laughed at nothing in particular, just the fact they seemed to know each other like old friends. All the way, they'd talked, exchanging daft stories and reminiscing as though they'd shared a childhood. Where Blair's tales had a perfect island backdrop, Autumn's were surrounded by concrete and graffiti. Still, they were of such a close age they both remembered the same TV programmes, characters, and fads. Even now, Blair had a thing for Pokémon, apparently.

'Glen Lodge, here we come,' he said.

'There's a quiz night later. You could come if you want. I need to text Richard and ask him too.' Autumn pulled out her phone. 'Seriously? The battery's dead. I was watching a YouTube film this morning about making candles, I bet I left it running.'

'Nearly there, you can charge it up. I can't come to the thing tonight, sorry. I do evenings in the Mishnish Bar, but we should keep in touch. I'm not spiritual or anything, but I feel something between you and me.' He peered at her. 'I don't mean in a lovey-dovey way, but there's something. Even if we're not related in the physical world, we might be cousins in another dimension.'

'You're funny.' She smirked as he chuckled.

Arriving back at the Glen Lodge with Blair, Autumn got out of the car and stretched. A tall woman trotted down the front steps and opened the boot of a silver Land Rover.

'Is that a seaplane?' asked Blair.

'Yeah, it's cool. Shall we walk down and have a look?'

'Sure, why not? I've got an hour or so before work.'

As they passed the woman at the Land Rover, she slammed the boot shut and squinted round. 'Oh, hi,' she said to Blair.

'Hi,' he said. 'It's Beth, isn't it?'

'Yup, that's me.'

'How's the roof working for you?'

'It's good, thanks.' Beth tucked her dark hair behind her ear.

'I'm trying to change careers. I do some joinery work on the side,' Blair told Autumn. 'I'm just learning, but this lady took me on to fix a barn roof.'

'It's hard to get good tradespeople sometimes,' she said. 'But you did a good job.'

Autumn glimpsed Robyn coming out the front door with a tall man wearing his hair in a neat ponytail. Blair waved to him as well and said aside, 'that's Beth's boyfriend.'

'This island is crawling with eye-candy,' said Autumn through her teeth so only Blair could hear.

'You think? Come up to the Mishnish tonight and you might change your tune when Toothless Tam comes in for his pint.'

Autumn giggled.

'Hi, Autumn. Did you get on ok?' asked Robyn.

Autumn pulled a side pout. 'Well, I met Blair, and I got a free tour on the bus which I guess is pretty good. But no luck on the Mum and Mike front.'

'That's a shame, but you're getting around. This is Beth,' said Robyn. 'And Murray, friends of mine.'

'You went on the tour bus today?' said Beth. 'It's my sister who drives it.'

'This really is a small island,' said Autumn. 'Everyone knows everyone except for the whereabouts of my mum.' They shared a laugh, but seriously, it was ironic. 'So, do you live here too, or are you just visiting?' Autumn asked Beth.

'We live here. We're helping set up the quiz.'

'Yeah, Beth's good at weightlifting.' Murray smiled.

Beth's eyes flashed, and she smirked. 'He's just jealous because he still can't beat me at darts.'

'I hope you can join us tonight,' said Robyn. 'And you too,' she added to Blair.

'Sorry, got to work, but you should, Autumn. It sounds like a laugh.'

'Yeah, I'll come down.' As the others headed inside, she and Blair strolled over the wide lawn towards the beach. 'I'm all out of ideas. I only have two days left and the likelihood of me finding my mum is less than zero. At least I've had a bit of a break.' The shore curved round to an old pier and a floating jetty next to where the seaplane sat. 'They look weird on the land, don't they?' said Autumn. 'Kind of clumsy when they're so elegant landing in the water.'

'Yeah, but how cool. I didn't realise they were so big.' Putting his hands in his pockets, Blair strolled along, gaping at the plane. 'I work in the evenings, but during the day I'm not too busy, so if you want, I'd be happy to take you somewhere tomorrow. I know you don't have anywhere in mind, but I could take you around some villages, we could ask in the shops and things.'

Autumn toyed with her cuff. 'Actually, that might be a good idea. I mean, I can't get a car, and I can't ask Richard.' She stopped and bit her lip. 'I'd like it if he could come with me, but he's so busy.'

'Do you fancy this guy?' Blair tightened his ponytail.

Heat blossomed in Autumn's cheeks. 'I guess, I do. It's not that I don't appreciate your company, it's just… Gosh, that sounds terrible.'

Blair laughed and shook his head. 'It's not terrible. It's cool with me. Is he a bit sweet on you too?'

Autumn shrugged and didn't look up. 'I think he likes me, yeah.'

'So, are you gonna try to see him again?' Blair gave a little wink. 'You know, for the old holiday fling?'

'Hmm, I don't think Richard's a holiday fling kind of guy and I'm not sure I'm that kind of girl, though I've never tried.'

'Maybe now's the time.' Blair slung his arm around her shoulder and she leaned into him, accepting the hug, though not necessarily the challenge. A holiday fling? No, that could take her down a path she could easily get lost on, and finding the way back was too complicated to imagine.

CHAPTER 16

Richard

Richard approached the reception desk in the foyer of the Glen Lodge Hotel. A woman with ice-blonde hair came out a side door and smiled. 'Can I help you?'

'I, um, yes. A guest is staying here, Autumn Elworthy. I wonder if, well, do you know if she's here? As in, is she in her room?'

'Oh, you're Richard.' The woman paused.

'Yes.'

'I think she said she was messaging you about the quiz tonight.'

'I don't know anything about it, sorry.' He frowned; she hadn't messaged him all day. Jealousy was a bitch of an emotion, but he couldn't stop the serpent's green fangs rising inside. It was stupid to think he was unique. Of course Autumn would have made other plans, other friends. She was like that, funny, sociable, easy-going. *All the things I'm not.* And it hurt. He'd chosen to work rather than help her. The sensible choice, but not what his heart wanted.

'She's gone for a walk to the shore,' said the woman.

'Thanks.' Stepping outside, Richard hesitated, letting the cool breeze ruffle his hair. Should he go and look for her? His eyes answered, landing on her in the distance. Her auburn locks were easy to spot. And what was she doing wrapped in an embrace that certainly wasn't with a long-lost mother? A young, powerfully built man, with a thick mane of blonde dreadlocks, rocked her from side to side. Richard could almost hear them laughing. *Wow, just wow. It didn't take her long to move on to the next guy.*

Richard hopped down the steps. What should he do now? No need to overreact. He could accept the situation and move on. She was ok, no crashed rental cars or visible scars. She needn't know he'd ever been here. Holding his head high, he glanced back. One last look. Autumn had broken away from the man, but they were holding hands and swaying them back and forth like kids.

When Autumn's eyes fell on Richard, his jaw stiffened, and he turned away. *Just get in the car and go.* He wished she hadn't seen him.

Autumn was running across the lawn, her hair flowing behind. The man didn't follow. He strolled along with his hands in his pockets. Richard opened the door to the Freelander and got in. Before he could close the door, Peppy shoved his head through the gap to get his nose to Autumn.

'Oh my god, Richard.' Autumn panted, splaying her fingers across her chest. 'I'm sorry. I should have called, but my battery died. I got so carried away.'

'Yeah, it's fine.' He glimpsed the young man, who'd stopped some distance back, fiddling with his ponytail.

'That's Blair.' Autumn's cheeks reddened. 'He gave me a lift. I had a car disaster. You wouldn't believe it, I don't have my licence with me and I had to get a ride on the tour bus.'

Richard nodded, rubbing the back of his neck, not making eye contact. His insides closed down. 'Well, I, um, you should get back to him.'

'Why?'

'He's waiting.'

Autumn tilted her head. 'Are you listening to me?'

'What?' Richard frowned at Autumn's wide eyes, reflecting the clouds above as they skimmed overhead.

'That's what I'm trying to tell you.'

Richard glanced up to see the young man using hand signs to tell Autumn he was getting in his car. 'Who is he?'

'He's Mike's son. Not the right Mike, unfortunately, but he gave me a lift back from Croggan. Why don't you come inside? We can talk better and there's a quiz later, you'd be good at it. I think it'll be fun.'

'No, really, I can't do that. I have stuff to finish.'

Autumn's expression drooped. Her reasoning didn't explain why she'd been holding hands with Blair and Richard wasn't sure he dared ask.

'Isn't Blair going with you?'

'No.' She shook her head. 'He's working. I didn't ask him, I'm asking you.'

Richard pinched his lips together and looked away. Autumn leaned in and patted Peppy through the gap beside the open door.

'I missed you today.' Richard couldn't be sure if she was addressing Peppy or him. 'It was a good day. In fact, I've had a good week. I just wish…' Her fingers slipped off Peppy's nose and onto the edge of the driver's seat.

'What?'

'That we could have spent more time together. I'm glad we met, it's just a shame I couldn't have met you on a week when you were on holiday.'

Richard allowed himself a smile. 'Yes. That might have been better. But I have a deadline and…' He skimmed around, finally letting his gaze settle on Autumn. 'Maybe before you go, we could… meet sometime. I'll show you the lab, and you can experiment with the kelp.'

She placed her hand on his knee and squeezed it, making him inhale sharply, but she didn't release him. 'I'd love that, but when? I only have two more days.'

'I'll try to finish as much as I can tonight and tomorrow, then I might be free on Friday.'

Her smile was so wide it almost split her face. Seeing someone so pleased by something he'd said was unusual, but so pleasurable, he could barely contain the urge to hold her. Her hand twitched on his leg and he grabbed it before anything else could happen. Touching her soft skin sent pulses of insane thoughts directly to every synapse. 'I'll be lonely without you,' she said to his hand, not meeting his eye. 'And I'm sorry I didn't message you.'

'That's ok.' He squeezed her fingers. 'Now, I should go. I'll let you know about Friday.' He swivelled into his seat and her hand trailed away. She closed his door and waved. As he drove off, he glimpsed her in his rear-view mirror. So much for keeping away. His body flooded with warmth and lust slammed through him at the thought of seeing her again. Jesus, he had to keep his shit together. Would a couple of hours on Friday be enough? Was checking out his lab all she wanted? Why was he wasting time, driving home to spend a night staring at an iPad when a real living person wanted him? And he wanted nothing more than to be with her.

CHAPTER 17

Autumn

Autumn stared into the distance long after the Freelander had gone from sight. Friday. Well, the promise of Friday was better than nothing, but it was bitter letting him drive away so soon. Their time together was too short.

'Is everything ok?' Blair drove up, lowering his window.

Autumn nodded.

'He didn't think…' said Blair, 'You know, that we were hugging back there because we're hooking up or something?'

'I don't think so. Well, maybe he did a bit. I just wish I had more time to get to know him.'

Blair leaned out. 'Listen, if you feel that way, do something.'

'Like what? He's a guy I met a few days ago. I can't give up my life on a whim. If it turns out we're not compatible after all, I'm screwed. I don't have the money to hang about here indefinitely, hoping to find a way into his heart.'

'I think it's obvious he likes you,' said Blair, 'he's shown you that much. Why not tell him? I know it's hard to talk about stuff like that, but what do you have to lose?' He checked the time on his phone. 'Heck, it's getting late. Work calls. Message me if you need anything and give me a bell tomorrow if you still want to go searching. But tonight, call

Richard, and talk to him. He's a guy, trust me, everything he's done for you tells me he likes you a lot.'

'Thanks.' Autumn squeezed his shoulder through the open window. Friendly warmth poured between them. So much love flowed through the world in different ways with different fits and she was getting it all this week in bucketloads. It was overwhelming – in a good way.

'You better go in,' said Blair. 'It's getting chilly, looks like another storm's brewing.'

Clutching her arms tight around herself, Autumn watched as Blair drove off. Now everyone was gone.

Robyn was at the desk in the foyer when Autumn claimed the warmth inside. Before either could speak, the door to the dining room opened and Carl came out carrying a box of tartan blankets.

'We need Georgia,' he said. 'No matter how we throw these things around, it's a mess. Oh, hi, Autumn.'

'I used to dress shelves,' said Autumn, 'though not always with much success.' Thoughts of shattered glass pinging around the floor leapt into her head. 'I could lend a hand.'

'That would be lovely,' said Robyn, 'but you're a guest, so don't feel obliged to. If you need some R and R, you take it.'

'I'd like to help, but I need to go up and change and put my phone on charge.'

'Sure,' said Carl. 'Join us when you're ready.'

Her room was bright and airy and she marvelled at the way hotel staff made the beds so perfectly. She fixed herself a quick coffee and cradled the mug as she gazed out the window towards the sea, trying desperately not to think about anything, just to let her brain rest. After plugging in her phone, she nipped back downstairs. In the dining room, Beth and Murray were piecing together large wooden blocks to make a stage.

Carl headed over with a wave. 'Hi, I was thinking, if you're coming tonight, you could team up with Georgia. The two of you could pair up with either Robyn and me, Beth and Murray, or Kirsten and Fraser.'

'I don't mind who I go with, I'm hopeless at quizzes.' Autumn raised her palms.

'Then stick with Robyn, she knows everything.'

'So does Murray,' said Beth. 'Don't you?'

'Well, not everything.'

'But you like to win.'

'Says the queen of darts.' Murray smirked at Beth. 'But sure, you can come with us. That makes more sense because Robyn shouldn't be allowed to win if she's in charge, it looks fixed.'

Beth grinned at Autumn. 'You see, not competitive at all.'

Autumn glanced between the two of them and chuckled. 'How did you meet? Are you both from the island?'

'No,' said Murray. 'I'll let Beth tell you about it, but I will say it had something to do with a highland cow and quite a lot to do with me being a boorish mainlander.'

The corners of Beth's mouth curled up. 'Yeah, I'll tell you about it later.'

'Sounds intriguing. Where do you want these blankets?'

Carl led her over to the other side of the room and explained his vision. After spending about half an hour laughing, chatting to the others and helping, Autumn relaxed, but she couldn't shake the Richard-shaped niggle gnawing a hole inside her. It was no good thinking he was some random guy she'd bumped into and could just let go again. She was floating in limbo with so many possibilities, but most of them short term and all of them crazy.

'Hello!' The door burst open and Georgia sailed in, pulling off a pair of gloves. Her bright red coat and tousled blonde bob gave her a Grace Kelly look with a modern twist. 'I hear there's some decorating to do.'

'Autumn has it under control,' said Carl.

'Oh, this looks great,' said Georgia, peering over what Autumn had done. Autumn stepped back and tilted her head. 'If we add a few branches, it'll be perfect.'

'A beautiful Autumn display,' agreed Georgia, taking Autumn aside and whispering. 'So, did you find out anything else?'

'No.'

'Hmm, maybe someone here tonight might know something. I'll do some snooping. Everyone knows I'm a gossip, so it won't be unusual.'

Autumn took some time to get ready, putting on tight black jeans and a floaty purple top. Back in the quiet of her room, she sat on the end of her bed, reading Richard's message from earlier. The pile of emotions inside her jumbled about like clothes in the washing machine, tangling into one big churning mess. Downstairs were some people she hardly knew, who'd welcomed, included, and embraced her into their little troop. And somewhere on the island was a man she desperately wanted to talk to… and maybe more. The craving in her heart wouldn't go away despite all the fun she'd had… Or maybe because of it.

She thumbed out a text.

AUTUMN: Can't wait until Friday. I'll be quite desolate until then. XX

She tried to make it jokey enough for him to dismiss if he wanted to, but true enough for him to get her meaning. Maybe she was overthinking the whole thing, which was so unlike her. Her thumb hit send. She jumped to her feet and looked in the mirror, checking for nothing, just trying to stop thinking about Richard. If it was this bad already, what would it be like in a few days when she was back in London?

A bustle of people arriving downstairs greeted Autumn in the foyer. She slipped amongst them, scanning around for familiar faces. Close to the bar was Kirsten, the bus driver, next to a dashing dark-haired man in a kilt. That must be the pilot. Autumn headed towards them, enjoying another bit of eye-candy.

'Oh, hi,' said Kirsten.

Autumn gave an awkward wave. 'This looks fun.'

'I hope so. This is Fraser, by the way.'

'Hey.' He stretched out a muscly forearm and shook hands.

'Nice to meet you. I hear you fly the seaplane.'

'Yeah, I do. How long are you here for? I could take you up before you go.'

'I leave on Saturday.'

'I'm not sure I have a window before then.'

'That's ok, another time. I'd like to come back.'

Georgia found her and led her to a table where Murray and Beth were seated.

'It's quite good if Kirsten sits with Robyn,' said Georgia. 'They didn't get on for a while but now they have a chance to bond, it's sweet.'

Autumn sat opposite Murray. He smiled at her, then turned back to Beth, his arm resting along the back of her seat. Everywhere people were happy together. Autumn's sense of loneliness increased, and she shivered.

'I heard you were looking for someone called Mike,' said Murray, his hand still on Beth, tracing a pattern on her shoulder.

'Yeah,' said Autumn, though it didn't seem to matter any more.

'I work at the West Mull Woods,' said Murray, 'and the land next to that is owned by—'

'A prat,' said Beth.

'Yeah, well, his name is Archibald Crichton-Leith,' said Murray. 'I know you can't help the name you're born with, but it says everything about him. He's full of his own self-importance. Anyway, that aside, he owns a lot of cottages around the estate and I met a guy from one of them the other day. I think he said his name was Mike, but, you know that way, sometimes you hear something but you're not sure. I was more interested in what he was telling me about Crichton-Leith, so I must say his name didn't fully register, but I'm going to say I'm eighty per cent sure he said Mike.'

'Oh wow. So where does he live? I don't know where the West Mull Woods are. I guess in the west, but I'm an island novice.'

'They're south of Calgary, heading towards Ulva Ferry.'

'And is this somewhere I can get a bus to?'

'Not really,' said Murray.

'It's annoying,' said Georgia, 'most weeks I could help you but the next two days I'm part-hosting an online conference for photographers. It's a massive thing for me so I can't get out of it.'

'That's ok,' said Autumn. 'Blair said he would help me tomorrow. He doesn't mind.'

Blair could drive her and no doubt they'd have a laugh, but he couldn't replace Richard. At the interval, Autumn left the room to go to the loo. Sitting at the bottom of the steps in the foyer where it was cool, she checked her phone again and stared at it, hoping to see a reply.

The door opened and Georgia came through. 'Oh, hi. Is everything ok?'

'I don't know.'

Georgia sat beside her. 'It's ok. Of course, you're emotional. Your mum's missing.'

'Thing is, that's not even what's bothering me.'

'Then what?'

'Richard.'

'Who?'

'This may sound stupid.' Autumn looked up. 'He's the guy who's been giving me the lifts, and I know it's crazy, but I really like him.'

'Wow.'

'Crazy, isn't it?'

'Not really. Sometimes you just have an instant reaction to someone. My parents insist they fell in love at first sight. There's obviously something about Richard that's attractive to you. Does he feel the same?'

'I think so.'

'Then why not call him and chat? See where it goes from there.' With a brief smile, Georgia patted her knee then nipped round the corner, into the loos.

Autumn pulled out her phone and held it. Would he want to talk if he was busy? Before heading back inside, she tapped out a text.

AUTUMN: Please call me, if you have a minute. X

As she stood up ready to return to the main room, the front door opened and Autumn's shocked gape morphed into a smile so huge, it hurt. 'Richard, you're here.'

He blinked, toying with the zip on his navy gilet. 'Yeah, is that ok?'

'Oh, my god, yes, more than ok.' She bounded up to him and embraced him around the middle. 'I just messaged you and here you are.'

With the ghost of a laugh, he placed his hands on her back, splaying his fingers. His chin pressed the top of her head. 'Sorry, I'm late. I wasn't sure if…'

'You're not late. Well, you are, but it doesn't matter.' She closed her eyes and breathed in the puffy fabric of his gilet. 'I'm just glad you're here. Why did you come?'

'For you.'

Goosebumps erupted over Autumn and her stomach flipped. Words failed her for once in her life. She tightened her grip around his waist.

'I don't know what use I'll be,' said Richard, releasing her and adjusting his glasses.

'I don't care if we don't get any questions right, at least I'll have company.'

'Don't you have company?'

'It's not the same as having someone all to myself.' She took his hand; his palm was burning hot.

Georgia was on her way back in as they reached the door and Autumn grinned, dragging Richard along like a puppy. 'Look who showed up.'

'Excellent.' Georgia smiled. 'Is this Richard?'

Autumn nodded, keeping a tight grip on him.

'Well, you can join our team,' said Georgia. 'I think technically it's teams of four, but as the prize is a box of Smarties, I don't think anyone will mind.'

As they crossed the room towards the table, Murray looked up with a flicker of recognition. Autumn sat, tapping the seat beside her for Richard. 'This is Richard,' she said as he took off his gilet and hung it over the back of a chair. 'He's helped me loads this week.'

'We've met before,' said Murray. 'You worked for the Crichton-Leith's in the spring, didn't you?'

'I did. Quite an unusual case.' Richard pushed up the sleeves of his oatmeal sweater.

'Tell me about it,' said Murray, glancing at Autumn. 'Crichton-Leith had it in for me. It all turned out ok, but he made my life a misery for a while.'

'I'm not sure he knew what he was doing,' said Richard. 'I'm not defending his actions, but I don't think he'd been in his role long. He made a lot of rash decisions, which he later regretted.'

'I hope he did,' said Murray.

Autumn shared a smile with Georgia, unable to express in words how it felt having Richard here, sharing this fleeting bubble of joy. Georgia seemed to understand.

When the quiz restarted, Richard was on fire. 'How do you know all this stuff?' asked Autumn.

'I just remember…'

'I'm a right dipstick next to you.'

He leaned fractionally closer. 'You just know different things.'

'Yeah, well sadly that doesn't include the capital of Syria.' Autumn pulled a face at him then looked at Georgia.

'It's on the news all the time,' said Georgia, snapping her fingers, 'but I can't remember, it's on the tip of my tongue.'

'Damascus,' said Richard.

'That's it,' said Georgia.

'Sounds like somewhere in the bible,' said Autumn.

'It is,' said Richard.

'What? The bible is set in Syria?' Autumn frowned.

'Well, all over the middle east.'

'I'm so bad at geography. What I need is a quiz on Netflix binge-watching or celebrity gossip,' Autumn huffed.

'Or an atlas,' said Richard with a wink.

'Yeah, do you actually think I could make any sense of that?'

Richard's hand was resting beside hers on the table. He pushed out his little finger, so it brushed the edge of hers. Autumn stared into his eyes and he smiled. 'You have other talents,' he murmured so only she could hear over the chatter in the room. 'Like making grumpy men smile, you're very good at that.'

Warmth radiated through Autumn and her hand trembled as she looped her little finger around Richard's. Even if this lasted only a few more days, she wanted to nurture it and make it grow. It was the most significant emotional connection she'd ever felt and she didn't want to break it.

They came joint first place. 'Which means we get approximately four Smarties each,' said Georgia. 'Bonus if you get an orange one.'

Autumn laughed with her but couldn't concentrate on anything. Everything she knew about body language was kicking in. Richard's proximity, the breadth of his pupils, and the way his knee kept bumping with hers made her tummy flip and sent her brain cartwheeling. The desire spilling from every pore didn't have brakes, and it was careering forward on an intercepting path with Richard. If he didn't put up a blockade, nothing could stop it.

As people started getting ready to leave, Autumn fidgeted with her quiz sheet, glancing at Richard, not able to find the words for everything she wanted to say. The moment hadn't quite arrived as Murray had moved beside him and was talking about land surveys. When Beth tapped him on the shoulder, he spun around and realised it was time to go. Richard stood up too, and Autumn followed him into the hall, saying goodbye to everyone. They wished her well and hoped to see her again.

Richard hung back. 'So, you're ok for tomorrow?' he said.

'Blair said to message him.' She cast her eyes round. 'Richard, I…' She swallowed before continuing. 'Will you stop here for a bit?'

'You mean stay?'

'Yeah.'

He ran his hands through his hair. 'Well, ok, but not too long. I've got an early start.'

'Ok, ten minutes. Why not come and see my room? I got it on Wow-Deals, it has a sea view and a four-poster bed.' Her foot was on the second step when she glanced back, sucking on her lip.

'It's dark, it won't have any view,' he said. 'And as for the bed…' He rubbed his eyebrow.

Heat rose up her neck. 'I just meant the room in general. We can chat.' Her heart raced as she hopped up the stairs. Chatting would do to start with, but there was so much more she wanted. She half expected to turn around on the landing to see him still at the bottom, but he was behind her.

She clicked open the door to her room and flicked the lights on.

'Wow,' said Richard, scanning around and pacing to the window. 'Very… nice.'

'I thought you'd like it.'

'I do, and… Well…'

'What?' she swallowed.

He fiddled with his cuffs. 'I also like you.'

Autumn's heart stopped. 'Really?'

He stepped up and gently pushed a strand of hair behind her ear. 'Of course I do. That's why I'm here.'

'I like you too,' said Autumn, a flood of heat rushing through her. 'A lot.'

'I worked that out,' said Richard.

'Because you're a genius?'

'No, I'm not. I'm not particularly good at reading body language, but… Well, it seemed like you—'

Autumn held her finger to his lips. 'You're a smart guy.'

'I might be intelligent but I'm not sure I'm wise,' he said, taking her hand.

'Why?'

'Because a wise man would walk away.'

'Walk away from someone he likes?' Autumn slipped her hand from his and placed both her palms on his chest, sliding them up to his shoulders.

He inhaled sharply. 'From a situation he knows isn't going anywhere in the long run.' He clamped his hands on top of hers to stop them moving.

She pushed up on tiptoes, slid her hands from his and placed them on his rough cheeks. 'Let's live this moment. Who cares what happens tomorrow, or the next day, or ever? No one knows what's around the corner, let's be happy just now.'

'I'm not sure I know how.'

'Let me show you.' She pulled his head towards her, pressing her lips firmly against him, knitting her fingers into his hair and closing her eyes as he gently returned the kiss. Snaking his arms around her, he bent down, holding her tight. Autumn matched him, kissing desperately, curling into him. He drew her impossibly close, twining one hand in her hair, sending shock waves through every nerve in her body. His other hand splayed on her back. 'Mmm,' she murmured, lips still touching. She slid her fingers from his hair onto his shoulders.

'If we keep going like this…' Richard whispered. 'Well, we both know where it's heading, and I'm not saying I don't want to, but I'm not prepared. I already have a child I have barely any contact with. I'd rather not make another one in some crazy moment.'

Autumn massaged his broad shoulders, fixating on the taut curves. 'I've got that covered.'

'You do?'

'Sure.'

He pulled back and peered at her.

'Come on. Let's not stop.' Autumn stepped forward and rubbed her thumbs up his back, under his jumper. She'd done this so many times with Josh when they'd been rushed trying to fit it in around his *real* life, it had lost all meaning, but this was different.

Richard removed his glasses, set them on the dressing table, and cupped his fingers round her cheek. With a gentle tug, he drew her towards him, kissing her again. All-consuming lust blazed through her. The intensity of both the physical and emotional bond sent an electric current surging to every nerve end.

'Oh, god,' she panted.

'You're so beautiful,' said Richard. 'Inside and out. I want to make this special for you.' He straightened up, looking slightly dazed, and flicked off the lights. When Autumn found him again, she melted into his arms and his lips locked with hers. Their clothes got dropped around the room, while they stayed joined at the lips. It was hasty and desperate, but not rushed like it had been with Josh; the need to get it done fast because he didn't have much time. This was raw energy and desire. Each touch brought them closer. Richard's hands were so warm, so firm. Autumn was wrapped in his arms and she didn't want to be anywhere else – ever. She nuzzled his neck and he guided her backwards.

By the time they reached the bed, she was so ready for him, she could hardly breathe. He gently lifted her onto the soft pillows and she gasped for air. It was just the two of them, living in the moment. Everything else in the world disappeared.

CHAPTER 18

Richard

When Richard woke, he was hot, feverish in fact. Trying to unravel sense from the delirium, he located the source of the heat. Another body was wrapped tightly across him. *Shit.* He closed his eyes again, his head sinking into the pillow. Autumn's mass of curls was sprawled over his torso. His burning palms rested on her smooth back. What was he doing here?

Enjoying the moment? He'd more than done that. Autumn stirred, moulding against him so completely he was trapped in a blissful prison. She did everything with joy and flare. Her infectious smile which had melted him from the start had undone him. What had started fast and urgent had developed over the evening as they'd realised there was no rush. They had time to enjoy every second. Their bodies and souls were so in sync he wasn't sure how he'd functioned without her or how he could go back to that. She lit up his world and filled every cavity of his soul. Memories swam before him, still fresh: her breathless giggles as he'd kissed her tummy button; the intensity of her eyes as they'd locked together; the overwhelming sensation of being wanted. Richard stroked her hair from his chest, uncovering her face and touching her rosy cheeks with his fingertips; warmth infused him deep within.

He didn't want to break this bond of perfection, but he couldn't stay. He'd left Peppy at home and he had an early start. Plus, he wasn't sure he could face the aftermath of this. He was digging a hole so big it would take months to crawl out. This went far deeper than sex. He kissed her forehead, remembering her tears the night before as they'd flopped into the pillows. 'What's wrong?' he'd asked with a tremor of fear.

'I'm just so happy.' She'd laughed through her tears. So was he, but what the hell could he do about it?

Autumn had woken a new world, made things wonderful, but it had to stop. They'd already taken it too far and the lines which had barely even been drawn were blurry and indistinct. He'd mistaken sex for love before and he couldn't afford to do it here. But separating mind from body this time would be like trying to split an atom.

'I have to go,' he mouthed to the canopy of the four-poster. This was how the world worked. People hooked up for a night, then walked away. It happened all the time. He'd done it with Lorraine, though she'd never wanted him to stay after. His job was to do the business and leave. More fool him for ever thinking he could make her care. He gently peeled Autumn off him. Their skin was stuck together with a thin layer of sweat, a sweet reminder of the night before. With a forceful tug, he extricated himself from under her. The cool air swept over him, not relieving the feverish sensation but chilling his heart. This was the cold emptiness waiting for him when Autumn boarded the ferry on Saturday. She stirred. How long had they been asleep?

He stretched his hand out and fumbled around for his phone on the bedside cabinet. It was six o'clock. *Shit.* He'd been here all night and slept. That was the first night he'd slept this long in months. *So that's the key!* He'd meant to leave straight away, but the emotions were too powerful. He'd stroked and kissed Autumn to sleep, allowing her happy tears to morph into contented sighs, then he'd drifted off himself.

'Where are you going?' said Autumn. Her cool hand landed on his wrist. 'Are you leaving?'

'I have to,' he said. 'I need to let Peppy out, he's been in all night.'

'Oh, yes. I forgot. Will he be ok?'

'Yeah, cross-legged, but fine.' Richard sat on the edge of the bed. Autumn switched on the bedside lamp and screwed up her face. Her bedhead was quite magnificent, her skin pale, apart from her rosy cheeks. Richard pulled the cover across his legs, and turned away, feeling completely exposed.

'So, is this it?'

'I don't know.' He kept his back to her.

'Oh, god. I'm sorry… Did I…?'

Richard looked over his shoulder. 'It's not because of you. But everything we do makes it harder to leave.' In spending the night with her, he'd given himself permission to unleash his affection, desire, and admiration for a short period. Everything had been real, but now he had to stopper the outpouring, push those feelings back inside and return to normality.

'I know.' She sighed, rubbing her forehead. 'I just… Like you being around.'

'I like that too, but…' He raked his hair.

'Can we still meet tomorrow?'

'How about…' He was about to suggest something there was every likelihood of regretting, but he couldn't cork the bottle. Not yet. 'How about I take you later, after I've finished?'

'Ok.' Her smile returned as wide as ever and, damn, he wanted to kiss her again. 'Or could I… Well, could I come with you?'

He looked towards the door of the dim room and a little sigh escaped him. 'I don't know.'

'I'm sorry, I guess I just get in the way.'

'No, it's fine. Come with me. I'll be back about eight, but I really have to go for Peppy.' Leaning over, he planted a kiss on her cheek. He didn't dare do anything else. Falling back into the bed beside her would be too easy. Instead, he bustled around locating his glasses and picking up his clothes, feeling Autumn's eyes burning into his bare flesh.

He'd barely pulled on his jeans when he felt her cool hand touch the warm skin on his back.

'Thank you.'

'It's ok, I want to help.' He cast her a glance.

Her returning smile split every rational thought into oblivion. 'You're just—' She didn't finish but reached up, cupping her fingers around his cheek. Her eyelids dropped as he sealed his lips on hers. She melted into him like she belonged nowhere else. And that was fine with him.

A rattle of wind at the window woke him from the fantasy. He pulled away with a slight cough. Autumn didn't open her eyes. The temptation to carry on was strong, but with an effort he stepped back and looked around the floor for his shirt.

'That's how I dreamed of waking up,' she said.

'Go back to bed and dream some more.' He dragged on his shirt. 'I'll see you at eight, I really have to go.'

At the bottom of the stairs, clattering sounds in the kitchen told him some staff were in, getting ready for breakfast. The air outside was arctic, blowing off the sea in great gusts and shuddering the trees. Richard jumped into the Freelander and put his foot down.

It seemed to take forever to get back, even though it wasn't far and he didn't pass any other vehicles. Peppy greeted him at the front door and sniffed him all over. 'Yeah, don't ask,' he said. 'You don't want to know what I smell of.'

The water in the shower washed it all away. Gone was the lingering aroma of Autumn. Memories slapped his face along with the water. It reminded him of how it had been with Lorraine. They'd hooked up and carried on like this. When he'd made the move to push things on, she'd laughed. How the hell did people ever know if this was the real deal or not?

Feelings had never entered the equation with Lorraine. He'd wrongly assumed their relationship was progressing, while she was only in it for the sex. What was Autumn in it for? A holiday fling? How could he find out? If he asked her, would it sound naïve and open him up to the same ridicule as the last time or would she be insulted? Was there anything more that could come of this?

'I wish I knew what to do,' he told Peppy as he opened the Freelander.

Was it worth the risk?

CHAPTER 19

Autumn

Autumn had to move. Her body, however, wasn't complying. The bed was too warm and the memories too fresh. For a man of few words, Richard knew how to use the ones he did use to perfection. Phrases like 'your smile is so beautiful' and 'do you like this?' would never have tripped off Josh's tongue – especially not during close encounters. Josh thought he was a gift; what woman wouldn't like what he had on offer? Autumn let her eyelids slide shut. After the intensity of last night, she wasn't sure anyone else would measure up ever again. Her body tingled at the memory and ached at the loss. The raw connection she'd experienced looking Richard in the eye as she hit an emotional and physical high had induced tears of joy. When had she ever done that? Not with Josh. He wouldn't have understood and would have been offended to think she was disappointed with his performance. After last night, she realised she should have been. Richard seemed to comprehend her inner needs on an atomic level – even the tears. After she'd asserted they were happy tears, he'd held her all night. Another first. He hadn't jumped and run as soon as he was done. He'd stayed. Present in mind and body. She brushed her cheek over the pillow, relishing its softness.

Never had she felt so emotionally safe. As she'd buried herself in his chest, enjoying the gentle strokes of his palms, she'd known a haven of warmth and compassion. Soon it would all be left behind.

Holiday fling… Tick. But it was way beyond that now. Her heart flipped. The gap between how she felt and what she had to do had grown so wide she was in danger of falling through. All these sensations and desires would be great if he happened to be a guy who lived in London, not someone from a world so remote and distant from anything she'd ever known. She couldn't live here, could she?

Did it matter where she lived? Nowhere so far had felt like home. Was taking a gamble on a guy she'd only met on Saturday worth the risk? Less than a frigging week ago. Shit like this wasn't supposed to happen.

For all his warmth, was it possible Richard was cool with this just being a quick fling? Maybe any hint of something more would send him running. But she'd felt so much in him; he hadn't needed words to express how deep his feelings were last night.

Eventually she dragged herself up, showered, dressed and took a quick breakfast in the dining room. Neither Robyn nor Carl were about which was a shame, she wanted to talk though she wasn't exactly sure what to say. She sent a quick message to Blair, thanking him but explaining that Richard had offered to help. She hoped Blair would understand. He replied almost straightaway with the thumbs up and a wink.

That's great! Enjoy and keep in touch X

When Richard pulled up, she jumped into the Freelander. Something about the look he gave her made her think again that maybe she was just a distraction. Perhaps she shouldn't have invited herself along. Was that a step too far? And if it was, surely anything more would be even worse.

He'd done so much for her already and made her feel incredible. Was this how she repaid him? What if her craziness caused him to miss a deadline or make a mistake? She might be responsible for the islands being ravaged by a fleet of kelp dredgers.

'Are you sure this is ok?'

'Yeah,' he said.

'What happens if parliament doesn't accept your research?' She pulled a lock of hair under her chin and twiddled it.

'It depends. It might go to appeal. It might be deemed inconclusive. There are several possible outcomes, but one bridge at a time.'

'I hope I haven't messed it up for you.'

'You haven't.' Richard leaned on his side window. 'In fact, you can help me.'

'Can I?'

'Yes.' Richard flicked her a brief grin. 'I need to swim out today, so you can look after Peppy while I'm in. Normally, I have to leave him in the car or enlist Ron. This'll help.'

'Wow, great. I can definitely do that. Do you need to take oxygen tanks and things like that?'

'No, I'm not going in that deep.'

'Are you taking your boat?'

'No.' He cleared his throat. 'Maybe if you come back another time, I could take you for a sail.'

'I'd like that.'

Yes, she could always come back, but would it be the same? She couldn't leave him waiting, the way Josh had done to her.

Silently they drove for several miles. Autumn contented herself watching the road she was getting to know so well. She tried to force her brain into imagining what it would be like to live here and if it would be any worse than living in London without being able to see Richard.

'I wonder,' said Richard. 'Why do you think your mum came here in the first place? What was her motive?'

'I'm not sure.' Autumn gave a dry laugh. 'Maybe she was trying to detox. Or maybe she really likes this guy.'

'People do crazy things when, well, you know…'

'When they're in love.' Was love enough? Were these crazy feelings bumping around in her head love? Something had swollen her heart to unknown proportions and when it deflated it was going to hurt so badly.

'Something like that.' Richard rubbed his neck and pulled on the wipers as a few drops of rain spattered the window.

By the time they reached the hidden beach at Fionnphort, the sky was clear again and sun shone through the white clouds. Richard had a different set of bags, including a neoprene one containing his wetsuit.

'Are you going to change into that here?' Autumn asked, parking herself on the giant flat boulder.

'Well, yeah… Under a towel. It's a bit windy for the tent.'

'Should I avert my eyes?'

'Hmm, you've seen it all before, don't tell me. But yeah, look the other way, preserve my dignity and all that.'

Trying to wipe the smile off her face, Autumn turned around, sensing him shuffling his way into the wetsuit.

'You can turn round now… if you want.'

She did. Her eyes travelled over him and she didn't feel the need to reel them in. He was well aware how much she liked his physique. She hadn't held back in letting him know last night. 'Tasty.'

'Autumn, please. I really do have to work.'

'I know. I'm sorry. That was…'

He dropped down beside her, the glimmer of a smile on his lips. 'Listen, why don't you go and find some more things to put in your candles?'

'Is there any point?'

'Of course there is.' He put his hand on her knee. 'You could open a shop. Autumn's Sea Kelp Emporium, selling all your kelp needs.'

She looked away, watching the gulls circling. 'I've thought of doing crazy stuff like that before. I once dreamed of a beach cabin in Cornwall.'

'Well, maybe you could do it here.'

When she looked at him, his eyes were fixed on her. She wasn't sure what to say. Was that an invitation or just an idle comment? Neither seemed likely from him, but before she could probe further, he stood up and rubbed his hands. 'I'll be in for at least an hour.'

'Ok. I'll take Peppy a walk and see you when you come out.'

Richard chapped her shoulder. 'Thanks.' He headed down the beach. Baywatch had nothing on this. It was her own private show, though she felt a tad voyeuristic as Richard smoothed back his hair and waded into the sea. That had to be freezing, right? But he didn't flinch. He got smaller and smaller and the sea higher up his body until he vanished under. Seconds later, he bobbed up again and swam towards a rock poking above the surface.

'Come on, Peppy,' said Autumn. 'Let's leave him to it.' Together they trekked across the grassy plain towards the beach. Peppy bounded ahead, tossing his nose high and loping through the long tufts onto the dunes. Wind battered Autumn's hair, tangling it high and she dug her hands into her pockets, striding along the raised shore, looking down on the turquoise sea. Richard was still visible in the distance, close to the rock.

'What should I do?' she asked Peppy, clapping her hands in front, trying to warm them. 'Do you think he really wants me to stay? Was he just being funny? Or did he just say that but not really mean it at all? Is that why he clammed up?' She threw her head back. It was impossible to know. Her heart was sending her messages, but could she put her trust in someone she knew so little?

Not knowing how long she'd walked for, it was a surprise to turn back and see the tiny figure of Richard back on the beach. As she got closer, she saw a towel wrapped around his shoulders, covering his otherwise bare torso. An iPad was on his lap and he was hunched over it. She broke into a jog and arrived beside him out of breath.

He glanced up as Peppy nosed him and turned to watch Autumn landing next to him. 'Are you ok?' he asked.

'Yeah, I ran, but I'm out of training. Did you get on ok?'

'Fine. I'm just emailing some data to the team. We need to see if it's consistent for each area and analyse the differences in the regions already affected by the dredging.'

'I hope it works out.' Autumn leaned on his towel-covered shoulder. He dropped his head so it was on top of hers; she felt his damp hair on her own.

'You know,' he whispered on to the top of her head. 'I want to thank you for bringing me along for the ride.'

She grinned. 'You don't need to thank me. You're the one who's given up so much time and energy to take me. I'm the one getting a ride.'

'I mean figuratively.'

'Maybe I did too.' She couldn't help giggling.

'Yeah, funny.' He rested his hand on her leg. 'You've helped me to remember what it's like to feel and that it's not always a bad thing. I've found something new in myself, and that's thanks to you.'

Autumn rubbed her head into his shoulder, letting the soft towel caress her cheek. 'I just wish we had more time.'

Richard freed his arm and put it around her. The addictive smell of the sea was all over his bare chest. He placed a soft kiss on her cheek. 'I feel so much for you,' he whispered in her ear.

'I do too,' she said, 'but I'm scared.'

He tightened his grip and she melted into him. The heat from his chest was intense. How could he be this warm, sitting half-naked on a beach in Scotland in October? Her ear nestled over his pounding heart. He stroked her arm through her coat. 'It's ok.'

'It is now.' This was home, where she wanted to be.

'I've got food,' he said. 'Shall we eat something. I've got a couple more things to do, then we can head off and look for your mum.' He stood up, pulled on his t-shirt and a soft grey shirt over. After raking about in one of his bags, he laid out some sandwiches.

'Tell me something,' said Autumn resting a foot on a rock and looking down on Richard as he sat on the boulder. The novelty of feeling taller than him made her smile.

'About what?'

'Yourself. Your family… parents, siblings, friends. Anything, just talk to me.'

He glanced out to sea. 'Well, my father's dead. My mother is sixty-five and has arthritis, though it doesn't stop her writing me long letters. And I have two sisters, who don't approve of their reclusive failed-at-life brother.'

'Why?'

'Long story.'

Autumn dropped onto her knees beside him and leaned her arms along the boulder. Settling her chin on her hands, she gazed up at him. 'Tell me.'

He stroked his fingers over her curls. 'You really want to know?'

'Of course, I do.'

'Apparently, when we were children, I was my father's favourite. He was old-fashioned, and because they were girls, he didn't give them the same opportunities as me. They've always held it against me. I didn't see it. I believed he nurtured my dreams because he thought I had a talent, not because I was the only son.'

'Ouch.'

'When I was married, my sisters came round for a while.'

'That was good then, wasn't it?'

'Ha, no. My sisters loved Ruth, my ex. She's like them; they're all strong, goal-orientated women.'

Autumn quirked her lip to one side. Was that the kind of woman he usually went for? She couldn't aspire to that. Her goal was just to get through a day without any major drama. 'I guess they weren't pleased when you split.'

'They were thrilled. It proved everything they'd said about me was true. I was the awful man they wanted me to be. It showed all their anger in just the right light. They'd always maintained I was undeserving, and I handed them the proof on a plate. They still idolise Ruth, while hating me.' He caressed her hair and Autumn leaned into his palm with a sigh. How would it be when she was too far away to feel his soothing touch?

'I sympathise. My family's a messed-up bunch as well.'

'I've learned to expect nothing, then I'm not disappointed when it goes wrong.' He sighed, still running her curls around his fingers.

'Tell me about Adam,' she whispered.

He removed his hand from her hair and took out his phone, swiping through it. 'There.'

Taking the phone from him, Autumn scanned the photograph on the screen. 'He looks so like you.'

'He doesn't like having his picture taken.'

'He's beautiful.' She ran her finger across it. 'Why does he live in America?'

'His mother's American. She and I…' Richard laced his fingers together. 'We had a troubled relationship. We divorced three years ago. She's a workaholic.'

'So are you.'

'Precisely. When Adam was born, we both worked in the oil industry and we lived in Aberdeen, and while most mothers like getting a year's maternity leave, Ruth didn't. She wanted to be back at work, but Adam was a difficult baby. When he was two-years-old, he was diagnosed with autism. It's unusual to get diagnosed so young, but he's on the top edge of the spectrum. His brain is wired differently, he doesn't see or react to the world like most people.'

Autumn slipped her hand over the top of his entwined fingers. 'That must be so hard.'

'It is. Ruth found the demands on her overwhelming and because I worked off-shore and for such long hours, I wasn't there to help. She blames me for the way he is. I have some tendencies myself, though nothing diagnosed or extreme, just oddities. You might have noticed.'

'Kind of, but it just seems like part of you.' She ran a fingertip across his knuckles. 'And I wouldn't change it.'

'Ruth wouldn't share your view. She has two more kids now and they're "normal".' He freed one hand to air quote. 'So she insists Adam got the gene from me.' As he lowered his hand, he brought it to rest on top of Autumn's and rubbed his thumb across the soft spot at the base of her thumb. Autumn inhaled slowly and deeply. 'That's why he lives in Chicago,' Richard continued, still stroking her, and Autumn struggled to keep her shit together and listen. He was sending her all sorts of places – again. 'His mother's from around there and her family has a country estate where it's safe for him. He's part of some progressive studies, and Ruth's parents are very good. Plus, they have a team of childcare workers to do the job while she works.'

'I see,' Autumn whispered.

'Ruth felt I'd absconded from my rights by not being there enough for Adam.'

'But she works herself?'

'Yes, but she doesn't see the correlation. Our relationship was complicated enough. When she came up with the plans for Adam, I signed the documents, though I knew I was signing away my son. I let her take him.'

'Why?'

'I thought I could make it work. I moved to Chicago for a while, but it was impossible to do my job without causing huge ructions to Adam's routine. Getting work visas in America is notoriously difficult and marine jobs in Chicago are non-existent, so it meant a lot of travel and uncertainty. It infuriated Ruth that my visits set Adam off. The home I had wasn't suitable for him. All my efforts were the worst thing for him. So, I came back here and hid myself away.'

Autumn bit her lip. 'Oh, Richard. That's sad.'

'I told you it wasn't a pleasant story.'

'It doesn't make you heartless though. You made a tough choice. If you'd chosen not to let them go, you might feel the same amount of pain, only in different ways.'

'Maybe.'

She extricated her hand and got up from her slightly numb knees. 'Don't beat yourself up.'

'I try not to, but it's hard. I feel powerless.'

'I think you made a brave choice.'

'Really? I've always felt like a coward.'

'You chose the path that was best for Adam.'

'Yeah, maybe.' He lifted a long piece of kelp from the boulder. 'Do you want some more of this?'

She guessed that was the subject closed. 'Is there any point? I still haven't worked out what to do with it.'

Richard sucked his lower lip. 'Let's swing by the house later and have a go in the lab. If we work it out, I could always mail you the dried kelp.'

Mail me? There it was. He either didn't expect her to stay or want her to. If she stayed it would mean a whole new level of courage and despite her love of spontaneity, she'd never done anything adventurous in her life… except making this trip. And had she made it for nothing?

CHAPTER 20

Richard

Richard stared into Autumn's eyes. They were a liquid turquoise colour, a perfect match for the sea. He'd pinged the ball into her court, suggesting she came back to his house and testing the water to see if she'd be interested pursuing her dreams here. So far, her response had been vague. There was no doubting the pull between them, but was it strong enough to last after the weekend? Or was Autumn happy with her fling?

Richard finished up his studies and Autumn helped him tidy up. 'So, time to go mum-hunting?' he said.

'Let's do it.'

He hoisted on his backpack and Autumn lifted another one, before turning to him, pushing onto her tiptoes and planting a kiss on his cheek. Her long auburn curls bounced around her lightly freckled cheeks as she sank back onto the sand.

'What was that for?'

'Because I like you.'

'Likewise.' Richard ran his fingers down her cheek. 'How about I make you dinner tonight?'

'Ok, sounds amazing.'

'Any special requests?'

'Now there's an offer.'

'To eat,' he clarified, but he smirked. Having Autumn in the long run might be impossible, but he could steal her for one more night. Even if it broke him tomorrow. No part of his anatomy other than his brain should be allowed to make decisions, but his brain wasn't giving the right answers.

'I'm a vegetarian, but other than that, no,' said Autumn.

'Well, so am I, so that's good,' he said, walking towards the machair.

'No way.'

'Yes way.'

'How bizarre. But good. At least I don't have to explain myself.'

'Peppy isn't unfortunately, so if you really can't stand meat, stay away from his bowl.'

'No, I can handle that. It's the snidey comments I don't like. My dad's girlfriend once came shrieking into the living room when I was visiting and told me to get off the sofa. I thought I'd punctured it with a stud on my jeans or something, but no. It was leather and Krystina decided to make a big thing of it that some vegan friend of hers didn't approve of leather, so she assumed I'd be the same. She wanted me to sit on the floor.'

Richard gave a dry laugh. 'Just as well our families won't ever meet, we seem to have collected quite a bunch between us.'

Autumn giggled, but as their eyes met, their smiles faded. Was this about to come to an end? There may be fireworks and fun, intimacy and ecstasy, but it couldn't last. Was he just torturing his mind by gratifying his body? As they walked, Autumn's silence was ominous. Peppy trotted along happily by their side.

White breakers crashed home, lifting high and wild as the wind tossed around. Richard hopped over a couple of stones on the path, waiting for Autumn to catch up.

'Richard, sorry if this is nosey, and you can tell me to shut up if you want, but when did you last see Adam?'

Richard shook his head. 'Last week.'

'Last week? I thought you never saw him. You said he lived near Chicago.'

'He does. It was his annual review meeting. Ruth invited me, but it never feels like it's out of kindness. I guess it's a formality, but it just reminds me of my failings. It was terrible timing workwise, but I travelled over. That was me on my way back when I met you on Saturday.'

'You'd been to Chicago?'

'Yup. The flights were delayed and I arrived late. My work phone rang in the middle of the meeting. You can imagine how popular I was.'

'Eek, that sounds painful. But you got to see Adam.'

'Yeah, as I'd travelled all that way, they allowed me one controlled visit. He doesn't know me now. So my being there wrecked his day and sent him into an episode. I shouldn't have bothered; I just make things worse.'

'But it's not your fault.' Autumn's sparkling eyes were full of conviction. 'You showed them you haven't given up.'

'But what's the point? If I hadn't gone, I'd be damned; when I did go, I was damned. Whatever I do changes nothing for the better. Not for Adam. The best thing for him is for me to stay away, which hits me right here.' Richard threw his fist into his chest.

'Then write him letters, send him cards or games. Do something else. It may seem like a cop-out, but at least you're doing something and in a way that doesn't throw Adam's world upside down and irritate the people he lives with.'

'I already do that. I send him birthday cards and presents, postcards, lots of things. It just never seems enough.'

'I get what it's like to be on the other side. My mum walked out on me as a child and I still don't really know if she loves me or not. At least when Adam grows up, he'll have evidence you didn't disappear. You made a choice to let him go with his mother and get the day-to-day support he needs, but you're still there, just a Facetime away. You've acknowledged his birthdays and shown you're still there for him. My mum didn't do that for me and she only lived a few streets away. Even when I was living in the same house as her, she forgot my sixteenth birthday. She told me she'd get me something at the weekend, but whatever it was, I never got it.' The wind tangled Autumn's hair as she jogged along. 'She was always too busy with her boyfriends.'

'Maybe throwing herself into new relationships gave her some sense of… something. I don't know.'

But Richard did. After losing Adam, he'd leapt into Lorraine's bed. The divorce papers weren't even signed, but it was a distraction… For a while.

'You didn't do that, did you?'

'No,' he said convulsively. 'Well… I didn't sleep around, no. I did have another relationship, but… Well, never mind.' Perhaps Autumn sensed he didn't want to talk, she went silent and Richard didn't offer anything further. Dragging up the past was his least favourite subject and this was skirting treacherously close to places he didn't want to visit ever again.

After packing up the Freelander, Richard jumped into the driver seat and headed north. 'So, where are we going to find this Mike?'

'It's near Calgary on an Estate called Ardnish,' said Autumn with a little laugh. 'Listen to me, talking like I know what I'm on about. Murray wrote it down for me.'

'I know it. I did a job there.'

'This is probably a wild goose chase and there's nothing to stop it being a disaster all over again.'

'Yeah, there is. I have no intention of falling down a ravine for one.'

'You're funny.' She patted his thigh.

'If you say so.' He rubbed his neck, trying to ignore the spikes of lust her touch sent ricocheting through him. 'So, which cottage is it on the estate?'

'Gardener's Cottage.'

'I don't know the estate well. My work was focused more on the neighbouring land, but let's assume Gardener's Cottage is close to the walled garden. I know where to find that.'

'You see, you're a genius.' She pulled her shoulders in tight and grinned. 'But you know that, right?'

'Goes with the territory.' He gave a side nod, gazing across the dismal grey panorama. Rain clouds were blowing in thick and fast. It was over an hour later when they reached Ardnish, and the wipers were going haywire.

'This weather sucks,' said Autumn.

'This is Mull.' Rain was part of the package. 'And this is Ardnish. The main house isn't visible from the road. It's down a long track, right by the sea. Once we turn in the main gate, if we take the track south, it goes to the walled garden. Mr Crichton-Leith gave me a tour, but I didn't pay close attention.' Richard eased the Freelander through the austere stone gateposts and turned left. The suspension jolted and they lurched along a stony track on a barren hillside. 'Look that way, you might spot the main house.' He pointed out his window, and Autumn squinted through the blustery rain, across the bleak plain.

A tumbledown stone wall came into view.

'This is not what I expected,' said Autumn. 'I remember going to a walled garden on a school trip once.'

Richard shook his head. 'Yeah, I don't think this estate is in the best of nick.' Rugged wilderness surrounded it. The wall was crumbling in several places and nothing inside resembled a garden; it was more like a storage area for old farming equipment. At the corner closest to them, a cottage was built into the wall. On its far side, it would have a sea view and on the inner, it must look into the garden. Maybe at one time, it was a stunning place to live, but it looked tired and forgotten. As Autumn and Richard got out, the wind whipped up, almost scalping them.

Without thinking, Richard took her hand and squeezed it. 'Even if this isn't the right place, it doesn't matter. At least you've tried.'

'I know.' She clutched his hand. 'And I have a nice dinner to look forward to.'

'You do.'

'But I am a bit nervous.'

Richard gave her a sideways glance as they rounded the corner. 'It'll be ok.'

The front of the cottage appeared more loved. Plant pots adorned the doorway, and although they'd blown over, it had a homely air. With very little idea of what Autumn's mum was really like, Richard couldn't speculate whether she was likely to be here. An old jeep was parked on a gravel patch. It shuddered in the wind. Behind, the sea fizzed with huge white breakers swelling around in a pell-mell of foam and spray.

'Are you ready?' he asked as they stood on the doorstep.

Autumn took a deep breath and knocked. 'As I'll ever be.'

After a few silent seconds, the door opened. An older man, somewhat rough around the edges, peered out. He ran his fingers over his short grey hair and frowned at them. 'Are you lost?' he said.

'No,' said Richard, squinting through the misty rain.

'Eh, hi,' said Autumn, tightening her grip on his hand.

'How can I help you? Is it Ardnish you're after?'

'I'm looking for someone called Mike,' said Autumn.

'Oh, yeah. What's it about?' The man folded his arms and peered at Autumn, eyeing her over, his brow furrowing.

'Actually, it's my mum I'm looking for.'

'Pardon?' said the man.

'Her name's Vicky.'

The man blinked and nodded, then glanced away. 'Aye, er yeah. I know who you mean.'

'Is she here?' said Richard.

'Um, no.' The man twisted his hands, his brow crinkled.

'Has she ever been here?' Richard pressed.

'Aye, but she's not wanting to be found.'

'What do you mean?' asked Autumn. 'I'm her daughter. If she's here, I want to see her.'

'Sorry, lass. She's er…' He looked around with edginess in his eyes. 'She's gone off.'

'Where?' Desperation flared in the word.

The man mouthed something before finding his voice. 'Er, don't you live in London?'

'Yes.'

'She talked about you.' The man squinted at Richard then back to Autumn. 'She said you had a boyfriend, the married chap. I'm glad it's worked out in your favour.'

'What?' said Richard. He furrowed his brow and stared at Autumn. Her cheeks were very flushed. She had a boyfriend who was married? Seriously? He loosened his grip on her hand but she clung on.

'Sorry, lass. I'm sure your mum will contact you when she's ready.'

'When was she here?' Autumn asked.

The man shook his head. 'I don't know. Sorry.' With a vague shrug, he closed the door.

Autumn stared at the door. 'That was weird. Should I knock again?'

'I don't think there's any point' said Richard, letting go of her hand and making his way back to the Freelander. 'So, you have a boyfriend…' He took his seat and buckled up. 'Maybe you should have told me that before, well, before last night anyway.'

'No, Richard. I don't. We split up. Truth be told, we weren't really together, not in the traditional sense.'

'Because he was married?'

'Yes, he was. We dated when I was a teenager, but he was older, he left, got married and moved on. Then he came back, full of promises.' Autumn massaged her temples. 'And I believed him. I waited and waited, basically letting him use me.'

'Autumn.' Richard let out a sigh. 'That's awful.' Why had she put herself through it? Not that he had a right to judge. After all what had he been to Lorraine other than a toy?

'My own fault.'

'No, really. You're not an object. Jesus, that's terrible.'

'My friends told me I was stupid, that I was besotted and should cut clean, but I didn't listen. I followed my heart and it led me into a trap.'

'It doesn't excuse his behaviour. I'm glad you've cut him loose. He doesn't deserve you.'

'I hope that's a compliment.'

'Of course it is. You were young. It's dreadful he used you like that.'

Autumn flicked her hair out of her eyes. 'I just wanted some security. Though seeing someone who's already married isn't exactly great for that.' She rubbed her face. 'And now I've spent several hundred pounds on a hotel room only to find Mum isn't here. I could have saved myself the bother. What a bloody mess.'

'Hey.' Richard took her hand and stroked it. 'Life is messy.'

She smiled at him; the trademark grin which turned his insides to jelly.

'Do you still want dinner?'

'Yes, please.' Autumn fastened her seatbelt before lavishing some attention on Peppy. Richard started the engine as Autumn glanced back at the cottage. 'What was that man all about? I guess it means Mum was here, but it's just weird.' Raking back her hair, she pinned it to the top of her head. 'When he opened the door, I had a weird feeling like I'd seen him before or I recognised him somehow.'

'Did you? He didn't look familiar to me, but it was all very odd. You and your mum seem to have a lot in common.'

'Seriously? That's not a compliment.'

'Yeah, sorry. But it seems like she's made some rash decision to come up here with a guy she met online, but the reality was nothing like what she imagined, so she left.'

'Yes, it seems like that.' And where did that leave them? Surely this would put Autumn off making a rash decision of her own.

CHAPTER 21

Autumn

Richard drove silently. The ever-changing scenery rolled by like a slideshow. Autumn couldn't take it in. She wanted to enjoy it but it was too fleeting. Just like her time with Richard. Last night she'd been his princess and his goddess; loved, desired, cherished, and worshipped. Ever since they'd met, he'd been kind, respectful, helpful, but what did it all mean?

They headed south, around a rugged coastline. From the lofty road, the sea and some smaller islands were visible with an impressive mountainous backdrop. 'Is that still Mull over there?'

'Yes, this road goes around a sea loch. Loch-Na-Keal.'

Trees swathed in gold lined the road as it clung to the coast. It was lush compared to the bleak ruggedness of Fionnphort. The sea rushed upon wide stretches of beach. Thick grey clouds looked both dramatic and foreboding.

Opposite the shore was a hedgerow with scrubby green fields and low peaks running along behind. Rising from a low promontory was a spectacular house with a glass-walled extension to the front. 'Oh my god, check out that house. It's stunning. I bet the view is amazing. I wonder what lucky sods live there.'

'That house?' Richard swallowed. 'Those lucky sods would be me and Peppy.'

'That's your house?' Autumn's mouth fell open. He was one big bag of never-ending surprises. 'Bloody hell.'

'Yup.' Richard rubbed his neck, then turned up the inclined track.

As Autumn got out, the wind smacked her hard. Her jaw nearly hit the floor. The sea crashed beyond. In the shelter of the garden, flowers grew, adding sparks of red and gold around the rambling green lawn. 'Wow, this is just, well…'

'Far too modern for me.'

'No, well, yes. But not in a bad way. This has got to be the most amazing house I've ever seen.' She followed him over a gravelled area to the door. Richard opened it to an entry porch, messing up his hair and scanning around.

The lilt of the waves and the high whistle of a curlew were the only sounds. The beauty sent Autumn's imagination whizzing. Oh, to be sitting inside, surrounded by candles, wrapped in a blanket, and watching the waves. It all looked rosy just now, but life here wouldn't always be like this. If she were to stay, what would she be giving up? Shops, theatres, work? Could she do it? And for what? Just Richard? Maybe that was what home meant. Being with a person not in a place.

Richard pulled off his boots and Autumn did the same with her bashed old things, ruined from their island escapades. Pushing open the interior door, Richard let Peppy in and the dog trotted into a bright corridor, stairs at one side and a couple of doors on the other. Light shone through the open door ahead. Autumn followed Peppy into the modern, open-plan extension. The room was L-shaped and a kitchen area was in the foot of the L, adjacent to the corridor she'd just come down. In front of the kitchen was a huge dining area and at the opposite end was a lounge seating area with comfortable sofas and a rectangular coffee table. A wall of glass ran the length of the whole room and the dining side too. On the side wall of the lounge area was a beautiful rustic stone fireplace and wood burner.

Autumn gaped towards the sea. 'Wow.'

'Yeah, it's a powerful view, but it's a bit chilly. I'll light the fire.' Richard threw some logs onto the burner and soon had a blaze going.

'This is such a cool house. Did you build the extension?'

'No.' He flopped into a sofa, crossing his long legs. 'I haven't done any of it. I haven't even finished decorating it. There's hardly any furniture. I don't really need a house this big. I thought, well, I dreamed one day Adam might visit, but you're the first visitor I've had since I arrived.'

'And when was that?'

A wry grin spread across his face. 'Three years ago.'

'Richard, I'm not even going to ask if you're being serious. What are you like?'

'I like my privacy, that's all.' He patted the empty space beside him. Autumn slipped into the soft fabric of the sofa and closed her eyes as Richard settled his arms around her. 'Why did you come all this way to find your mum when she's treated you so badly?'

'An excuse.'

'What do you mean?'

'I needed a reason to get away. I told myself and my friends it was what I needed to do, but what I really wanted was to get away.'

'Why?' He rubbed her shoulder and a drowsy calm flowed through her, like he was slowly hypnotising her.

'I've made a mess of things. I spent all that time waiting for Josh. Then I discovered his wife was pregnant. We hadn't seen each other for months. I had this feeling he was going to turn up and "need" me again. I didn't want to fall back into his arms, but I didn't know how to stop it. I couldn't let myself wreck their family. I know too well what that's like.'

Richard didn't speak but continued to gently smooth his palm up and down her arm.

'I dread going back,' said Autumn.

'Then stay.'

Maybe if he hadn't been softly sending her into a trance, she'd have been shocked, but she let out a sigh. 'I don't know… It's so different here.'

'Yeah.' His hand stopped moving. 'I understand. I didn't mean to put you in a difficult position.'

He got to his feet, leaving Autumn shivery and exposed. She rubbed her arms and squinted about, uncertain.

'I'll make the dinner.'

'I can help,' said Autumn.

'No, just relax. I've got a book you can look at. Two minutes and I'll get it.'

Autumn waited as he left the room. He'd just asked her to stay and she'd said no without thinking. It was such a huge idea, she couldn't make sense of it, just like she couldn't make sense of her feelings. In amongst all the jumble, they'd made something beautiful and she clung to that. When he returned, he was holding a large hardback book.

'It's all about the uses of kelp. You might find something useful in it.' He passed it to her and she smiled.

She was no great scholar, but why not? As he headed for the kitchen area, she opened the book and started leafing through it.

CHAPTER 22

Richard

Richard set about making dinner. He straightened his glasses and snuck a glance at Autumn. She was still ensconced on the sofa in the lounge area, leafing through the book on kelp. Where did they go from here? Did she still want to spend the night with him, playing out one last island fantasy before their separation? Irresistibly, he was reminded of Lorraine. They'd spent days like this, working together, then evenings of passion. None of those encounters had produced feelings like this, not reciprocated ones anyway.

Autumn shared his feelings, he was certain, but she didn't want the change in lifestyle. He couldn't blame her. He'd done it himself and it was awful. Life in Chicago wasn't for him, just as life on Mull wasn't for Autumn. Onions sizzled in the pan and Richard carried on prepping the veg, chopping with more ferocity than was strictly necessary.

'For candles, I think you have to dry the kelp first,' said Autumn. Richard looked around. Autumn had taken a barstool on the opposite side of the breakfast bar. She spread the book across the black granite worktop. 'There seem to be a few different ways to do it.'

Richard poured a glass of wine and placed it in front of her. 'I forgot to show you the lab. It's a bit dark now though it has lights if you're desperate.'

'Maybe not tonight.' Raising her glass to her lips, Autumn took a sip. 'That's good wine. I need to come back one day, there's too much to take in.'

'Yup.' Richard rolled up his sleeves and loosened his shirt. Darkness had settled outside, and great gusts howled past the thick stone walls, rattling the glass-fronted extension and whistling over the roof.

'I'm so glad we met,' said Autumn. 'I know this is just a brief moment but it's been special.'

'Yeah.'

'Can we keep in touch?' she asked. 'I'd hate to think we'll never see each other again after Saturday.'

'I'll try.' So this was it.

'Sign up to Facebook. We can be online friends and you can post pictures of edible seaweed and jellyfish.' She tilted her head and pleaded with those sparkly turquoise eyes. Like those online methods would ever replace the real thing.

'I'm already on Facebook, but I hardly ever look at it. I friended Ron and Anne because it's easier to contact them on messenger than texts. Well, you know what reception is like here.'

'I'm learning.' She took out her phone and scrolled through it. 'Is this you? Richard Linden, University of Aberdeen.'

'Yes. I should probably update that.'

'And no picture? Seriously, Richard.'

'I don't like having my picture taken.'

Autumn held up her phone. 'Go on, let me take one. Just so I don't forget what you look like.'

He leaned on the breakfast bar and gave his best attempt at a smile.

'Looking good,' she said. 'I'll message it to you as soon as you accept my friend request, then if you're feeling brave, you can upload it to your profile.'

'Hmm, maybe.' Lifting his own phone from the breakfast bar, he accepted her request and laid it back down. 'There you go, we're officially friends.'

'We're definitely that.' She raised her glass.

Yes, they'd reached online friends and if that was the extent of things it wouldn't go much further. Richard knew his limitations and social media had never worked for him. He didn't buy into the culture of posting the minutiae of his life for everyone to see.

'Why don't you sit at the table? I'll bring the food round in a minute.' Richard suggested, adding sauce to the pasta simmering on the stove.

'How about I put out the cutlery?' Autumn came around and started checking through drawers.

'That one.' Richard directed her to the right place and she bustled about setting up, looking a bit too at home. Maybe becoming online friends had eased her mind more than it had his because she seemed quite chilled as she laid out the cutlery and speculated about where her mum might actually be.

'She's probably gone back to Phil, though I seriously hope not. I feel sorry for Phil, but he's his own worst enemy. All the hoarding, it's awful.'

'Yeah. It's something I've never understood. I'm possibly the opposite. You should see the spare bedrooms. There's nothing in any of them except a clothes airer. I haven't even bought furniture.' Richard dished the food onto the plates, half wondering why he was telling her stuff like that, but as always, she seemed interested and her open expression invited confidence.

'I'd love to do up a house, but I own nothing. I usually rent furnished places. My rent's almost up on my latest flat. I need to get a job as soon as I get back or I'll be evicted.'

It was on the tip of his tongue to suggest she stayed again, but no, he'd tried that already. 'I'm sure you'll find something.'

After serving up, they both ate in silence for a moment. Autumn sipped her wine, watching him. 'I'd like to come back,' she said. 'But…'

'But what?'

'I just… You know, you and me.'

'I'm not sure I do. We've had a good week, but where does it leave us?'

Autumn poured more wine, her hand shaking slightly. 'If I was braver, I could get a temporary job here and see how it goes.'

'That's not really fair on you.'

Toying with her glass and remaining food, Autumn's words seemed to have run dry. After finishing, Richard got up and cleared the table. Autumn followed, helping him to load the dishwasher.

'Autumn, I like you a lot, but I don't want you to have to make some kind of sacrifice for me.'

'Not just for you, for us.'

'But we don't know where this might go.'

A distant, high-pitched, metallic scraping sound echoed from outside. Richard straightened up from putting in a plate and he spun to the window. 'Did you hear that?'

'What was it?'

'I don't know.' He padded towards the glass wall. The dishwasher door shut with a thud and Autumn appeared at his side. Together they squinted out. Richard crossed the room and switched off the lights, then held his face to the glass, but he couldn't see a thing except for the raindrops. 'I'll go and look from upstairs.'

He dashed up to his bedroom, leaving the light off as he wound around the bed to the window which, like the corresponding room below, had floor to ceiling glass. Peering into the thick darkness, he strained to focus on anything but the lashing rain and swaying trees in the garden.

'Can you see anything?' Autumn whispered, moving in behind him.

He jumped and stumbled into her. 'Jesus. I didn't hear you come up. I can't see anything.'

She edged in front of him and peered out. 'What do you think it was?'

'I'm not sure.' In the dark by the window, they stood silently for some time, trying to glimpse anything. The sweet scent of Autumn's perfume in the darkened room played havoc with his thought process. 'Probably something blowing over. Let's go down. Do you want dessert?'

Turning to face him, she pushed onto her tiptoes and wrapped her arms around his neck. 'Yes,' she muttered, reaching up and nipping his lower lip.

Bending, he kissed her, their open mouths melding together. Tremors of need ran through him. What tomorrow might bring was so low in his priority list right now he simply didn't care. He couldn't express how he felt in words, but he could show her how much she meant to him. Her fingers were in his hair, pulling him ever closer. The rustling wind built into gusts, a spatter of rain peppered the windows. In the distance, waves crashed in a crescendo. Richard pulled back and took off his glasses, setting them on the bedside cabinet before he unbuttoned the first few buttons of his soft grey shirt, hoisted it over his head, and discarded it. His t-shirt followed suit.

'You are so fit,' Autumn murmured, gliding her fingertips over his chest, sending tingles through every nerve end. Slipping her hands around his neck and under his hair, she nuzzled his shoulder. His stomach flipped at her touch and he ground in closer so he could feel every part of her.

His hot blood obscured every thought not related to their immediate pleasure. He was losing himself again. Blasting wind roared along the front of the house, pummelling the windows. The bunching muscles at his shoulders rolled under Autumn's super-soft lips. She broke away with a soft moan and Richard skimmed his mouth over her cheek.

'I really do like you… So, oh… very much,' she moaned, leaning back, exposing her neck, as he followed its gentle curve with his lips

'Likewise, you're—'

A deafening bang made him stop dead. Peppy started barking.

'What was that?' said Autumn.

'No idea,' mumbled Richard. 'Something blowing over.' He leaned in, placing a kiss on her warm collarbone, finding the slender curves of her back with his palms. The thudding came again, louder and heavier. Peppy's barks increased.

'I think it's someone at the door.' Autumn's lips grazed his ear as she spoke.

'It can't be. No one ever comes here.'

A cacophony of bangs followed. Richard straightened up, his eyebrows contracting.

'That's definitely someone at the door,' Autumn whispered.

Who the hell could it be?

CHAPTER 23

Autumn

'For heaven's sake, no one has ever knocked on that door before except the damned postman.' Richard disentangled himself from Autumn and rubbed his forehead. 'Peppy! Hush,' he shouted out the door.

Autumn sat on the bed and breathed for a second, trying to make sense of what was going on. Who was at the door? What could matter more than the feelings they were sharing right here and now? They were the most important things in the world. This was what it was like being loved and cared for. Who dared burst the bubble?

'Tonight of all nights someone decides to come hammering. You couldn't make it up.' Richard grabbed his glasses from the bedside table, snatched his shirt and made his way downstairs. 'Hush, Peppy.'

Autumn followed to the landing, leant on the bannister and peered over. Her heartrate escalated. Whoever wanted in was giving the door a right pounding.

Richard opened the door, fumbling to fasten his shirt. A squat woman tumbled in from the porch, dripping wet from her sodden hat to her saturated boots. Peppy sniffed her.

'Oh, Richard, I'm sorry to bother you,' she shrieked in a frantic voice, clutching a soggy scarf. 'I really am, but I don't know where else to go. I've called the police. They're on their way, but I can't wait.' Water ran off her waxed coat. Her eyes bulged from her wide face. 'Can you come and help?'

'With what?' He groped for his buttons.

Autumn craned her neck, furrowing her brow.

'It's Neil, he's had an accident.' The woman panted. 'Oh my, I don't know what happened. He must have swerved, trying to miss something. He's on the rocks and can't get out. He phoned me and told me to get help. Please come. I'm terrified he gets swept away. I drove along, but I can't get to him. It's so windy out there I could hardly stand.'

'Ok, ok.' Richard raised his hands. 'Let me grab some clothes and some boots.'

'Oh yes, thank you, thank you so very much.' She fussed Peppy as Richard ran up the stairs.

Autumn met him on the landing.

'Did you hear that?' he muttered from the corner of his mouth, his eyes darting downstairs. 'That's my neighbour.'

'Yes, I'll come too.'

'No, you stay.' He edged forward. Autumn backed into the room. With Richard's bare chest visible under his haphazard buttoning, the sea breeze smell was impossible to miss, reminding her of his kisses, his warmth.

'I want to come with you.'

He put his hand on her cheek. 'I'm sorry.'

Closing her eyes, Autumn held her breath. 'I'm coming with you, no matter what you say.'

'I know. I meant I'm sorry about the interruption.' He let his hand fall, switched on the light and glanced towards the bed. Grabbing two jumpers from his drawer, he threw one to her. 'Wear that, you'll need it out there. Now, let's go, it sounds serious.'

Autumn bounded down before Richard to where the woman rocked, muttering to herself. She lifted her pallid face, furrowed her brows, and drew back. 'Oh, hello.'

'Hi.' Autumn hopped off the bottom step. 'I'm coming to help.'

The woman fixated on Autumn with her jaw hanging loose. 'Good lord, um, I'm Joyce. I thought I heard voices. I'm sorry, I didn't know anyone else was here.'

'Come on,' muttered Richard, his feet heavy on the stairs. 'Where's Neil?'

'Not far, on the rocks over there.' Joyce pointed wildly.

Richard handed Autumn his waxed jacket and pushed Peppy back into the house. 'You stay here, boy, it's not safe.' They dashed out and Joyce lumbered along behind.

'It's past the house, a bit further,' she shrieked over the wind. 'I hope he's all right.'

'I see it.' Autumn pointed. Richard held his huge torch towards the rocks,

Joyce clutched her face. The vehicle shone, silvery, suspended between the craggy rocks. One move could send it flying.

'Oh, hell.' Autumn put her hand to her mouth. 'How can we get him out of there?'

Thousands of raindrops twinkled in the beam from the torch. The wind buffeted round. Richard strode across the rocks. Autumn slipped and slid, following the bobbing torchlight. She caught him as he searched around the car and grabbed his arm.

'Go back, this is not safe.' Richard clutched her frozen hand. 'Please.'

A sharp gust rattled the car, throwing icy raindrops into her face. She squinted through them. 'I'm staying here.'

Richard turned to the car and prised open the passenger side door, holding the torch high.

'If he phoned, he must be conscious,' said Autumn.

'Neil, are you there?' Richard called into the crack.

'Yes,' croaked a man's voice.

'Are you hurt?'

'I don't think so, but I daren't move. If I do, I might tip it too far. Are you a policeman?'

'No, I'm Richard,' he shouted over the gusts.

Faint shrieks whisked around on the wind. 'Someone's shouting,' said Autumn.

'Go back and find out what's wrong.' Richard raked his hair, examining around the car with his torch, bending to check underneath. 'Use the light on your phone.'

'I'm staying here.'

'Please. It might be important.' He straightened up, looking directly at her. 'Joyce can't get over here, go and help her. She'll be terrified.'

'Ok, but…' Shivering all over, Autumn bit her lip. Richard pulled her close and kissed her rain-streaked forehead.

'Take care,' he said, crushing her. 'I don't want anything to happen to you. I love you.'

She was too shocked to respond. Picking her way across the rocks, she couldn't be sure if the water on her face was rain or tears. Further along, up high, the lights from the house twinkled and Peppy stood silhouetted. *Why can't I still be there? Safe, warm, and happy, wrapped in the arms of someone who loves me.* He had just said that, hadn't he? Slimy seaweed moved under Autumn's feet. She lost balance jumping onto the shingle and aggravated her ankle again, hobbling the last few feet.

Joyce's nails were gouging dents in her cheeks. 'The police are stuck, there's a fallen tree on the road, someone's coming to cut it, oh god, this is awful.' A tremendous wave crashed close to the car, and it wobbled. 'Oh no. This is it. I know it.'

Autumn peered into the distance, her legs shaking. 'Wait here. I'll go tell Richard.' Her heart pumped.

'No, stay here,' shouted Joyce. But Autumn couldn't. She scrambled back over the rocks, seaweed slipped under her feet, but she had to get there. She stumbled, seeing Richard's dark outline, his torch shining from the ground. He grabbed her wrist and pulled her the last few feet. She wanted to hug him and pull him back to safety, but she couldn't move, his grip was so firm.

'The police are stuck; they might not get here in time.'

A nerve twitched under Richard's eye. 'That last wave nearly hit the car, I tried to lean in but I can't reach him. Another wave might hit any second, we could be washed out to sea.'

'Can you get me out?' yelled Neil. 'I need to get out!'

'We're trying,' muttered Richard.

'I'll lean in and pull him,' said Autumn.

'No way. I'm six foot four. If I can't get him, there's no way you can, you're tiny.'

'I know, but listen.' She tugged him round to look at her. 'If you hold on to me, I can climb in and help him. You can pull us back.'

'That is crazy.' Richard rubbed his forehead.

'We can't stand by and watch, not when we're this close.'

'Please, get me out,' shouted Neil.

Richard rocked on his feet for a second, then spoke into the slightly open door. 'Ok, we're going to open the door wide again. Autumn will climb in and help you out.'

'Who? What?'

'Never mind, just get ready to move, ok?'

'I'm ready.'

Richard prised open the door. Blood pounded in Autumn's ears. The car creaked. The wind tore past. She wobbled. Richard seized her by the arm, leaning his opposite shoulder on the open door. 'This is going to be impossible holding you and the door. I can hardly hold it against the wind. I'm not sure this is a good idea.'

'I couldn't live with myself if we didn't try.' Taking a deep breath, she broke his grip, leaned in and fumbled for Neil. Her feet were off the ground. Richard clung to her back.

'Come on,' she yelled. Neil scuffled and the car swayed.

'Autumn!' Richard tugged her jacket.

She pulled Neil's sweaty palm. He scrabbled about, struggling to get across the gearstick. 'Come on.' Autumn gritted her teeth. Placing both her hands on the front of his jacket, she clenched it tightly. If the car moved again, they'd all fall. She pulled until her arms ached and her shoulders stung.

Suddenly, Richard's arms clenched around her waist. He hauled her back. The car shuddered. Autumn clung to Neil, her nails digging into his jacket. With an immense surge of adrenaline, she yanked at him. His frantic kicking and scrambling wobbled the car even more. Her heart almost stopped. She clung to him frantically.

'Let go.' Richard braced himself against the open door. It buffeted in the wind. 'Put your back on the door, I'll get him.' He grabbed Neil under the arm, dragging him out the rest of the way in a fireman's lift and all but dropping him onto the rock as soon as he was clear of the car. 'Let the door go. Move!' The car creaked and scraped. Richard grabbed Autumn as she jumped away from the car and the door banged shut. 'Let's get away from the sea.' He held her hand painfully tight. 'Then we can breathe again.'

Shaking and unable to think, Autumn struggled to the other side of Neil and pushed him, while Richard attempted to shoulder him. Hauling him up, they started to walk. 'Go back to Joyce and get her to the house, it's freezing. I'll bring Neil,' said Richard.

Autumn extricated herself from Neil, who lolled about panting. After stumbling over the rocks, guided by the tiny light on her phone, she found Joyce sobbing.

Autumn put her arm around her broad back. 'He's all right, we got him out, come on, let's get to the house. He's ok. They're coming, they're ok.' She intoned the words over and over, *they're ok, they're ok*.

Leading Joyce towards the house, Autumn struggled forward, pushing across the road. Barely able to see a thing, Autumn dropped her head against the ferocious wind. Horizontal rain hit hard as they advanced towards the door and Joyce staggered along. Autumn's numb fingers fumbled with the door handle. The door to the porch burst open and she sagged inside. Her hands shook as she removed the sodden waxed jacket and kicked off her boots. Peppy's wet nose hit her the second she stepped into the main house. She rubbed him over and he licked her wet face, making her want to cry.

Joyce leaned on the wall with a sigh. 'We should call the police and let them know. They tried to keep me on the line, but I lost the connection.' She turned to Autumn and stopped.

'Yes, do that.' Autumn peeled strands of wet hair from her forehead. 'There's better reception in the front room.'

Joyce's eyes popped, and her mouth fell slack. Was there any need to stare so obviously? After what they'd been through.

'Maybe you should sit down,' said Autumn.

'No, no. I'm quite all right. I'm just shocked.' She peeled off her wet hat, revealing wispy grey hair stuck flat to her scalp.

'It's understandable. That was a terrible thing to happen.'

'What? Oh, yes.' Joyce rubbed a mole on her chin. 'No, I meant. Oh, I do rattle on. You must be Lorraine.'

'Who?' Autumn frowned.

'Richard's girlfriend.'

Richard had a girlfriend? No. What was the woman talking about? This must be shock. 'No, I'm Autumn.'

'Oh… right. My friend, Anne, told me she'd read something on that Facebook thing about Richard having a girlfriend called Lorraine. A very pretty girl with red hair, she said. I saw your hair and well…'

'He… No…' Lights flashed by the window. 'Here they come. Could you boil the kettle?'

'Of course. Where's the kitchen?'

'Through there.' Autumn pointed, but she was looking at the main door. Richard staggered into the hallway, his glasses askance, Neil's arm draped over his shoulder. Peppy bounded up, wagging his tail. With a shaky smile, Autumn caught Richard's eye. He barely returned it, dragging Neil's bulk forward. On seeing him in the light, she stared. How had they pulled him out? He was so big. Richard was tall, but Neil was bulky and possibly weighed twice what Richard did. He hauled him down the corridor, into the living room, and laid him on the rug beside the fire. Neil grumbled as Richard straightened, flexing his shoulders and rolling his neck.

'You need to stay lying down. We shouldn't really have moved you, but it was too dangerous to stay out there. Can you get some cushions and put them under his feet?' Richard glanced towards Autumn. She grabbed some from the sofa and pushed them under as Richard lifted Neil's legs.

Taking off his soaking glasses, Richard shook his wet hair and held it off his forehead. Autumn wanted to hug him, but he threw her a warning glance and shook his head. His eyes shifted to the kitchen area at the sound of the tap running. His fists balled as he saw Joyce.

'Oh, gracious.' Joyce shuffled in, stopping at the sight of her husband on the floor. 'Is he all right?'

'He will be.' Richard dried his glasses. 'But call an ambulance, I know the road's blocked, but he should go to the hospital. He's in shock.'

'I'll do that,' said Autumn. 'So you can stay with him.' She patted Joyce on the shoulder.

'Oh, thank you, dear, and you, Richard, I can't thank you enough.'

He waved off her words, replacing his glasses. 'I'll get hot water bottles.' He went into the corridor.

Autumn followed. 'What's your house called?' She took out her phone.

'Creel Lodge.' Richard didn't look out from the cupboard under the stairs.

Autumn made the call, keeping Richard in view. Wherever the hot water bottles were, he made a meal of finding them and didn't emerge until she'd finished talking.

'He weighed a ton.' Richard moved his head from side to side as if testing his neck.

'I don't know how we did it.' Autumn sighed, returning her phone to her pocket.

'What a nightmare.' Richard pinched the bridge of his nose and closed his eyes.

Joyce peered through the door. 'Do you have the bottles?'

Richard's jaw tightened. Autumn removed the hot water bottles from his clutches and smiled. 'Here they are.'

'I'll get some blankets.' Richard dashed upstairs and Autumn followed Joyce into the kitchen.

'The police are en route again,' said Joyce, filling a bottle. 'The tree's been moved.'

'Good.' Autumn leaned on the breakfast bar. The weight of what had happened pressed on her shoulders, making her shaky, but one thing was clearer. Her feelings for Richard. He'd said he loved her and, even if it was in the heat of the moment, it had to mean something. She'd heard those words trip off Josh's tongue more than was good for her but this felt different. But what about this woman? Lorraine?

As the kettle boiled again, Autumn whipped out her phone and opened Facebook. She scrolled onto Richard's page. He had only forty-three friends, and most of them seemed to be university and science types. Autumn typed in L, O, R and before she got any further, the name Lorraine Wallace popped up. Her profile was covered in photographs of beautiful locations and links to articles about marine engineering. She was a redhead all right with a striking angular face. Autumn ran a quick search for interactions with Richard Linden and she wasn't disappointed – well, she was. Her heart froze as she read. There wasn't a lot, but a couple of times, she'd posted on his timeline. One particular post caught Autumn's eye.

Can't wait to see you later, Big Boy. I have a birthday treat for you.

A row of winks and smilies followed, along with a picture of Richard and Lorraine both in revealing swimwear and looking a little too cosy, though his expression was grim. Richard hadn't replied. The date stood out – it was five years ago. Joyce and her nosey friend might not have noticed and just enjoyed speculating about his love life. As a handsome single man, they were probably intrigued. But five years ago? He'd only divorced his wife three years ago. Did that mean he'd had an affair? He'd been cagey earlier when he'd spoken about other relationships. Lorraine might not be his girlfriend now, but had Richard cheated on his wife with her? Autumn closed her eyes and held her breath. How did she always pick them?

The appearance of blue lights stopped her musing. She heard Richard's voice in the hall and she turned off her phone as two hulking police officers in hi-vis uniforms marched in. They spoke to Joyce and Autumn peered between the two of them. Richard's grim face was dark with five o'clock shadow. He raised his eyebrow in an expression of hopelessness. Autumn mirrored it. Her shoulders sagged.

After much discussion, the police left. 'What a night.' Joyce shook her head at Neil. He had progressed to resting on the sofa. She shifted her attention to Richard, then on to Autumn, her left eyebrow lifting higher and higher. 'So, Autumn, are you—'

'Maybe you should rest before the ambulance arrives,' Richard butted in.

'I'm making tea,' said Autumn.

'Yes, tea,' muttered Richard, joining her in the kitchen. With his back to the living area, he filled the kettle. 'She is so bloody nosey,' he hissed through gritted teeth. 'I'd rather she wasn't in my house. And don't say anything to her.'

Autumn took out some cups. 'About what?' she said with innocent eyes.

'Anything.' He craned his neck, checking Joyce wasn't watching from the living area. 'You did good out there.'

Autumn lifted her shoulders and brows in tandem. 'It was mostly you.'

'The hell it was. Don't you know how brave you were?' Their eyes met. Richard glanced back at Joyce. Autumn waited. 'You're the bravest person I've ever met. What you did tonight… I don't have the words. Just amazing.' He took a step forward, Joyce laughed loudly, and he turned away, opening a cupboard and lifting out a box of teabags. He smacked them on the worktop beside the mugs. Shoulders dropping, Autumn plopped in the teabags.

'Richard, tell me about—' Before she could say the name Lorraine, the ambulance arrived. Paramedics burst in to check Neil and the moment was lost. It felt like weeks ago she'd found the curious man who knew her mum. And hours since she and Richard had been on the verge of another encounter of the exceptionally close kind. Holding her elbows, she applied pressure, desperate to assuage the hollow ache inside. She had to accept this wasn't going anywhere. They'd had their fun and trying to crush in a lifetime of feelings just wasn't going to happen. If Richard had cheated on his wife, who was to say he wouldn't do it again? Autumn rubbed her face. Emotional exhaustion was making her think like that. She had nothing to prove Richard was a cheat, but it was too painful to think that he loved her or cared for her. Not when she couldn't have him without an unimaginable change in lifestyle. What if she tried and he turned out just as bad as Josh? Once a cheat and all that… She couldn't risk her heart after so short a time. It was too insane, even for her.

'There's no blood loss or sign of injury, but we'll take him in for observation,' said a paramedic.

'Should I come too?' asked Joyce.

'There's space in the ambulance for one family member.'

'Oh, good.'

'Just go home,' grumbled Neil. 'If you come in the ambulance, how will we get back? And who will feed the dog? I'll be fine, it's a lot of fuss about nothing. I've got my phone, I'll call you. You can collect me tomorrow. Stop fussing. Oh, and thank you, you two.'

'Go with him,' said Richard. 'I'll follow with the car and drive you back later.'

'Would you?' said Joyce.

He nodded.

Joyce chased the paramedics to the hall. 'Wait, I'm coming too.'

'Maybe you should take me back too,' said Autumn.

'What?' Richard frowned.

'To the hotel, remember.'

'Oh, right. Yes, if you want.'

Looking slightly puzzled, he moved into the hallway. As Autumn patted Peppy, tears welled. 'It was nice meeting you.' He rolled over and let her stroke his long bristly tummy. 'But I've let this go too far.'

Rain slapped Autumn hard as she dashed for the Freelander, following Richard. She got in and quivered, numbness spreading all over. Richard pulled out behind the ambulance. It shuddered in the wind. Her island dream was over, she couldn't see a way to save it.

CHAPTER 24

Richard

Richard crunched the gears. 'I thought you wanted to stay with me tonight.'

'Is that what you want me for?'

'Pardon?' How could she say that? Was that the impression he'd given?

'Nothing.' Autumn looked away. 'Tell me about Lorraine.'

'Who?'

'Lorraine Wallace. Did you have an affair with her?'

A chill ran through Richard's veins. 'How do you know about that?'

Autumn shook her head. 'Never mind. I probably don't want to know.'

'Look, she's ancient history. I don't know where you've dug that up from, but it's not relevant.'

'Maybe not, but I… I can't do this. Let's be honest, this whole you-and-me-thing isn't going anywhere, is it?'

Richard stared forward. Did she want reassurance? How could he give it when he didn't know the answer? Or did she want him to agree so she could walk away guilt free? 'Well, you live in London, I live here, and we have totally different lives. So, I suppose it wouldn't be easy.'

'And you've had a whole life without me that you haven't told me about.'

'Well, excuse me, but so have you. I don't know all the details of your past. I've only known you a few days. But you know what, you're probably right. Let's not drag this out.' His feelings were so bloody big, he couldn't cope with them. His temper rose to shield him from the pain and disappointment. 'I should never have let this happen. It's got so out of control. We can't behave as though there's no tomorrow because there is. And my tomorrow involves working here, while your tomorrow involves going back to London. Of course, we don't have a future together. It's not real. This kind of thing doesn't happen.'

'Exactly. Let's quit now, we've done enough damage as it is.'

'Damage? Wow.' But she was right. His heart would never be the same after this, it felt bludgeoned.

Eyes firmly forward, they sat in silence. As they approached the hotel, lights flickered in the windows and the silhouettes of trees swayed violently in the wood behind the small wooden cabin in the grounds. Bushes shuddered back and forth.

'Goodbye.' Autumn opened the door and jumped out. Water splashed. 'Shit,' she muttered, looking at her boots.

'Goodbye, Autumn.' He swallowed, wishing he could say something to save the situation, but anything he said would just prolong the agony.

'And… I hope Neil's ok… Maybe you could—'

'Text you. Sure.'

She slammed the door and Richard watched her dash for the hotel entrance, head bowed against the wind. Then she disappeared inside. It was possibly the last time he'd see her. He didn't move despite the pain in his chest, threatening to crack him open. She'd shut the door without a backward glance. With a nod and a sigh, he drove on towards the hospital.

His heart, that wretched, blackened muscle inside his ribcage, ached. But tonight, tomorrow, Saturday, whichever day she chose to leave, it would be the same. So why delay? He was used to this kind of pain. Eventually, it would go away or, at least, become so much a part of him he wouldn't care. *Yes, you will*, said the angel. Of course he cared, but how else could he protect himself? And her? He'd fallen into the pit of idiocy which he thought he'd weaned himself away from. For years, he'd taught himself to deal with social situations, but no. Once again, he'd demonstrated his emotional naiveté. Autumn liked him, enjoyed his body, took pleasure in their interactions, but he wasn't emotionally equipped for this. *Why the hell did I lose control so badly?* It wasn't like he hadn't known what was going to happen. How Lorraine's name had been dragged into this was a mystery. She had nothing to do with anything, but if that was what Autumn needed to see past him, he'd accept it.

By the time he arrived at the hospital, Joyce was already inside, tapping her foot in the waiting room. He joined her. 'Where's Autumn?' she asked.

'I dropped her off at her hotel,' he mumbled.

'Oh. Isn't she staying with you?'

'No.' He took off his jacket.

'I'm sorry,' said Joyce. 'I might have put my foot in it. I thought she was your girlfriend. Anne told me you had a girlfriend called Lorraine who was a striking redhead, so I assumed it was her.'

Richard shook his head with a frown. 'Where do people around here get their information?'

'Anne saw something on Facebook. She was very intrigued; she's so nosey, but she has a good heart. She just wants you to be happy.'

'Facebook?' Several pennies dropped and the pieces fell into place. 'Right. I haven't posted anything on there for years, so unfortunately her information's out of date.'

'Oops. I hope I didn't speak out of turn with Autumn. She seems so nice.'

'She was the person looking for Mike.' He paced, running his fingers through his hair. 'I was helping her out, that's all.' Yup, that was all it should ever have been. Who'd have guessed helping a lost stranger would lead to pain like this a few days later?

Joyce sighed and together they waited until she was called to see Neil.

'Damn, damn, damn,' Richard muttered at an NHS-24 poster. What had he done? He thrust his hands in his pockets and paced – why, why, why?

Neil came out sometime later, smiling. Engulfed by his thanks and Joyce's clucking, Richard craved air.

'Maybe you could give us Autumn's address, I'd like to send her something,' said Joyce.

Richard shrugged. 'I don't know it.' He tapped out a quick text, informing Autumn Neil was ok.

'Oh.' Joyce raised an eyebrow.

Richard didn't need special training to read her thoughts. Now she suspected him of fooling around with random tourists. Maybe she wasn't far wrong. Why had he agreed to give Autumn a lift that first day? He should have let her wait for the taxi. His heart shrivelled to prune size. He couldn't have left her. Even then he'd seen something in her he liked. Now she was gone.

They helped Neil into the Freelander and as Richard climbed in, his phone flashed.

AUTUMN: Good to know. X

He winced: could she stop sending him kisses, please? More than enough kissing had taken place that week.

Seventeen times fifteen equals… he couldn't bloody remember. He wanted to smack his head into the windscreen until every thought shattered.

*

The following morning, Richard had sorted his head out enough to realise he had to at least explain about Lorraine. Without agenda, he just wanted to make it clear that she played no part in his life any more. He called in at the Glen Lodge on the way to Fionnphort. Settling this like an adult couldn't be that hard, though his pounding heart suggested otherwise.

'I'm sorry, Autumn checked out about half an hour ago,' the woman at reception informed him.

Richard checked his watch. She'd be boarding the ferry now. There was no way he could catch her. Back in the Freelander, he tapped out a text.

RICHARD: I called into the hotel, but you'd already left. I wanted to apologise in person, but this will have to do. Last night, if it came over that I was only interested in you for sex, then please forgive me. I'd be a liar to say I didn't enjoy our time together, but it was part of a much bigger deal for me. I just don't know how it would have worked. I've tried long distance before with no success and I didn't want to freak you by expecting you to move here or seem like I was moving things too fast when we had so little time.

One thing I need to explain is about Lorraine. I've checked through Facebook and worked out where you got that information. Lorraine and I were in a relationship years ago, after I split with Ruth. I haven't seen Lorraine for years and I assure you, I have no feelings for her. I understand our island gossips leapt on the discovery and made up an intriguing story.

I'm sorry things ended as they did. No matter what happens now, I'd like to wish you well. You've changed me in so many ways I can't reconcile them all yet and only time will tell how I can best move forward.

I hope you find the happiness you deserve.

After sending it, Richard began muttering, 'Nineteen times six is… one hundred and fourteen. Nineteen times seven is… one hundred and thirty-three.' He turned up the heating dials as he recited. He wanted to shut down and learning the nineteen times table was a good place to start. Taking a bend sharply, he continued, 'nineteen times eight is… one hundred and fifty-two.'

Peppy let out a sorrowful cry. Richard sighed as he passed the ferry terminal, the boat was sailing away. Autumn was on board and who knew if he would see her again. As he reached the Glen Road, he listened for the sound of a reply, but there was nothing. Pulling into a passing place surrounded by imposing mountains, he rested his elbow on the windowsill as he waited for a truck to labour up the long twisty road. He tried to ignore every distraction looming on the horizon. *Why does even the damned season have to share a name with her?* Every silly little thing put her back in his head. The red leaves recalled her hair. The vibrancy of her laugh echoed in the colours. The changeable sky mirrored her spontaneity, and the sea gleamed like her bright, wide eyes. She was everywhere, yet nowhere. Richard thumped his fist on the windowsill. He glanced at his phone and a new message flashed with a buzz. After tugging on the handbrake, he opened it.

AUTUMN: Thank you for your message. I decided just to leave. Sorry if I overreacted to Joyce telling me about Lorraine. Of course you've had relationships, and that's fine. What I found hard to stomach was one of Lorraine's messages to you that was somewhat suggestive and clearly written at a time when you were married. I think you'll understand my reason for being upset at the idea you'd have an affair. Having lived that life for so long as "the other woman", I couldn't contemplate the idea of falling for someone who'd cheated. Not again.

And I did fall for you. It felt like no one in my life had ever understood me as well as you, which makes this so hard to swallow. I felt things for you like I'd never felt before. But as we both know, I'm the idiot who reads everything into nothing while you read nothing into anything without unequivocal proof. When you said you loved me, I took that at face value and decided that was all I needed. Of course, that was crazy.

But for what it's worth, I loved you too. XX

Richard read it twice, his heart pounding. Shit, shit, shit. Seriously? He'd ploughed in, opened his mouth and made a mess of everything again. For a few too-short days, Autumn had filled the gaping hole in his soul where he'd once had a wife and son. Now the abyss was wider and darker than ever. He'd learned to shut it down before, to hide away where no one knew him, and walk amongst normal people and look normal himself. Could he do it again?

As he gathered his equipment in the car park, memories flooded back. A few days ago, Autumn was there, asking him questions, smiling. He shook his head to disperse the thought. Nineteen times… oh, for god's sake.' He slammed the boot shut and bashed it with his fist. Peppy stared with huge, sad eyes. 'I'm sorry.' Richard fussed the dog's bristly nose.

Striding towards the descent to the beach, the sound of his name distracted him. Mary MacLean hobbled up from her cottage with her little shopping basket, waving her bony hand at him.

'I was hoping to catch you.' She panted. 'I'm not very quick and you go at some speed.'

'Oh, hello.'

'How is Autumn? I wonder if she's had any luck yet?'

'She found the man but her mum wasn't there so she's gone back to London.'

'Dear, dear. I am sorry to hear that, I really hoped to see her again. I wish she could have stayed.'

'She doesn't belong here.'

'Oh, I don't know. Sometimes it's not about the place but the people. If her mum had been here, she might have stayed. Sometimes people have to make big sacrifices for their loved ones, but no point in her staying if her mum isn't here.'

As Richard said goodbye, he swallowed the empty pang in his stomach.

Dropping his equipment on the hidden beach, his resolve to forget evaporated. He parked himself on the boulder where not so long ago Autumn had sat talking non-stop, and put his head in his hand, tugging at his hair. 'Oh god, I want her.' He looked up in desperation. He should have played things differently, but how? A skein of geese skimmed overhead; their melancholy cries mingled with the gentle lilt of the waves. 'I miss everything about her. I love her so much, I'm crazy about her.' He stood up with an urge to cleave open his head on the edge of the rock.

He pulled out his phone. Writing a considered and meaningful reply could take time. Time he didn't have. Work was pressing, but he needed to do this.

RICHARD: Thank you for your message. Perhaps what happened between me and Lorraine was an affair. Technically I was married to Ruth when we started seeing each other, but we'd been separated some time and Ruth was already with someone else. I didn't cheat on her and have never cheated on anyone. I can understand your gut reaction, but please be clear on the facts.

You didn't read anything into the situation that wasn't already there. I said I loved you because that was exactly how I felt. If I'm honest, I still do. I don't see that stopping any time soon. I just can't see a favourable outcome for that just now. You made it clear this life wasn't for you and a life in London doesn't work for me. As we'd only known each other such a short time, it seemed silly to pin hope on a long-term outcome.

Everything I said to you and did with you, I meant with all my heart. I agree that ending things before we got too close made sense, though in reality, it was too late for that. You will always be a very special person to me, even if only in memories. Believe in yourself, follow your dreams and never stop being you.

Could you please send your address? Joyce would like to send you something.

Safe onward travels.

X

He hit send without rereading it. This had to come from the heart, though he'd barely scratched the surface of how he truly felt.

The following morning, as he made his way down the beach near his house, he received her reply with her address and a brief message.

AUTUMN: I'm sorry, I misread the whole situation. My head feels like a muddle. I don't see a favourable outcome either. Not without a big upheaval and it scares me. But I meant everything too. X

His stomach turned over. Nothing could break the bond of feelings except the distance between Mull and London. Another familiar pang. How many years had he lived away from his son unable to share the love he felt? He couldn't expect Autumn to make that upheaval. If he wanted it, he had to do it himself.

Barely a mile along the beach, he spotted Joyce floundering along after her dog. She was making a beeline for him. 'Peppy!' Richard's call fell on deaf ears as the dog hared towards Joyce's four-legged companion.

'I was hoping to see you,' shouted Joyce, waving her arms. 'I never had a chance to thank you properly. I left you a bag of goodies. I hope you got it.'

'Yes, I did, thanks.' He'd found the letter and the basket. Chocolates, wine, cheese and shortbread. 'All very nice.' But nothing to fill the emptiness.

Joyce advanced, puffing. 'We really appreciate what you did. The car's going to be recovered, but it's a write-off. Neil's on the lookout for another one, he's using mine until then, which is highly inconvenient.'

Richard nodded, eyes darting around.

'And how's Autumn?'

Richard scratched a mark in the shingle with his boot. 'Back home. I have her address now if you want it?'

'Oh, yes.' Joyce took out her phone, still chattering as Richard pulled up the message. 'I was chatting to Beth McGregor yesterday, and she informs me Autumn is from London. I hear she's gone back, and never found her mum. What a mystery.'

'I suppose it is.' Richard rubbed his neck. Joyce was fishing, perhaps wanting to add another chapter to her saga on his love life. Her version – the one that came nowhere near the truth and caused happy havoc. He read out Autumn's address for her to type it in. He didn't dare forward any of the messages. It would be just the thing if he forwarded the wrong one; Joyce's gossip radar might short circuit with glee. 'Listen, you don't happen to know who lives in Gardener's Cottage on the Ardnish Estate, do you?' he asked.

'No, I'm not sure. It was empty for a long time. Some of the properties on that estate are almost uninhabitable. I could try to find out.'

'Thanks. If you do, can you let me know?'

'I most certainly can.'

Richard whistled Peppy and strode back to the house, waving his hand behind his head.

His phone rang shortly after he'd logged onto his laptop. His heart leapt. Autumn? But an incoming call registered on his laptop seconds later. With a sickening jolt, he saw the name, Ruth Millard. He clicked the answer button on his laptop, dreading what was coming. Was Adam ill? Ruth hadn't called for ages. This couldn't be good.

'Well, hello, Richard.' Ruth's sharp face filled his screen. Richard ran his hand through his hair, hating the picture of himself in the corner. *I look rough.*

'Hello.' Keeping the dialogue to a minimum was essential. Ruth was a merciless lawyer and used every syllable he'd ever uttered in evidence against him. Her knowledge of legal jargon and technicalities had made sure she got what was best for herself. For a few short months, he'd been the prize she craved. He'd married her despite preferring Lorraine, but Ruth had talked him into believing it was for the best. Years later, she'd done the same with Adam. Perhaps their son had what was right for him now, but he'd never know an alternative.

'I need to fill you in on a couple of things that have come up after your visit.'

Richard exhaled. Ruth's words sent a shiver up his spine, which he associated with imminent pain. 'So, what have I done now?'

'What indeed.' She paused. He waited; his fists balled. 'Adam got very agitated after your visit. He doesn't like disturbance to his routine.'

'Yes, I know,' said Richard. Why did she say everything in that patronising tone? Like he didn't know or care. 'And I fully sympathise. God knows, I don't want to disrupt his life. That's why I live here, alone. Remember.'

Ruth gave a little smirk. 'Yes, Richard, and we all appreciate the sacrifice, but maintaining a routine is one of his core requirements.'

Or yours, thought Richard. Ruth, despite all her love and concern, often treated Adam's autism as an illness or something to be cured. She'd never comprehend it was inherently part of him, or if she did, she'd be in denial. *Just as she never cut me any slack for my idiosyncrasies.*

'So what's the problem?' There was no point in dragging out the subject. He knew she did everything she could to make Adam's life as good as it could be, while his role was to keep away. No matter how much they argued, it wouldn't change, but the pain constantly burned the edges of his heart, charring it and searing him with bitterness. Some of which he threw in Ruth's face, often without meaning to.

'Well, after his spell of agitation, I managed to calm him down and Lana, his carer, worked out some days later some of what he was trying to communicate seemed to revolve around your visit.'

Richard rubbed his fingers across his chin. 'What about it?'

'His language is difficult to understand at the best of times.'

The fact he used language at all was something to applaud; he'd been nonverbal for years. 'But?'

'She reckons he was saying *dad* and when she showed him a photo of my husband, he shook his head and got annoyed. So I found a picture of you and showed it to him and that seemed to interest him.'

Richard leaned into the screen, disbelieving.

'Would you like to talk to him?' asked Ruth.

'Now?'

'Well, when he's ready. I can't make any promises about what will happen if I put him on to a chat like this.'

'I'll try. Whenever. Of course, I want to speak to him.' He stared at the screen. 'And thank you. I know I've done nothing practical to help, that's what makes my side of the deal hard for me. I'm not meaning to belittle what you do for him every day, but I miss the chance of any kind of interaction.'

'I know.' She ran her hand down her slick dark hair. 'And maybe this will help. If we can offer this to Adam as something positive then who knows where it might lead.'

Who knew indeed, but with that prospect, Richard felt buoyant. Here was an opening. Although they hadn't arranged an exact time, as it would have to fit with Adam's mood and routines, it was there. The fact Ruth had considered him gave him a little bubble of hope. Perhaps they could work together rather than fight. They both had Adam's interests at heart after all and a partnership seemed better than the constant tit for tat.

Returning his focus to his screen, he scrolled through his research notes, entering the data and figuring out how best to present it. With the kelp industry having the backing of large companies, environmental groups were being shafted left, right and centre. Richard shuddered at the way things had been done in Norway. Huge forests had been lost. This work was for a client, but it was something he believed in. He made a team call and spent most of the afternoon working through the final data and checking for any gaps and places they needed further samples.

'I envy you,' he told his co-worker, Johan who was based on Harris, but had taken a trip to St Kilda for the latest round of tests. 'You don't get much more remote than that. One day I need to visit it.' Unbidden, a vision of sailing his boat towards the remote pinnacle with Autumn at his side shaped in his mind. Sharing the awe of the approach with her was so vivid, he couldn't imagine the reality of doing it one day without her.

A loud thumping on the door set Peppy barking.

'Let's end there for the day. There's someone at my door. If you email me the reports, I'll read them next week and see where we stand after that.' He shut down the call and got to his feet.

Peppy padded out the door first and into the corridor, sounding surprisingly brave as he mingled a little growl into his barks. Richard followed and gave him a pat. Who was knocking at this time? He was painfully aware of the consequences the last time someone had come hammering on his door. As he pulled it open, he frowned. *You again?*

'Hello,' boomed Joyce. Peppy nosed forward and sniffed her.

'Hi. Is everything ok? No accidents?'

'No.' Joyce chuckled. 'I've been out for afternoon tea with my friend, and I did a bit of snooping. Would you like to know what I found out about the residents at Gardener's Cottage at Ardnish?'

'Oh, yes.' Richard swallowed and stepped back. 'Come in.'

'Very kind, thank you.' Joyce entered the hall and took off her hat. Richard showed her into the living room and she took a seat by the window. 'So,' said Joyce, beaming. Her wide eyes bulged as she cut to the chase. Richard perched on the edge of a chair, waiting. 'Gardener's Cottage has been empty for a long time, but a couple of months ago, a man moved in. He's an islander, but he and his wife have split up, and I understand this was the only place he could find.'

Richard rubbed his hand over his chin, waiting for her latest gossip wagon to grind to a halt. 'Do you know his name?'

'That's the interesting part.' Joyce grinned, clearly enjoying the big reveal. 'His name is Mike.'

'Hmm. I wondered. When we spoke to him, he wouldn't give his name.'

'Well, it's Mike Robertson. I thought there was a Michael Robertson if you recall, but I muddled him with Michael Anderson. Anyway, his wife is Lynne Robertson, she's a bit of a character herself, been seeing a man on the mainland for months by all accounts. And they have a son – Blair. He lives somewhere on the island too. But I haven't told you the juicy bit.'

'Hang on. Did you say Blair?' Richard's brain whirred round at a ludicrous speed. As in *the* Blair? The one Autumn had met. She'd already discounted that Mike because Blair had told her it wasn't him.

'Yes, Blair. But that's not the good part, or, should I say, the curious part. My friend, Joanne, the florist – you might know her – goes to Ardnish to get plants and she reckons Mike isn't living alone. Apparently, he's acting cagey and doesn't say much, but Joanne has seen a woman hanging about there. She's been out working in the walled garden and walking on the beach with Mike, but they always go back to the house if people approach them. Now, is that suspicious or what?'

Richard ran his hand down his face and peered out the window to the now pitch-black sky. He wasn't good at gossip and chitchat, but if Joyce's words represented facts, then there was something worth investigating. 'It sounds curious.'

'I'm not sure why you wanted to know about him. Is he Autumn's father or something?'

'No, he's not. Listen, if you're in touch with Autumn, please say nothing about this. I want to investigate before she finds out. In case it's nothing. I wouldn't like to get her hopes up.'

'I wish I knew what it was about, then I could help some more.'

'It's not my place to tell you, but what you've said is definitely helpful. Thank you.'

Richard closed the door as she left, his mind teeming with possibilities.

CHAPTER 25

Autumn

Lining up cans of baked beans wasn't as fulfilling as dressing the glass shelves in luxury homewares. But none of it had ever satisfied Autumn's desires. The city which had been home all her life now felt like a dirty, unwelcome place, noisy and unforgiving. Everyone was busy, pushing their way here and there.

She slammed a can of beans onto the shelf and shook her head. The result of her little island sojourn had been the same as everything else. Disappointment. 'You'd think I would have learned by now,' she muttered. Putting trust in others always backfired. And now she was here, back in a dead-end job, only this time one which didn't begin to cover her rent.

By the end of the month, she'd be out. Priya had offered her a spare room until she got her shit together, but none of it seemed to matter. When she was here, she stared at rows upon rows of products. When she was at home, she looked over the concrete side of more flats. A far cry from the white sandy beaches of Mull.

After leaving, she'd tried to stay in touch with her new friends, but it wasn't the same. Distance was real and messenger could be diverting, but it didn't replace tangible human contact. At the thought, Autumn ripped up an empty cardboard box and flung it in her recycling cage. The person she wanted contact with the most was the one she was least likely to see ever again. She pushed her cage forward, wishing it was as simple to push him out of her mind. She'd allowed emotions to rule her as always without thinking things through. Richard was as bad as Josh. Her heart shrivelled. No, he wasn't. She could try and trick her brain into thinking that. It eased the pain, but it didn't change facts. All he'd done was act rationally to her knee-jerk reaction to Joyce's gossip. She just didn't have the guts to go after what she wanted.

During her break, she threw herself into one of the threadbare chairs and checked her messages. One from Blair caught her eye. She had to read it about six times before it sunk in.

BLAIR: Ok, read this when you're sitting down. Your mum is on Mull, living with my dad! Apparently, she was there the whole time you were too. Dad says she's very fragile as she's gone cold turkey. Then he had a visit from your friend Richard. Anyway, dad realised there was no point trying to hide it any more. I went to see them. Your mum's in a bit of a state. I'm still shocked that my dad was ever online dating! What is happening in the world?! Hope you're ok. At least you know your mum's safe.

Mum was on Mull? With Mike? And Mike was Blair's dad. Richard had visited them but not told her?

She hit call on the phone.

'Blair? Your message.'

'Ha! Yeah, can you believe it?'

'I'm struggling,' said Autumn. 'And my mum was there when I called around.'

'Yup. We seem to have landed bang in the middle of some worldly weirdness.'

'Haven't we just.'

'But you know what?' Blair's voice was full of mischief. 'If they're together, does that make us brother and sister for real?'

Autumn giggled through her brain stupor. 'That would be cute, but weird!'

Blair hummed the opening notes from *The X-Files*.

'Crazy.'

Where did this leave them? Back to the status quo? Only with her mum on Mull instead of across London. Would Vicky cope? Would she last? The day couldn't end fast enough. Autumn was desperate to talk to Priya, or Georgia, or anyone. Someone who might be able to make sense of what was going on.

As she sat on the bus on her way home, she averted her eyes from the early Christmas displays appearing in the shops and checked her phone. A message head popped up and she recognised Richard's photo in it. The one she'd taken in his kitchen.

RICHARD: Hi. You may hear this from Blair or someone else, but I returned to Gardener's Cottage yesterday. Your mum was there with Mike, who also happens to be Blair's dad. I know how confusing and upsetting this must be. Your mum said she didn't feel up to seeing or speaking to anyone until a day or two ago. She wants to contact you, but I don't want to give out your number without permission. So, I will send you her details and if you want to call her, it's up to you.

I miss you, and the island isn't the same without you.

Please recognise this as my terrible attempt to keep in touch.

Richard X

Autumn bit her lip and stared out the window as the bus rolled around a corner and stopped. So dead slow and stop compared to her rollercoaster island ride. Richard missed her? He was trying to keep in touch. She wanted him, but not as a pen pal or message mate. She needed him close to her, talking to her, holding her. She ached to be back on the beach, picking up kelp, laughing with him.

AUTUMN: I don't mind if you give Mum my details. I need to talk to her. Saturday is my last day in my flat and it's my birthday. I'm not sure where I'm going to be living after that, so best she doesn't send me anything in the post (not that it's likely!).

I miss you too. X

She put her phone away, rested her head on the window and closed her eyes. Yes, she missed him and the island. Now faced with an eviction, the idea of going back didn't seem farfetched or beyond her. Surely there would be island jobs? She could pretty much do anything, she'd never been fussy or career-driven.

As she let herself into the main entrance of her block of flats, mulling over possibilities, voices echoed in the stairwell. Her mouth fell open as her gaze landed on a pair of four-inch heeled, red stilettoes, and travelled upwards over a slim figure, pulling a white fur coat tight. Beside the woman was her dad, a stocky man with an almost bald head.

'Dad. Krystina. What are you doing here?' said Autumn.

'There you are, my beauty.' Brian Elworthy smiled at his daughter. 'We just came by to see how you were. We're on our way to the cinema, but I haven't clapped eyes on you for an age. How you doing, my darling?' He hopped down the concrete stairs and embraced her.

'I'm fine.' Autumn gave him a brief pat on the back and pulled away.

'It's cold out here.' Krystina screwed up her nose as she teetered down the steps. 'Let's not hang about.'

Brian cocked his head. 'Autumn, darling, my beautiful little girl. How's work going?'

'Work? Oh, it's fine.' He probably didn't remember she'd lost a few jobs lately and was now stacking shelves at Waitrose.

'Good, good. Well, I have something grand to tell you.'

Autumn rubbed at her eyelid. 'Oh?'

'Your mum has finally signed the papers. We're officially divorced and Krystina and I have a wedding date.'

'That's great.' Autumn mustered a smile. 'But how did you get mum to sign them?'

'Her lawyer sent them to us.'

'Apparently, she is living on that bizarre little island,' said Krystina, picking at an inch-long glittery scarlet nail. 'I suppose she's hiding from fat Phil. Unsurprising, he's a slob. Or maybe she's trying to come off the bottle, that'll hit her hard.'

'I don't think Vicky'll give up the booze until her liver packs in,' said Brian.

Autumn let out a sigh. 'I just hope she's ok. It's a big thing making a move like that.'

'Don't you go worrying, my little chopstick.' Brian clapped her cheeks. 'She'll be back here before long. Never could stick with anything.'

'You heard our other plans?' said Krystina.

'Er, no.'

'Yeah,' said Brian. 'After the wedding, we're planning on moving to Spain.'

'Spain? Wow.'

'Yeah, always wanted to,' said Brian.

Autumn nodded. 'Oh, wow… that's cool.' Amazing how they made these decisions and treated her like an afterthought.

They left without coming up to the flat, which was good. At least Autumn didn't have to listen to them moaning about the chill. She'd turned down the radiators in an attempt to save money.

As she entered, she pulled out her phone and called Georgia. An idea had blossomed and she couldn't get rid of it.

'Hey,' said Autumn.

'How's it going?' asked Georgia. 'I heard about your mum. That's unreal.'

'Don't I know it. Listen, I wonder… You don't happen to know of any jobs going on the island? Anything… shops, hotels, whatever.'

'Not off-hand, but you could try Robyn. She'll know if there's anything at the Glen Lodge and her mum knows everyone in the hotel business.'

'Yeah, good idea.'

'So, are you thinking about coming back? Now you know your mum's here?'

'I am thinking about it, though maybe not for her.'

'Well, if you can't find a job, get an old boat, flip it over, and sell shells to passing tourists. What do you have to lose?'

'Actually, it's possibly the best plan I've heard in a while. I'm just not sure I'm cut out for island life.'

'You'll never know unless you try. And you'll have us as friends, plus your mum, plus Richard.'

'Assuming he wants to.'

'Try. Go on, you know you want to.'

Autumn laughed despite herself. It was surely worth a try. She'd never know otherwise. She had to find her courage and soon because eviction day was just a few days away.

CHAPTER 26

Richard

Richard knocked on Ron's door and stepped back to wait. From here he could see the ferry making its way towards the harbour. It was late afternoon but soon he'd be on that boat.

'Hello there.' Ron pulled open the door. Peppy's tail went crazy as Ron patted him. 'A'right, Richard mate.'

'Yeah, I'm fine. Thanks for doing this at short notice.'

'Ah, no worries, I'm happy to have Peppy anytime, yes I am,' Ron said, still fussing Peppy. 'Yes, you're always welcome here, big lad.' Ron glanced up at Richard. 'Oh, now, don't let me forget, I have your books. I'll get them for you, don't want to be in trouble with Autumn again.'

Ron bustled off and Peppy followed him into the house. Richard smiled, glad Peppy didn't spare a backward glance for him; it was good to know he was happy here.

'Here we go.' Ron returned with a pile of books and handed them over. 'How is Autumn, by the way? Are the two of you still together?'

'I eh… Maybe.'

'Maybe? You don't want to let someone like her get away.'

'She lives in London.'

'Ouch,' said Ron. 'You're not upping and leaving, are you?'

'I don't know. I might have to. I think I've found a way, but nothing's set in stone. If I did, it would mean long periods away from here… And Peppy.'

'Ah, right, I see what you mean. Well, you can count on me. Anne and I will take Peppy any time for as long as you like. We've only got the one son, Calum. He's grown and flown the nest long ago, but I miss the company. I keep saying one day I'll get my own dog but taking Peppy in the meantime is always a treat.'

'Thank you, that's good to know.'

Armed with that knowledge, Richard gave Peppy a quick pat and headed for the boat. His car was in the same long stay car park where he'd left it a few weeks ago for his trip to Chicago. This trip could be almost as foolhardy and for a man who prided himself on planning skills, he'd been spectacularly spontaneous this month. With a wry grin, he pulled out his wallet to check for his ticket.

Travelling had been part of his life for so long that making trips like this wasn't daunting. In years gone by, he'd have flown from Aberdeen to London several times in a year. This had a sharper feel to it. On the train, he was keenly reminded of sitting here opposite Autumn. Even that first moment he'd seen her, something about her had drawn his eye.

It was late when he reached Glasgow and took a taxi to the airport hotel where he checked in for the night. The bed was hard as a rock but it didn't matter, his flight was early the next day. By ten o'clock he'd be in London. He had Autumn's address and a glimmer of hope.

After reading in her last message that she missed him, he couldn't stand it any more. If they both missed each other that much, then damn it, they had to be together, at least to talk and to give it a chance. She was going to be evicted on her birthday and didn't know where she was staying. He wouldn't allow it. No doubt she had friends who would put her up, but she needed more than that. He was going to make certain she was ok and he sure as hell wasn't going to leave her on the streets.

CHAPTER 27

Autumn

Everything was packed and ready to leave. Autumn didn't feel a thing as she looked around the flat. Her life here hadn't exactly been filled with happy memories. Most of her days had been working, and her evenings waiting. Waiting and hoping Josh would call or come around. But no more. She was off on an adventure. With her life packed into a suitcase, she scanned around the flat one more time, checking she'd left nothing.

A knock on the door drew her attention and she bit her lip. Her landlord? Had he come to make a last check? Everything was tidy and clean, but there was that one bit of bubbled lino in the kitchen where Autumn had once upended the mop bucket. Hopefully, he wouldn't notice and if he did… Well, she'd lose her deposit. And what did that mean? Another few hundred pounds deducted from her already non-existent bank balance.

She pulled open the door, and her jaw almost hit the floor. 'Josh? What the hell are you doing here?'

He pushed in before she could stop him. With a sharp movement, he grabbed her shoulder. 'I can't stand not seeing you, it's killing me.'

'No, Josh.' She pulled away from him. He looked rough; his fair hair was messed up and his stubble was too much to be smart and too little to be a beard. 'We're finished.'

'We're not. I had to lie low a bit with the pregnancy and all, but now Debs is obsessed with that, she won't even notice. In fact, once the baby arrives, it'll be the ideal time for me to leave. That way I can share custody and you and me will have plenty time together.'

'No. Jesus, Josh.' Autumn pinned her hair to the top of her head. 'You can't be serious. I'm not getting back together with you.'

'But I love you.'

'No, you don't. You love getting what you want from me when your wife's not interested, but that's not the same.'

Another knock on the door had never been so welcome. Autumn was ready to kiss her landlord. She swung open the door and her eyes almost popped out of their sockets. 'Richard?'

'Hi.' He moved to put his hands behind his back, but Autumn flung her arms around him.

'I'm so glad you're here.'

'Wow.' A little stiffly, he returned the hold, pressing something into her back, it felt like a book. Autumn realised he'd spotted Josh when he tried to pull back, but she didn't let go.

'Who's this?' said Josh.

'He's my boyfriend and I'm going to live with him.' Autumn expected Richard to bristle and recoil at the fib, but he didn't, he just stroked his free hand down her back.

'What?' Josh gaped.

'And who are you?' said Richard.

'That's Josh,' said Autumn, moving away from Richard but still keeping an arm around his waist. He returned the favour with an arm over her shoulder and she nestled under him.

'I see,' said Richard. 'And why are you here?'

Josh gaped at him. 'I've come to see Autumn.'

'And you're just leaving,' said Autumn. 'Because I told you, I don't want to see you again.'

'But Autumn—'

'There's the door,' said Richard, pointing with the package in his hand.

With a moody glower, Josh stalked passed them. Autumn slammed the door behind him. 'Oh, my god. I don't know what the hell you're doing here, but your timing is so bloody good.'

He gave her a brief smile and held out the package. 'I came to deliver this. It's a birthday present.'

'You remembered. And you came all this way… for this?'

'No. I came to see you. I said some harsh things after Neil's accident. Instead of addressing the way I felt and how to make things work, I pushed you away and I'm sorry, truly.'

Autumn bit her lip. 'I did quite a bit of pushing myself… I'm sorry too.'

'There's a job going on the south coast.' Richard glanced at his feet. 'I could easily do it and I feel quite confident I'd get it. If I did, I could base myself here, and you and I could get together… If that was something you still wanted.'

'What?' She gazed at him. 'You'd come and live here?'

'For you, I would.'

'Well,' said Autumn, thumbing the package.

'I've lived all over the place. I found a modicum of happiness on Mull, but it won't ever be the same without you.'

'I'm pleased you feel that way and you'd be willing to do that for me, but it won't be necessary.'

Richard's jaw tensed and he looked away. 'Right. Ok. I understand, of course. You have every right to feel that way.'

Autumn smiled. 'I meant because you're talking to the Glen Lodge Hotel's new receptionist.'

'Pardon? You mean… What do you mean?'

'Didn't you hear what I told Josh? I'm moving to Mull to live with my boyfriend. I'm going to give it a go.'

'But…'

'No buts.' She held her finger to her lips. 'I want to do it… for us. I just wish I'd told you so you didn't have to come all this way.'

Richard shook his head and moved closer. Autumn put her arms out and embraced him.

'I'd do anything if it means we can be together.' He rang his fingers down her spine. 'And if it doesn't work out, if you can't adapt to life on Mull, I'll still come here with you.'

She let out a contented sigh and withdrew to finger the package. 'Can I open this?'

'Of course, it's your birthday.'

She pulled open the paper to reveal a book on how to make your own candles. 'So perfect.' She smiled.

After leaving the flat and clearing everything with the landlord, Autumn synced her ideas with Richard's plans. Instead of staying with Priya, she spent the night in the airport hotel with Richard.

Sitting on the end of the bed, she scrolled through her phone cancelling her train ride while Richard booked her on a flight with him. A text pinged in.

PRIYA: You dumped my mad house for a hot night in a hotel with a handsome scientist. Wow, I'm so offended.

Autumn smirked at the long row of laughing faces.

You know I'm joking! Enjoy yourself, Lovely! X

She intended too, just as soon as Richard put down his phone. Her arms snaked around his neck and she kissed his cheek. 'I've missed you so much.'

Richard slid his phone onto the bedside cabinet and took off his glasses. 'Me too.'

Autumn straddled him and slipped her fingers across his cheeks, pushing them into his hair. 'Can I have my birthday treat now?'

'Sure.' Richard pulled her close and kissed her. Autumn melted in, savouring the moment. She didn't stop until they fell asleep – well after midnight.

*

By the time the ferry docked the following afternoon, Autumn was nursing a jumble of nerves. While spending time with Richard again was wonderful, the idea of seeing her mum was causing all sorts of confusing emotions.

'What will I say to her?'

'Just be yourself,' said Richard. 'You don't owe her anything. Just talk. You know how good you are at that.'

'Nice.' They proceeded along the covered walkway and Richard led Autumn past the bus stances and across the road to a car park surrounded by bright orange trees. Leaves were scattered over the ground and the cars.

'I need to nip in and get Peppy,' said Richard. 'Ron's got him, but his house is just over there.'

Richard gave her the keys to the Freelander and she headed for the car park. Five minutes later, Richard strode towards her with Peppy loping alongside, both of them lean and long-legged.

Peppy greeted her with so much joy she almost cried. 'You're such a great dog.'

Richard drove off and before long, they passed the Glen Lodge Hotel.

'Aren't we going in? I told you I'm staying in a cabin on the grounds there.' It was all part of the deal. Autumn got accommodation with the job. It had seemed best to arrange everything in case Richard hadn't wanted to see her. How could she ever have thought that?

'Let's go see your mum first. Once that's done, you can relax. The cabin isn't going away.'

The uneasy sensation in Autumn's tummy increased. *Yes, get this over with.* Watching the scenery go by was food for the soul. 'Richard… I'd like to think we have a future. I know it seems fast, but this is real, isn't it?'

'Yes.' He stretched out his arm and placed his hand on top of hers. 'I don't want to imagine my life without you. I've spent enough time living that life.'

'Me too. I shouldn't have waited around believing in Josh, I should have gone and done something long before now.'

'Well, now you have.'

He smiled at her, still watching the road, and she fake punched his shoulder. 'We're a team.'

As they pulled up at Gardener's Cottage, the sun was getting low, producing a stunning red glow over the sea. Autumn put out her hand, inviting Richard to take it. Holding her gaze, he leaned down, cupping her cheek in his free hand, and slowly kissed her. The gentle pressure on her lips, followed by the increase in intensity, had Autumn letting out a moan of desire. 'You're amazing, and you can do this,' whispered Richard.

'I didn't come back here for my mum, not really. I came back for you,' said Autumn, her words falling on his chest, as she allowed his warm hands to infuse her with strength.

'I'm glad you did. You're a special person. My special person. Now, let's do this.'

Leading her by the hand, Richard knocked on the door. 'That's Blair's car.' Autumn recognised the bash on the side.

Mike opened the door and Autumn held firm on Richard's hand as they entered the dingy hallway.

'Hey.' Blair bounded up as they entered the sitting room and lifted Autumn off her feet. 'Good to see you again.' He leaned in and whispered in her ear, 'Big sister.'

'Haha, let's see if that works out.' Peering past Blair, Autumn spotted a thin figure sitting by the fire. So there she was. Mum. This was the first time Autumn had seen her for months. 'Hi, Mum.'

Slowly Vicky raised her eyes and blinked. 'Hi, Darling. You're looking beautiful, as always. She's a beautiful girl, my daughter.'

'Yes, she is,' said Richard, then whispered in her ear, 'Inside and out. Listen, why don't we leave you to it? So you can work things out in peace.'

'We'll be in the hall,' said Blair.

Richard gave Autumn a fortifying hug around the shoulder before pulling away. Autumn watched him, Blair, and Mike retreat, then sat opposite her mum. Clasping her fingers in her lap, she waited for Vicky to speak.

After a prolonged silence, the floodgates opened, and the words tumbled out. Through Vicky's tears and Autumn's brain overload, it was hard to take it in. Was it an apology, a cry for forgiveness or an expression of hope? Or just the jumbled mess that was her mum? Autumn tilted her head to one side as the frail woman struggled to find the right words.

'It's ok, Mum. I don't blame you for anything any more. What you did when I was twelve upset me for a long time. I didn't really understand. Now, I do and I want to move on. You're still young, and so am I. It's not too late.'

'You're a good girl, I should have looked after you properly, but something in me was crooked.'

'It sounds like depression, Mum. You could have got help if you'd been diagnosed. But what about now? Are you going to stay here?'

Vicky nodded. 'I like it here. It's not what I'm used to, but I don't mind. Mike's a good man and that boy of his is a sweetheart too. I want to learn to drive and get a job cleaning holiday lets. There are loads around here. I love cleaning. I let it slip with Phil because I didn't see the point. I'd clean something and two minutes later, he'd chuck crap on it. Then he started bringing home all sorts of rubbish. I lost the will to live. Thank god I found Mike.'

'I wish I'd helped you.'

'It wasn't your job to help me. I had to do it myself. But I'd love it if you stayed here.'

'I am staying.'

'You are?' Vicky smiled and through her pale waxy skin, a little colour returned.

'Yes. Listen, I'll come back tomorrow if someone can give me a lift and we can talk properly. It's getting dark, we should go.'

'Ok, darling. And thank you. Thank you for caring enough about me to do this.'

After their farewells, Autumn jumped into the Freelander with Richard and was delighted to feel Peppy's nose on her shoulder. She stroked it. As Richard drove along the bumpy track towards the estate gates, Autumn woke her phone and tapped out a message. 'I hope there's reception here.'

'Probably not. Who are you messaging?'

'Just Georgia.'

'One of your new friends.'

'Our new friends. I'm going to drag you kicking and screaming out of that shell of yours.'

'Really?'

She giggled. 'No! Well, maybe once in a while. But I'd rather keep you all to myself.'

Richard glanced over with a smile before pulling out the main gate. 'How did it go with your mum? Are you resolved, or will it take time?'

Autumn pulled up one shoulder and sighed, finishing her text and hovering the phone around, hoping to conjure some reception. 'I think we're ok. We're both in a better place to make a new start.'

'Good.'

They'd almost reached the Glen Lodge Hotel when Georgia's reply came in.

GEORGIA ROSE: Hooray, you're back! Guess what? There's a Halloween party on Friday. It can be your first island party.

Autumn smiled at Richard.

'What was that message about?' he asked.

'Georgia telling me about the best parties for the week.'

'And you expect me to come along to them all.'

'Only one this week.'

'Hmm, I might manage that.' Richard pulled up in front of the hotel and crunched on the handbrake. 'So, is this goodbye for tonight?'

'Seriously?'

'Well, you might want an evening alone to settle in.'

'I need you to help me take my stuff in. Also…' Autumn reached up and stroked her finger across his cheek. 'It's dark and lonely down there. I could do with some company.'

With a slight nod of his head, Richard smiled. 'Is it indeed? Well, off you go and get the key.'

Autumn ran up the stairs and into the foyer. Robyn and Carl were no longer on hotel-sitting duty. An older woman with very short, cropped hair introduced herself as Maureen. 'I'm Robyn's mum. And I'm happy to have you here. I'll let you relax and settle in then show you around the hotel tomorrow.'

'Brilliant, thank you.' Autumn took the keys as Maureen chatted and asked about her journey.

'Can I help you with anything?'

'No thanks, I've got someone helping me.'

'Oh, that's good.'

'See you tomorrow,' said Autumn, and she headed back outside. The wind whipped up and the trees behind the cabin swayed. She jumped back in the Freelander and Richard rolled it down the track, stopping outside the cabin. 'It's a bit stormy.'

Inside it was homely and warm, with a red glow coming from a stove on one wall. It had a kitchen area in the main room and a small bedroom on one side. A compact bathroom area was neatly hidden in an alcove near the front door. 'Oh, it's cute,' said Autumn. 'Though I'm not sure it's a long-term option.'

Peppy lay in front of the stove with a contented groan.

'Well…' Richard stood in front of Autumn and swept her hair behind her shoulders. 'It doesn't have to be long term. You could stay with me.'

Autumn stepped in front of him, placing her hands on his shoulders. 'I'd like that, but after you've done all the kelp work. I've done enough hindering of that.'

'It's a deal.' Richard coiled his arms around her. 'Then you can help me furnish the house properly.'

'Oh, so exciting,' She beamed.

'Well, after three years of living there, I'm running out of excuses.' He lifted a strand of her hair and tucked it behind her ear.

'Stay with me tonight.'

'Ok,' he whispered in her ear.

She cocked her head, grinning, and he returned it, his face brightening.

For a moment they looked at each other and a new world of possibilities travelled between them until Richard pulled her close. She wound her arms around him. The heat from the stove permeated into her cheeks as she leaned on him. Everything had gone quiet. Only his heart was audible, just a beat too fast.

'I love you, I really do.' She glanced up. 'I can't think of anywhere I'd rather be, or anyone I'd rather be with.'

'Me neither, Autumn.' He breathed on the top of her head. 'Me neither.'

She blinked as he kissed her gently and she threw her arms around his neck. As their lips touched, she dropped her eyelids. Richard held her close, and she twisted her fingers into his hair. If it lasted forever, it wouldn't be long enough. Red glowing embers fizzed from the stove, and Peppy let out a contented sigh from his place on the rug. Autumn and Richard stood together, wrapped in the moment, a moment that could last for as long as they wanted.

EPILOGUE

Richard

Getting over the novelty of having Autumn on the island wasn't going to happen quickly. Concentrating on deadlines became almost impossible, but Richard still had to read all the team's reports. Autumn's job meant she wasn't around all the time, which gave him time – hours he could hardly wait to finish until he saw her again.

A nagging worry tugged at him. Somehow he'd got off the hook. After psyching himself up for a move to London, it was like a reprieve at the scaffold. From his desk at the window of his study, he glanced up as a pink van drove by. Everyone on the island recognised that van, though Richard had only recently discovered that Georgia was its owner. A few minutes later, the back door opened, and he heard chatting. Autumn had been off somewhere with her new friend.

'Boo!' She bounced in the door and before he could turn around, she jumped on him from behind, strangling him and placing a kiss on his cheek. The office seat wobbled dangerously.

After listening to the story of where she'd been, Richard looked about, considering. 'I feel like I've got off lightly. You made this big move while I haven't had to change anything.'

Autumn sat on the desk and stretched her hands out. 'You came to London, and I believe you would live there with me if it came to it.'

'I would. If you tire of Mull.'

'Well…' Autumn lowered her head and theatrically batted her lashes. 'I'm not tired of it yet, but I do have something I need you to do.'

'And what's that?'

Autumn jumped off the desk and disappeared for a few seconds. Richard frowned at the sound of rustling from outside the door. When he swivelled around, Autumn sailed in, holding a long black cloak on a hanger. 'I need you to wear this tomorrow night. We're going to the Halloween party and you're going as Count Dracula.'

Richard's mouth fell open, taking in the cloak's high collar and the red lining. 'You are joking?'

'Nope. And remember, it's a lot easier than moving to London. Just wear the cloak, come to the party, and maybe dance a bit.'

'An apartment in London is looking more appealing by the second.' He smiled with a little shake of his head. 'And what are you going as?'

'A pumpkin witch.'

'Of course you are,' said Richard as Autumn ducked out and returned holding an elaborate concoction of orange and black lace, net, ribbon and frills.

'Georgia made these. She's amazing.'

Richard walked over to Autumn, took the costume from her and hooked it over the door handle. 'She is, but not half as amazing as you.' He slipped his arms around her waist and pulled her in for a long, timeless kiss. 'I knew almost as soon as I saw you you were trouble.' He brushed a strand of her auburn hair around her ear. 'I just didn't realise quite how much.'

'I think you're the troublesome one, you just hide it better than me.' She winked.

'Hmm. We'll put it to the jury some other time, but, before I forget, I got something for you. It arrived earlier.' From his desk, he lifted a large box and handed it to her.

'What's this?'

'A box. Open it and find out.'

With her eyes wide, Autumn lifted the sides and pulled out the smaller boxes and packages inside. 'What is all this? Is it a chemistry set?'

'Not exactly.'

'Do you want me to help you take kelp samples or something?' Autumn lifted a jar and a packet containing ten pipettes.

'You're getting closer. It's everything you require to make your own candles.'

'Oh my god. Really?' Her smile was so huge and her excitement so palpable Richard couldn't help laughing.

'Yes, really. There's plenty of kelp here, not to mention heather and lots of other plants you can use. It's ideal.'

'It is.' She set the box aside. 'Thank you.' Autumn gazed into his eyes and he opened his arms to her.

'I'm glad you chose to live here. I'm learning a lot from you. Home is a place, but it's also about people,' he said. 'People you love. And I love you more than I can ever say.'

She rubbed a slow circle on his back and he drew a deep contented breath. 'I know. I felt it right from the start. I knew there was something about you and now I know what it is. We've come home to the place we belong. Together.'

'Exactly.'

It didn't matter where they were. As long as they had each other, they'd always be home. Beyond the window, the golden sun dropped, leaving an ethereal haze. Richard pressed his lips to Autumn's forehead and stroked her hair. Her eyelids dropped, and she breathed slowly.

'Yes, always together.'

The End

SHARE THE LOVE!

If you enjoyed reading this book, then please share your reviews online.
Leaving reviews is a perfect way to support authors and helps books reach more readers.
So please review and share!
Let me know what you think.

Margaret X

ACKNOWLEDGEMENTS

As always, I'd like to thank my husband, Ian, for putting up with my writing talk 24/7 and supporting me in my quest to become a published author. His encouragement has helped me pull through tough times and keep going. Also to my son, whose interest in my writing always makes me smile. I'm so proud to be your mum.

Throughout the writing process, I have gleaned help from many sources and met some fabulous people. I'd like to give a special mention to the following people. Stéphanie Ronckier, my beta reader extraordinaire, for giving me phenomenal feedback on my writing and helping me see everything from a fresh perspective. My lovely friend, Lyn Williamson, for her continued support. And fellow author, Evie Alexander, for her no-nonsense style of encouragement and all-round writing fabulousness!

Also a huge thanks to my editor, Aimee Walker, at Aimee Walker Editorial Services for her excellent work on my novels.

A shout out also goes to Anita Faulkner and the Chick-Lit & Prosecco Facebook group, which is a wonderful community of supportive people and a fun place to hang out.

To everyone else in my family and to all my friends and online buddies, thank you for being there for me.

About the Author

I live with my family in the beautiful county of Perthshire in Scotland. With impressive scenery everywhere you look, it's hard not to be inspired around here.

I'm mummy to a precious little boy who loves stories as much as me and always likes to know what I'm writing today.

I've been a closet writer for several years and have written stories, articles and poetry. In 2012, I won a short story writing competition at Pitlochry Festival Theatre with a faerie tale, Out of the Frame. It was an honour to have the piece read live in the auditorium.

As well as writing, I'm a keen photographer, and I also enjoy drawing. If you're looking for me, I tend to be either clacking the keys, scribbling in a notebook or reading - preferably with chocolate.

I'm thrilled to introduce my first series Scottish Island Escapes.

Join me on an adventure to the wild and remote Scottish islands from the comfort of your armchair and cosy up for some heart-warming reading.

To find out more visit: www.margaretamatt.com

MORE BOOKS BY MARGARET AMATT

Scottish Island Escapes

A Winter Haven
A Spring Retreat
A Summer Sanctuary
An Autumn Hideaway
A Christmas Bluff

FREE HUGS & OLD-FASHIONED KISSES

A short story only available to newsletter subscribers. Sign up at www.margaretamatt.com

Do you ever get one of those days when you just fancy snuggling up? Then this captivating short story is for you! And what's more, it's free when you sign up to my newsletter.

Meet Livvi, a girl who just needs a hug. And Jakob, a guy who doesn't go about hugging random strangers. But what if he makes an exception, just this once?

Make yourself a hot chocolate, sign up to my newsletter and enjoy!

A WINTER HAVEN

She was the one that got away. Now she's back.

Career-driven Robyn Sherratt returns to her childhood home on the Scottish Isle of Mull, hoping to build bridges with her estranged family. She discovers her mother struggling to run the family hotel. When an old flame turns up, memories come back to bite, nibbling into Robyn's fragile heart.

Carl Hansen, known as The Fixer, abandoned city life for peace and tranquillity. Swapping his office for a log cabin, he mends people's broken treasures. He can fix anything, except himself. When forced to work on hotel renovations with Robyn, the girl he lost twelve years ago, his quiet life is sent spinning.

Carl would like nothing more than to piece together the shattered shards of Robyn's heart. But can she trust him? What can a broken man like him offer a successful woman like her?

A SPRING RETREAT

She's gritty, he's determined. Who will back down first?

When spirited islander Beth McGregor learns of plans to build a road through the family farm, she sets out to stop it. But she's thrown off course by the charming and handsome project manager. Sparks fly, sending Beth into a spiral of confusion. Guys are fine as friends. Nothing else.

Murray Henderson has finally found a place to retreat from the past with what seems like a straightforward job. But he hasn't reckoned on the stubbornness of the locals, especially the hot-headed and attractive Beth.

As they battle together over the proposed road, attraction blooms. Murray strives to discover the real Beth; what secrets lie behind the tough façade? Can a regular farm girl like her measure up to Murray's impeccable standards, and perhaps find something she didn't know she was looking for?

A SUMMER SANCTUARY

She's about to discover the one place he wants to keep secret

Five years ago, Island girl Kirsten McGregor broke the company rules. Now, she has the keys to the Hidden Mull tour bus and is ready to take on the task of running the business. But another tour has arrived. The competition is bad enough but when she recognises the rival tour operator, her plans are upended.

Former jet pilot Fraser Bell has made his share of mistakes. What better place to hide and regroup than the place he grew to love as a boy? With great enthusiasm, he launches into his new tour business, until old-flame Kirsten shows up and sends his world plummeting.

Kirsten may know all the island's secrets, but what she can't work out is Fraser. With tension simmering, Kirsten and Fraser's attraction increases. What if they both made a mistake before? Is one of them about to make an even bigger one now?

A CHRISTMAS BLUFF

She's about to trespass all over his Christmas.

Artist and photographer Georgia Rose has spent two carefree years on the Isle of Mull and is looking forward to a quiet Christmas... Until she discovers her family is about to descend upon her, along with her past.

Aloof aristocrat Archie Crichton-Leith has let out his island mansion to a large party from the mainland. They're expecting a castle for Christmas, not an outdated old pile, and he's in trouble.

When Georgia turns up with an irresistible smile and an offer he can't refuse, he's wary, but he needs her help.

As Georgia weaves her festive charms around the house, they start to work on Archie too. And the spell extends both ways. But falling in love was never part of the deal. Can the magic outlast Christmas when he's been conned before and she has a secret that could ruin everything?

MAP

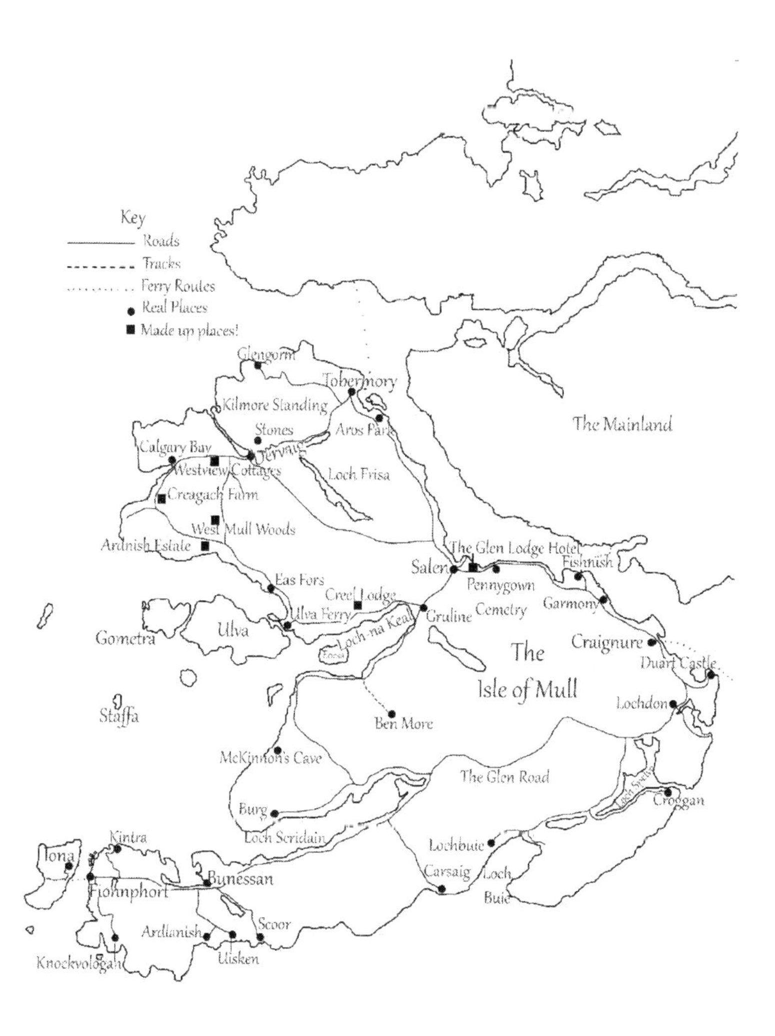
Key
Roads
Tracks
Ferry Routes
Real Places
Made up places!
Glengorm
Tobermory
Kilmore Standing
Stones
Aros Park
The Mainland
Calgary Bay
Westview Cottages
Loch Frisa
Creagach Farm
West Mull Woods
Ardnish Estate
The Glen Lodge Hotel
Salen
Fishnish
Eas Fors
Creel Lodge
Pennygown
Cemetry
Garmony
Ulva Ferry
Gruline
Gometra
Ulva
Loch-na Keal
Craignure
The
Isle of Mull
Duart Castle
Staffa
Lochdon
Ben More
McKinnon's Cave
The Glen Road
Croggan
Burg
Loch Scridain
Kintra
Lochbuie
Iona
Carsaig
Loch
Buie
Bunessan
Fionnphort
Scoor
Ardlanish
Uisken
Knockvologan